RAINBOW BRIDGE

First Published in Great Britain 2020 by Mirador Publishing

First edition: 2020

ISBN: 978-1-913264-71-0

Mirador Publishing
10 Greenbrook Terrace
Taunton
Somerset

Rainbow Bridge

By

Dan V. Jackson

Dedication

To everyone who has adopted, cared for, loved, been loved by, and lost
a beloved dog.

And on a personal note: to the Scooters, Tiqui, Abby, Bella, Sammie…and
Norman.

Table of Contents

Just this side of heaven is a place called the Rainbow Bridge.

When an animal who was especially close to someone dies, that pet goes to the Rainbow Bridge. There are meadows and hills for all our special friends, so they can run and play together. There is plenty of food, water, and sunshine, and our friends are warm and comfortable. All the animals who had been ill and old are restored to health and vigor. Those who were hurt or maimed are made whole and strong again, just as we remember them in our dreams of days gone by. The animals are happy and content, except for one small thing: they each miss someone very special to them, who had to be left behind.

The day comes when one suddenly stops and looks into the distance. His bright eyes are intent. His eager body quivers. Suddenly, he begins to run from the group, flying over the green grass, his legs carrying him faster and faster.

You have been spotted, and when you and your special friend finally meet, you cling together in joyous reunion, never to be parted again. The happy kisses rain upon your face; your hands again caress the beloved head, and you look once more into the trusting eyes of your pet, so long gone from your life but never absent from your heart.

Then you cross the Rainbow Bridge together...

—Author unknown

I.

FRISCO

I.1

Hot Springs, Arkansas—August 1978

He had been there a moment ago; now he was gone.
Something was terribly wrong.

* * * * * *

Frisco had diligently maintained his post throughout the morning watching over three-year-old Nathan Wilkinson as the youth played with a set of matchbox cars on his cluttered bedroom floor. For the border-beagle mix, this was less a responsibility than a pleasure and a privilege, allowing him to play an active role in his beloved human's development, growth, and overall well-being.

The four-year-old dog cut an elegant stature as he positioned himself by the worn auburn dresser adjacent to the bedroom door, his fifty-pound torso sporting a predominantly white double-coat with a sprinkling of black fur. While he appeared to be a mix of border collie and beagle, there were certain times that a smattering of other breeds was visible, including Australian shepherd and even a hint of Labrador. But the bloodline mattered not at all to the Wilkinson family; Frisco was their loyal, devoted, and lovable mutt, ever since he unexpectedly appeared in their backyard as a frightened young stray shortly after Nathan's birth. Sadly, callous owners frequently dumped unwanted puppies in populated Hot Springs subdivisions, leaving them to the elements where only the fortunate few would be rescued and adopted by neighborhood families. Nathan's mother found the starving pup huddled under the porch, nursed him back to health, and despite her husband's objections, insisted on making him a permanent part of the family. She never regretted her decision, especially after Frisco took an unusually spirited interest in the safety and well-being of their infant son.

Today's routine had been no different from those countless others, Nathan enjoying his pre-lunch playtime and Frisco patiently observing him, sighing affectionately at the boy's energy and creativity while ensuring that he remained safe and secure. But a moment later, the border beagle's acute hearing detected the rustling sound of a squirrel scampering outdoors through the branches of the front-yard oak. Centuries of instinct ignited; immediately Frisco shot through the bedroom door and down the modest one-story home's main hallway to the front window to investigate.

He pawed at the pane for several moments, emitting a low growl of frustration at his inability to secure the elusive prize. He eyed the squirrel one last time, then shook himself, pivoted and wandered back to the bedroom. Stepping inside, he was startled to find the room empty and eerily quiet.

He scanned the bedroom and adjoining hallway, listening carefully for the shuffling sound of a toddler on the move. Nothing. That wasn't right; Nathan should have been easily locatable in the modest, one-story home.

Annoyed at allowing himself to be so fixated on the squirrel that he neglected to notice the boy's movements, Frisco inhaled deeply in an effort to detect the boy's scent. It led out the bedroom and down the opposite end of the hallway to the screen door leading to the backyard. Frisco scurried up to the screen and peered through, yet he still did not see Nathan.

A combination of apprehension and anxiety set an inner alarm pulsating through his body. He spun about; his paws clattered against the linoleum floor as he headed back through the hallway past the entryway to the kitchen, to find Sally Wilkinson busily preparing her son's lunch. The late-morning sun shone through a torn curtain, bathing the tiny kitchen in a swaddling glow. Like so much else in their sparsely furnished home, the ragged drapes constantly reminded the family that money remained tight and left little room for indulgences.

The ever-present sound of the living room television blared in the background as Sally, brushing the light brown hair away from her eyes with the back of her hand, lifted a grilled cheese sandwich from the skillet with her spatula and deposited it onto the Star Wars–themed child's plate. Frisco yipped to draw the diminutive thirty-year-old's attention as she spread a handful of potato chips next to the sandwich.

"There you are!" She smiled when she saw him. "I'm surprised it took you so long to get here." She tossed a potato chip to him, but he ignored it; it split into pieces as it hit the floor. He yipped again, more urgently.

"Not hungry? That's not like you." She shrugged and turned toward the hallway leading to her son's bedroom. "Nathan! Lunch is ready!"

She set the lunch plate on the kitchen table, then took a moment to fill the pan with water and deposit it in the kitchen sink.

"Nathan?" she called out again. "Your lunch is going to get cold. Come on in now!"

Frisco whined loudly, shook himself in agitation, and scraped his paw on the linoleum.

"Yeah, I know. He needs to get out here." An irritated Sally untied her apron; Frisco scratched at her leg, then darted down the hallway to Nathan's door, where he stopped abruptly, turned, and stared at her with pleading eyes.

"Nathan! I'm not kidding. Come out here now!" Sally followed Frisco to the bedroom door and peered inside, seeing too that that the room was empty. She moved on to check the master bedroom, then the bathroom.

Growing increasingly apprehensive, Sally made her way back through the kitchen and into the living room, Frisco flanking her. Larry Wilkinson lay spread across the couch, clad in a faded army T-shirt and plaid shorts, eyes fixed on the blaring television. Even though it was not yet noon, the unshaven thirty-year-old was already swigging from a can of Budweiser.

"Have you seen Nathan?" Sally asked, a hint of worry in her voice. Larry eyed his wife disdainfully, annoyed at the interruption.

"I thought the dog was watching him."

* * * * * *

The bright sun and the gentle breeze set forth an ideal morning for outdoor exploration. But then, to a three-year-old, virtually every day overflowed with potential for new discovery.

Nathan Wilkinson paused a moment to gaze back at his house, which was now down the street, distant in the background. Frisco's rare moment of distraction investigating the rodent interloper had afforded the sandy-haired toddler the ideal opportunity to escape the boredom of his bedroom and seek a real adventure. Nathan had planned for this in the past and knew exactly what to do: he toddled down the hallway, slipped out the screen door into the backyard, and made his way around the side of the house. In moments, he had trudged up the front driveway to its point of intersection with Greenway Avenue. Aging starter homes adjacent to curving streets lined with plush Arkansan foliage crammed the subdivision known as Greenway Gardens. To Nathan's right was the same backdrop he always saw when his mom took him out in the car: his street ascending a hill to a plateau and disappearing beyond the horizon.

Nathan had long wondered about the strange hill. His mom always steered the car the other way. *Why was it there? Why did it make his road disappear? Did the road go past the top?* Today he was finally going to find out.

He turned right and tottered up the side of the street, past a half-dozen neighbors' homes. It took several minutes, but he finally reached the plateau—a long-sought and satisfying victory. As he stood at the summit, he gazed ahead and saw that the road did indeed continue ahead, though oddly enough, it started to decline and, in the distance, curved to the left and out of sight.

This was not what he had expected. He started up again, quickening his pace as he moved forward down the back side of the hill. After passing four more homes, he stopped again. Behind him the hill ascended; he could no longer see his own home past the plateau. So, wherever this mysterious road was taking him, he was well on his way.

* * * * * *

"Billy, we really ought to get back to school!" Marta shouted to her boyfriend over the roar of engine as the Buick GTX raced down Hot Springs's main thoroughfare.

"C'mon, it's just lunchtime," the sixteen-year-old scoffed, glancing at his watch. "We'll have at least thirty minutes at my house before my mom gets home from work. I'll have you back at school by fifth period."

~ 16 ~

"You better. My grades aren't as good as yours, you know. I can't keep missing classes."

"You can miss a few if you have a good reason to."

He grinned mischievously, his cherubic face lighting up as he glanced down at her short skirt and exposed thigh. She smiled back at him and squeezed his arm appreciatively; distracted, he let the car drift right and skirt the shoulder of the road.

"Whoa!" Billy abruptly jerked the steering wheel; the car's tires kicked up gravel as it righted its path back onto the street.

"You shouldn't be going so fast!" Marta cautioned.

"It's all cool. The sooner we get to my house, the more time we'll have. Now take off that seat belt and slide a little closer to me."

* * * * * *

Sally sighed audibly, irritated that her husband had yet to take his eyes from the television.

"Relax," Larry snorted. "He'll turn up."

An exasperated Sally turned about and noticed Frisco was no longer at her side. She peered down the hallway from the kitchen to see him pawing at the screen door to the backyard. That gave her an idea; she went to the screen door and pushed it open, yet before she could reach the first step onto the porch, Frisco lurched by her and shot into the backyard. In a second the manic, galloping border-beagle mix had disappeared around the side of the house and out of sight.

She paid no attention to the dog; a much more pressing matter lay at hand. Descending the final stair from the porch, she searched for but could detect no trace of Nathan in the backyard. Ever so slightly, she felt knots forming in her stomach.

"He's not in the backyard!" she said as she darted back into the house and to the living room.

Larry didn't even bother to look up; he continued to affix his eyes on the TV as he drank from his rapidly diminishing beer.

"Larry! Are you even listening to me?"

"Will you calm down? He's just being a kid, off playing somewhere."

"Well he's not in the house, and he's not in the yard. I don't like it when I don't know where he is!"

"So what am I supposed to do about it?"

"You can try getting off your butt and helping me look for him!"

"Fine!" Larry slammed the beer can down on the coffee table. "I'm telling you, he's just off playing somewhere. I'm tired from my shift last night, but I'll help look for him if that's what it takes to get you off my back!" He struggled to lift himself off the couch, his portly midsection weighing him down like an anchor.

"Just look through the house again. I'm going to go back outside." Sally turned away in disgust from the man she had married eight years earlier. She would deal with his attitude later; her priority was to find her son.

* * * * * *

It was darker here, in this strange place beyond the hill. Dense branches from the trees lining the street cast shadows over the neighboring yards. The homes appeared murkier, more ominous, in the shade. Nathan didn't like any of this; his young mind strained to fathom the creatures that might be lurking inside those unfamiliar dwellings.

The plush trees blotted out most of the sunlight, leaving only a patch gracing the center of the road. Nathan stepped into the street and to the light; feeling its warmth eased his apprehension, at least for the moment.

Then, just like that, this last patch of sunlight was gone, impeded by cloud cover. The trees tossed about in the strengthening wind; in the hazy daylight, the shimmying branches seemed more…foreboding. Nathan was startled by the sound of a crash behind him, wind slamming shut the porch door to a nearby house, after which an eerie quiet fell over the street.

Maybe I should go back, he thought. But where was back? He looked to his right; the road declined and curved out of sight. He looked the other way; it rose up toward the plateau. Was that the same hill that he had just come over? Which way was back home? He couldn't remember.

Where's Mommy? There was no Mommy here. Only strange houses, swaying trees, creeping darkness, and loud, scary sounds followed by silence. And what kind of monsters could be inside those homes? He didn't like this place anymore. He wanted to go home. But he didn't know where he was or how to get back.

And then, an overwhelmed Nathan Wilkinson sat down in the center of the street and began to cry.

* * * * * *

"Now, that's better," Billy smirked as Marta nestled up to him on the GTO's bench seat. "I always like it when you get close to me."

"If you like this, then just wait until we get to your house." She giggled, her hand reaching down to stroke his thigh.

Billy smiled again and pressed down on the accelerator. The engine roared, the speedometer jumped, and the GTX careened onto Greenway Avenue, briefly skidding and kicking away gravel from the partially paved road.

Marta leaned in and kissed him on the neck. Billy's grin widened as he relished the warmth of her lips. He depressed the accelerator again; the muscle car raced up the street toward his house, just over the plateau.

* * * * * *

It was still there. A visibly distressed Frisco sniffed vigorously, again and again. Though obfuscated by the pollen floating through the breezy airstream, he could detect the faint scent. Nathan had been here, minutes earlier.

Frisco stood in the front yard now, near the driveway's entrance to the street. Anxiety flowed through his body as he pivoted to his left and gazed down the hill. Nothing, only a car turning sharply onto the street from the intersection a half mile away.

"Nathan!" came a voice behind him. Frisco saw Sally by the side of the house, approaching the front yard, calling out to her son, palpable worry in her voice.

Then, Frisco's finely tuned ears detected what Sally's could not—the distant and faint echo of whimpering. It was Nathan. And Nathan was in trouble.

In a flash Frisco sprinted onto the street and up the hill toward the plateau, his paws crunching over the pebble-strewn asphalt. The border beagle crossed over the summit and yelped in relief and excitement at the sight of Nathan sitting in the center of the street, wiping the tears from his eyes.

But his excitement vanished when he heard the sound of that same car's engine, now approaching the plateau. His ears told him that it was already less than fifty yards away, at a high rate of speed, and within moments would be over the hill and upon them.

He glanced back to see the boy, sitting unmoving, still crying. Close enough that once the vehicle emerged from the plateau, there would be no time to stop.

Frisco's ears rang from the roar of the still-unseen engine. It was closing in, and rapidly. In an instant, his choice became all too clear.

A tear formed in his eye; he whined softly, then spun about and sprinted back across the plateau.

* * * * * *

Now it was Billy's turn. He buried his face in Marta's neck and gently kissed her tender, exposed skin. When he lifted his head again, he saw them passing by a woman who was standing in her front yard, calling out a name he could not discern. He snickered in amusement—*probably lost her stupid cat*—and once again planted his lips on Marta's cheek.

Marta closed her eyes for a moment and sighed in pleasure at the sensation. Then she opened her eyes again and glanced at the road ahead.

"Look out!" she shrieked.

Billy popped up his head and saw it in front of him, right as the car was reaching the plateau. A black-and-white dog, emerging from the other side, galloping directly at them. Billy slammed his foot on the brakes; the worn pads squealed as the tires dug into the asphalt. But it was not nearly enough to stop the momentum.

They both felt a thud and heard a howl of pain. The car slid to a halt.

* * * * * *

"Frisco!" Sally screamed.

She had witnessed it all: the car racing past her up the hill; Frisco's sudden reemergence on the plateau and into its path; and the violent, sickening collision. Frantically she dashed toward the scene, only to find upon arrival confirmation of her worst fears. Blood stained the stalled vehicle's grill and the nearby asphalt. Frisco lay on the gravelly roadside, his eyes open and his tongue hanging limply from his mouth. Remarkably, the dog was still breathing.

"I -- I'm sorry lady!" Billy sputtered as he rolled out of the car. "I didn't see him!"

"What were you thinking, driving that fast in a neighborhood!" Sally bent down to her stricken dog. "Oh, Frisco, my poor baby!"

"Is he okay, ma'am?" Marta asked sheepishly.

"No, he's not okay!"

Marta extended her arm around her ashen boyfriend. "Ma'am," Billy said tentatively, "this is all my fault. If there's anything I can do…" He stopped when he saw, emerging from the plateau's summit and running toward them, a young boy with sandy-brown hair.

"Nathan!" Sally exclaimed, catching the running boy in her arms. "Where have you been?" Nathan, relieved as he was to be in his mother's arms, started to answer before glimpsing a haunting sight.

"F-Frisco?" he croaked, pushing away from his mother and gesturing toward the border beagle. Sally grabbed his arm and hugged him again, trying to shield the boy from the grisly sight. But he shook loose from her grip and kneeled in front of the injured dog.

His vision blurring and his breathing labored, Frisco gazed forlornly at his young friend. He felt the comforting warmth of Nathan's hand as the young boy stroked the top of his head. In great pain, Frisco reached up and with what little strength he could muster, gave the boy a kiss on his cheek. Then he lay back down on the pavement and slowly closed his eyes. His chest heaved one last time, then finally stilled.

"Oh, Frisco," Sally moaned.

"What the hell is going on?" came a voice behind her. She turned and saw her husband running up the street toward them.

"Frisco got hit by this car. He—he's gone!"

"Oh God," a stunned Larry murmured. The dreadful sight gave him pause; though he had never been enthralled with the responsibility for the border beagle, it clearly didn't deserve such a fate.

"Mommy, is Frisco okay?" Nathan asked, fear in his voice, his eyes filling with tears.

"Take care of this, will you?" Sally said to her husband, then grasped her son's arm and lifted him to his feet. "Come with me, Nathan," she said, tears falling from her eyes. "Let me take you home, and I'll tell you about a special place where Frisco is going to go. It's called the Rainbow Bridge."

Holding Nathan closely, Sally turned away from the car and back toward the house, the surrounding silence broken only by the young girl's sobs as she buried her head in her traumatized boyfriend's chest. Then a haunting realization dawned on her. Nathan had emerged over the plateau in the middle of the street barely an instant after the accident. She didn't want to contemplate it, but as terrible as this accident had been, it just might have prevented something even worse.

* * * * * *

"Wake up, my boy!"

Lying in the lush grass of a rolling meadow, Frisco opened his eyes to behold the beautiful and familiar sight. The meadow's endless hills were lined with oak and magnolia trees, their branches swaying in the gentle winds. Patches of daffodils, chrysanthemums, and begonias in vivid colors lay perched throughout a landscape that was illuminated by an intensely bright sun. Late-morning dew lined the grass, mixing with the sun's warmth to create an intoxicating just-after-rainfall aroma. It was perfection, nothing short, and it filled Frisco with an overwhelming sense of contentment.

In the meadow's distance lay the entrance to a magnificent golden bridge. Fifty feet in width, its resplendent girders and suspension cables glistened in the shimmering sunlight. Only the entrance to the bridge was visible; the pathway protruded from the meadow and arched upward, eventually disappearing into a layer of clouds.

Frisco jumped to his feet to face an old man with a bushy white beard wearing a plain brown tunic and sandals, a cord fastened about his portly waist. The old man bent over and stroked Frisco; his soft hands brought a soothing touch as he rubbed the border beagle's favorite spot behind his pointed ears.

"It's good to see you again, Frisco." The old man smiled warmly. "You did superbly during your brief time on earth. It was a noble act, sacrificing yourself to save your ward. I'm very proud of you."

Frisco whined softly and kissed the man's outstretched hand.

The old man waved his arm toward the meadow. Frisco saw hundreds of dogs, cats, and other animals frolicking in the sunlight among the grassy plains and flower patches. Some played chase games, others napped under trees, still others drank the crisp water from the babbling ponds. Birds lazily glided above; crickets chirped happily inside their patches.

"I know that when I placed you with Nathan you wanted to spend a lifetime with him. Sometimes things don't work out the way you prefer. But what you did earned you the chance to play a very special role for him and his family in the years to come.

"Now, your friends have been waiting patiently for you to return. Go on and play with them. But don't be too long. I'm going to need you again soon."

Frisco yelped in appreciation, turned, and scampered off toward a band of dogs clustered underneath a maple tree.

The old man stepped over to a group of five other dogs waiting a few yards away: a tan German shepherd, a black miniature schnauzer, a stout Belgian Malinois, and two Labrador retrievers, one black, the other blond. They stood before him, tails wagging and tongues dangling from their mouths.

"All of you should have learned a valuable lesson from Frisco," the old man said to the group. "Love, honor, responsibility, sacrifice. It's why your human families need you.

"And young Nathan is one of our special cases. He is going to face many challenges in the coming years. I have chosen each of you to provide the guidance and support he and his loved ones will need. Now, who wants to be the next to help him?"

The German shepherd barked and gestured at him. The old man smiled warmly.

"Good boy, Shiloh. I thought it might be you."

II.

SHILOH

II.1

Chino Valley, Arizona—October 1986

"What're you still doing here, newbie?"

The menacing words echoed from behind as Nathan kneeled in front of his locker in Heritage Middle School's seventh-grade concourse. Recognizing the nasally tone, he pivoted to catch sight of three fellow twelve-year-olds flanking him in the crowded hallway. A pungent odor of worn sneakers and bleach permeated the school corridor, magnified by the stifling Arizona heat. His arms weighed down by textbooks, Nathan slowly rose to face the group's self-appointed leader, Tom Manogue.

Decked out in his trademark fashionably torn jeans and denim jacket, the light-haired, freckle faced Manogue glowered menacingly at him. "I thought after last Friday you wouldn't be showing your ugly face in this school again."

Nathan said nothing; his mind flashed to the previous week, in the schoolyard, where Manogue and his fellow ruffians had taunted him for his aged and ill-fitting jeans, then cornered him, dumped the books from his arms, and shoved him to the ground.

"Yeah," wheezed Manogue's pudgy sidekick, Travis Roach. "We thought you'd be back in Arkansas or wherever it is you're from."

"What do you want?" Nathan said uneasily as the boys moved closer to him.

"Is everybody in Arkansas as ugly and stupid as you?" Manogue barked.

Travis leaned in toward him, close enough that Nathan could not avoid the noxious combination of body odor and bad breath. "Nah," he scoffed in that unmistakable rasp again, his weight aging him beyond his years, "he's uglier and stupider than all of them."

"Leave me alone, you guys." Anger and humiliation bubbled within Nathan as he stepped away from the three tormentors. "I gotta get to science class."

As Nathan passed him, Manogue reached down, grabbed, and yanked one of the books tucked under his arm, causing the rest to dispense from his grip and scatter across the linoleum floor. The aggressors broke into laughter; other students walking between classes stopped to witness the altercation, none willing to intervene on Nathan's behalf.

"That's a heckuva mess you made," Manogue laughed. Nathan said nothing as he crouched down to gather the scattered books. "What you gonna do, start crying?"

"What a wussy," Travis snarled.

Nathan tried to ignore the taunts; outnumbered and outsized, he broiled inside, knowing he was no match for the three antagonists. He picked up another book as he heard the bell signaling the start of fourth period.

"See you soon, newbie," Manogue scoffed as the bullies backed away. Signing in relief, Nathan quickly finished reassembling his belongings. He paused as he smelled a wispy perfume and saw a pair of laced tennis shoes stroll by; he glanced up to briefly make eye contact with Darlene Tully, the raven-haired junior cheerleader with whom he shared math and history classes. Popular though she was, she still smiled warmly at him.

As Nathan tried to return her smile, he suddenly a felt a surge of pain from Travis's fist striking his arm. He gasped and dropped his books; again they scattered over the tile flooring.

Manogue triumphantly slapped Travis on the back, and they broke into a chorus of laughter as they strode down the corridor. Nathan glared at them with fury in his eyes and once again set about to gather his books. It was then that he noticed Darlene, and, in a flash of pain more cutting than the blow to his arm, he saw that she was laughing as well.

* * * * * *

As the afternoon wore on, Nathan sat sullenly at his desk, uninterested in the droning lectures, instead gazing out the window at the forlorn Arizona landscape. Chino Valley was so different from Hot Springs—hotter, drier, fewer stores, not a single movie theater, all compounded by his difficulty at integrating into his school's social network since his arrival earlier in the year. New students from different states were a rarity in the small town, a factor that directly led to the unwanted attention he was receiving from the class bullies.

He glanced down at the Lawrence Taylor sticker affixed to his notebook and drifted off into another of his frequent daydreams of gridiron glory. Surely no one ever picked on his hero, the menacing New York Giants linebacker, in middle school or anytime else, for that matter. He tried to turn his attention back to the lesson at hand, but the frustration building inside him prevented any meaningful engagement, which was sure to further damage his already-marginal grades.

At 3:15 p.m., the final bell rang. Nathan breathed a sigh of relief, sprinted back to his locker, stowed his books in his backpack, and bolted out the front entrance. He preferred to walk the short distance to his home, which had the added benefit of avoiding the tormentors who frequented the middle school buses. On the way was the town's only 7-Eleven, so he decided to stop in and use his leftover lunch money to purchase his favorite candy, a giant-size Tootsie Roll.

Departing the store with the chocolate treat in hand, he gazed downward as he stuffed the little remaining change in his pocket. Momentarily not paying attention to where he was going, he inadvertently strode right into Tom Manogue and his two buddies in the parking lot.

"Hey! Watch where you're going, newbie!" Manogue barked as he pushed him away, amused by the good fortune of running into his victim twice in the same day.

"What you got there?" Travis Roach said, eyeing the Tootsie Roll.

"Nothing." Nathan's stomach knotted as the frustration of once again allowing himself to stumble into a confrontation with his more numerous adversaries swelled within him. "Leave me alone; I gotta get home."

"Not so fast," Manogue said, stepping in front of Nathan to block his escape route.

"Yeah, I'm kinda hungry." Travis sneered and snatched the candy from him.

"Hey!" Nathan thrust his arm at Travis, but Manogue blocked him with his own arm. Nathan felt a spiking pain as Manogue closed his grip around his wrist; then the third boy shoved him forward. Manogue released his hold as Travis grabbed Nathan and yanked him to his side. The sharp movement tore Nathan's shirt and propelled him to his knees; his pant leg ripped on the gravel-strewn pavement. The frustration morphed into a combination of fear and apprehension; his mouth dried up, and he hid his hand inside so the other youths could not see the trembling.

"Thanks for the dessert, newbie!" Travis laughed.

"What a fag," Travis wheezed.

Manogue reached down, grabbed Nathan again, and lifted him to his feet, and punched him point-blank in the face. "And next time, be sure to get enough for all of us."

The boys sauntered off, laughing, as a seething and humiliated Nathan felt a throbbing wave of pain and blood flowing from his nose.

* * * * * *

He sighed audibly as he approached the run-down three-bedroom home on Briar Hollow Avenue, off Highway 89. Unlike in his Hot Springs neighborhood, no trees lined these streets; the only color derived from the occasional patches of St. Augustine grass that dotted the dirt-strewn yards. Paint peeled off the home's exterior siding; a detached gutter drooped over the front porch. Nothing appealed to Nathan about this home or neighborhood— except for one special someone.

Nathan gently cracked open the front door and peered inside, checking for a clear path to his bedroom. He shut the door behind him and crept down the hallway. Though he thought he knew every weakness in the aged wooden floor, his eighth step creaked loudly, echoing through the hallway.

"Nathan!" his mother called from the kitchen. "Is that you?"

"Yeah," he answered sullenly.

"It's about time you got home. Come in here now. I need you to set the table before dinner."

"Not right now; I have to get to my room."

"You can go to your room after you finish helping me."

"But I have homework to do."

"Stop making excuses and come into the kitchen now."

Finding himself out of options, Nathan warily approached the kitchen to find his mother, as usual, in front of the stove, apron drawn about her waist, stirring a pot filled with boiling potatoes. A buttery aroma floated through the kitchen and adjoining living room.

"Get the placemats from the pantry first, and—" Sally stopped suddenly when she saw Nathan emerge from the darkened hallway. "What happened to you?"

"Nothing."

"What do you mean 'nothing'?" She gestured at the torn clothing and the dried blood on his nose.

"I don't want to talk about it."

"You get beat up again?" Standing at the entrance to the living room, dressed in faded jeans and a Van Halen T-shirt, sporting the faint odor of moist armpit stains, Larry was home early from work again and already swigging from his usual Budweiser.

"No, I didn't," Nathan protested. "I—I just tripped over the curb outside the 7-Eleven, that's all."

"The hell you did. It's bad enough that you couldn't defend yourself. Don't make it worse by lying about it."

"Well, I didn't start it," Nathan snorted, humiliation and anger again building inside him.

"Did you fight back this time, at least?"

"There were three of them."

"So what? I keep telling you, even if you know you're going to get your butt kicked, at least try to get some licks in first. If you don't make them pay for it, they'll never stop."

"We should talk to someone at the school about this," Sally said to her husband. "Get them to make those bullies leave Nathan alone."

"No, Mom!" Nathan protested, understanding all too well the schoolwide implications of having his parents intervene on his behalf against Manogue and his gang.

"We're not going to do that." Larry took another pull from the beer. "If he rats those kids out, they'll never leave him alone."

He turned to Nathan. "You've got to learn to stand on your own two feet and defend yourself. Fighting back is the only thing that's ever going to make those kids respect you."

"I don't care about making them respect me! I hate everyone in this crappy town!"

"Don't you talk like that!" Sally snapped.

"Why did you make us move here anyway? You never asked me if I wanted to come here. I want to go back to Arkansas!"

"Well, you can't," Larry said. "I have a job here now, so we're not going anywhere. You just better make the best of it."

Nathan turned toward the door to the backyard, his eyes filling with tears. "Maybe I'll just go back by myself."

"Yeah, sure you will, you little crybaby," Larry sneered.

"That's enough, Larry!" Sally shouted. "Leave him alone!"

Larry continued to glower at Nathan. "You go outside now and come back in when you're ready to start acting like a man."

Nathan scowled back at his father for a moment, then bolted out the door to the backyard. Tears streamed down his face as he collapsed onto the bench by Sally's makeshift garden.

* * * * * *

And then, from the garage, he heard the ever-so-familiar squeal of his best friend. Out the door came Shiloh, bounding exuberantly across the yard toward his master and companion. The four-year-old German shepherd's tan-and-black double-coat ruffled in the wind; his tongue flopped with each impact of his paws on the sun-burnt lawn. His normally erect ears were pulled back, and he let out a whine as he jumped into Nathan's lap.

"Shiloh, no!" Nathan exclaimed, far too late, as he absorbed the full force of the sixty-pound canine. His mood brightening despite the pain as his dog crashed into his aching body, Nathan could not help but giggle as Shiloh happily shimmied and groped at him, his black nose pressing against the boy's cheek while he rained kisses on his face, washing away the dried blood and. expelling onto him the fruity and endearing scent of dog breath.

"Yes, yes, it's good to see you too." Nathan scratched vigorously under

Shiloh's chin, setting the canine to emit another high-pitched yowl of delight. "Thank God I've got you here at least. I hate this place so much. I've got no friends, I can't get away from Manogue and his pals, and my parents don't even care."

Shiloh kissed him again and jumped onto the ground. He turned back to Nathan and sat down on his hind legs, focusing his lively, intelligent brown eyes attentively on the boy.

"I mean, what is there to even do here? I miss the days back in Hot Springs when we used to hang out in the ravine with Brian and Oreo. I've got to find something to do here, or I'm gonna go crazy."

Shiloh abruptly laid his front paws down on the ground and crept forward toward Nathan, who watched in puzzlement as the dog wiggled under the bench, raising his hind legs to force his torso further beneath it.

"What are you doing, boy?" A moment later Nathan had his answer as Shiloh emerged from underneath the bench, grasping in his mouth a foot-long oak stick.

"So that's what you want!" Nathan laughed. "Give me the stick, Shiloh." He reached for it, but Shiloh deftly twirled away from him.

Puzzled at his companion's unwillingness to surrender the stick for their usual game of fetch, Nathan feigned disinterest for a moment and then lunged forward. But Shiloh gracefully dodged the assault, his muscular jaws closed tightly against the stick as he growled playfully, circling about Nathan.

"Taunt me, will you? I'm gonna get you now!" Again Nathan lunged at Shiloh, but the shepherd shimmied again and sped across the backyard toward the hiking trails leading into the foothills behind the subdivision. His sour mood now fully evaporated, Nathan took off after the canine, who ran to the trail, then turned to face Nathan as he again waved the stick in his mouth. Before Nathan could reach him, Shiloh pivoted, and together they dashed off toward the deserted footpath.

* * * * * *

"That dog always makes Nathan feel better." Sally sighed as she stood in the doorway watching the two cavort in the backyard. "I'm so glad Mrs. Purcell let us adopt him last year."

"If you say so," Larry muttered, riffling through the refrigerator. "All I remember is that no one else wanted him."

"Nathan wanted him. I'll never forget how he was drawn to Shiloh the minute he saw him in the Purcell's' living room. It's like those two were meant to be together."

Larry popped the new can and took a healthy swallow. "I'm kind of surprised you were willing to take in another dog, after what happened to the last one."

Sally hesitated, momentarily overcome by the horrific memories. "I did it for Nathan. And he takes care of Shiloh, just like you insisted."

"Yeah, he may feed him and bathe him, but I still have to pay for everything," Larry grunted. "And that dog food isn't cheap, you know. I could use that money for other things."

"You mean like that piece of junk that's parked in the garage?"

"Are you gonna bring that up again? Why can't I get something for myself once in a while?"

"I don't want to get into that right now. All I'm saying is that maybe one of those 'other things' should be making sure your son is happy. Shiloh is the only thing he has right now. He does have a point—moving out here hasn't been easy for him."

"Lots of things aren't easy. I didn't want to leave Arkansas either." He paused to again bring the bottle to his lips. "There may not be much in Chino Valley, but at least I was able to get a decent job here. So, Nathan's going to have to suck it up and make the most of it."

"And that goes for you too," Sally said. "That means not doing here what you did in Hot Springs."

"That wasn't my fault, and you know it."

"Yeah, right," Sally said dismissively. "Every time something bad happens to you, it's someone else's fault. For once, you need to take responsibility for your own actions. You had to come all the way out here to find an auto shop that would hire you. And I don't want to have to leave another state if you screw up again."

"I don't have to take this." Angered by his wife's hectoring, Larry turned abruptly and stalked off toward the garage, beer still in hand. He saw no point in rehashing that old argument again. Better to spend time on his own favorite

activity, putting his mechanic's skills to use while restoring the
that Sally had so erroneously characterized as junk.

As he entered the garage, he noticed a metal bar lying o.
the Mustang's left rear tire. The vision of Nathan, torn shirt and br.
flashed through his mind, triggering memories of the childhood schooly.
taunts he himself had faced. A cold fury built inside him, at the ruffians who
had been abusing his son and at himself for allowing it to happen. That was
going to change.

His plan taking form, he decided the Mustang could wait.

* * * * * *

A unique and lasting bond often forms between a young boy and his dog; a
bond of loyalty, of love, of endless and unflinching devotion. From the day
they came together, Shiloh proved to be friend and companion, playmate and
confidant, a key accomplice in the epic adventures of young Nathan
Wilkinson. Together they explored their Hot Springs neighborhood, Shiloh
trotting alongside the bike-riding Nathan through the twisting streets and
alleyways, over the plateau to the different quarters of Greenway Gardens.
Through the wooded ravines they ventured, chasing imaginary pirates and
battling enemy soldiers, sometimes with friends and their dogs, bounding
about the gullies with endless youthful energy, the adventure only ending
with the onset of dusk and Nathan's mother's distant call to come home to
dinner.

Now, relocated to this remote Arizona town, Nathan found himself more
and more in need of his friend's emotional support. The endless energy of the
bountiful greetings upon arrival home from school; the playtime outside and
through the new neighborhood; the relaxing downtime in his room—it all
made the transition to this new and unwelcoming community a little more
bearable.

The happy memories of times past raced through Nathan's mind as he
strained to keep up with his companion on the lonesome hiking trail. Shiloh
possessed the dual advantages of speed and endurance; occasionally he would
flip about, stick still firmly in his mouth, to let Nathan come within reach,
before pivoting again and darting away in a playfully taunting manner.

~ 33 ~

inally, they reached a clearing near the trail's summit. Nathan stopped to catch his breath, then gazed about at the plains of the Verde Valley. The rolling, sun-drenched peaks and valleys painted a spectacular portrait of beauty that he had never before noticed. The air was clear and crisp, tainted by the faint aroma of the surrounding lantana and hibiscus shrubs.

"I know, I know, you're too fast for me." Nathan panted as Shiloh approached him again. The shepherd pressed the stick into his hand; Nathan tried to pull it away, but Shiloh's iron grip proved unyielding. The tug-of-war commenced, with Nathan spinning Shiloh around and pulling the canine onto his hind legs in a futile effort to dislodge the stick.

"Too fast for me and too strong for me," Nathan sighed. "Just you wait—sooner or later, I'm gonna get that stick from you. Now, what do you want to play next? How about Soldiers at War?"

Shiloh whined in excitement, and off they went into the terrain, two warriors behind enemy lines seeking to engage and defeat the lurking enemy. It was Nathan's favorite game, as it allowed him the rare opportunity to be powerful and in control, and to emulate the one attribute of his father that he admired: the elder Wilkinson's military service. They darted through the terrain, Nathan occasionally discharging his imaginary rifle at the enemy fighters as Shiloh circled about to support and protect.

After a time, with the enemy vanquished and America once again safe and secure, Nathan and Shiloh set forth on their journey home. The distant, waning sun cast a dull glow over the Verde Valley's desert landscape as Shiloh led the way, maintaining a pace sufficiently brisk to keep Nathan straining in pursuit. Finally, bathed in sweat and gasping for breath, Nathan and his companion arrived in his backyard as the sun disappeared over the horizon.

"Looks like Shiloh put you through quite a workout," said his father, sitting on the back porch finishing off yet another Budweiser. "How far did you go?"

"To the summit and back."

"Not bad. You keep doing that, every day, and it'll tone your body good. But that's not all you need to do if you want to stand up to those kids. You're going to have to build some upper-body strength."

"How do I do that?" Nathan asked cautiously, taken aback by his father's sudden interest in his travails.

"Well, for starters, try pull-ups." Larry pointed to an iron pipe set against the roofline and extending three feet from the side of the house. "While you were gone, I installed this bar for you. Every day, before you and Shiloh go off on your run, go to the bar and do as many pull-ups as you can. Then, when you reach the trail's summit, drop and do as many push-ups as you have the strength for. Then when you get back, more pull-ups. Here, try some now."

Larry guided Nathan over to the bar and gestured to a stool set beneath it. Nathan climbed onto the stool, grabbed the bar, and struggled mightily to raise up his body. Shiloh barked in encouragement as his friend's head cleared the bar. Nathan managed two more pull-ups before finally letting go and dropping to the ground.

"Not good enough," Larry said sternly. "Within three months I want you to be doing fifty pull-ups at a time."

Nathan set his jaw at the words. *Fifty? No way I can do that many!*

"One of the things I learned in the army is that pull-ups are just about the best possible upper-body exercise. You build the arm strength to get to fifty pull-ups, and not many kids are going to want to mess with you." Then Larry kneeled and started directly into Nathan's eyes. "I bet you can do it."

"Okay." Nathan smiled, the reassurance fueling a resolve within him. "I'll do my best."

"I know you will, son. Between me and Shiloh, we'll get you in shape."

* * * * * *

His mind brimming with new purpose and drive, Nathan threw himself unreservedly into his new routine. Each day after school, he raced home to change into his shorts and running shoes before meeting up with Shiloh in the backyard. As his father instructed, he began his workout with the pull-up bar, after which, ferrying the ever-present stick, Shiloh took the lead as they raced up the hiking trail to the summit, where the push-ups and the tug-of-war awaited. Then back home to face the pull-up bar once again, followed by a shower and dinner, at which Larry quizzed him about his progress and implored him to do better, the combination of which serving to further strengthen his resolve.

Over the next few months, he rapidly increased the number of completed pull-ups and push-ups, as well as the speed at which he covered the trail. The lanky preteen, always a natural speedster, could feel his endurance escalating and his muscles tightening as he ran up and down the rugged trails. Though he still could not catch his running partner, with every passing week, he felt more fit and more confident, and the combination of push-ups and pull-ups gelled his upper-body strength to the point where he began to win his daily tug-of-war battles.

The daily workouts gave him something to look forward to, something to ease the tedium of middle school and life in his new hometown. He still kept mostly to himself during the days, sitting silently in classes, eating lunch at a cafeteria table by himself. Though he frequently noticed Darlene Tully chatting with her circle of friends in the hallways between classes, he could never find the right time or opportunity, not to mention the courage, to approach her. It would not have been worth the effort; he was convinced that she would never be interested in someone like him. His only real acquaintance was Darrian Lawrence, a tall, energetic classmate who sat next to him in history and social studies. Darrian's good nature and infectious smile made him popular among all the students, but unlike the bullies, he was amiable and convivial with Nathan, though their budding friendship had yet to extend beyond the classroom.

Nathan still occasionally drew the attention of Manogue and his gang. The taunts, the shoves in the school hallways, and the occasional book dumping still occurred, though a little less frequently as the gang turned their attention to other hapless targets. It was always the same—three of them versus one of Nathan, leaving him no ability to defend himself. And each encounter left him angry, humiliated, and longing for the day when he could make it end for good.

* * * * * *

Finally, the day arrived when he hit his magic number: twenty-seven pull-ups before his run and another twenty-five when he returned. After dropping from the bar, he ran excitedly into the house and to his mother, who was stuffing a load of laundry into the washing machine.

"Mom! Where's Dad? I have some great news for him!"

~ 36 ~

"He's still at work. He had to stay late, so he won't be home for another couple of hours."

"That's okay. I'll just go up to the shop and tell him myself."

Nathan dashed to the garage, strapped on his helmet, and pedaled his bike into town, Shiloh, as always, by his side. He rode along Highway 89 through two lights before arriving at the ramshackle body shop that employed his father. He parked his bike in the gravel-strewn lot, and together, he and Shiloh excitedly approached the open bay. But then they stopped abruptly when they heard an angry voice inside the alcove.

"And what exactly do you call these?"

Distressed at the tone, Nathan scurried to the side of the alcove and, along with Shiloh, slid behind an open door to conceal his presence. Gasping from the stench of motor oil, gasoline, and exhaust fumes, he peeked out to see a burly man with a bushy beard facing his father in one of the bays next to an SUV hoisted on a nearby lift. The man was grasping a plastic six-pack yolk, four rings empty, two securing Budweiser cans.

"I don't know what you're talking about," Larry protested.

"Don't lie to me, Wilkinson. I found these in a mini cooler at the bottom of your locker. You sure as hell better not be drinking on the job."

"I'm not! I just keep those for after my shift ends."

The man took a step closer to Larry. "Then why do you smell like a barroom right now? If you're soused when you are working on any of these cars, I could be liable for the damage you cause. It could put me out of business!"

"I haven't—I mean, I won't, not again."

"I should fire you right now. You're more trouble than you're worth."

"Please don't do that!" Larry pleaded. "I need this job. It took me four hours to replace that SUV's transmission, and I was just a little thirsty afterward, that's all. I promise, I won't do it again!"

The man glared at Larry, then scratched his beard. "Since you have a family, I'll look the other way. But just this once. You're on pretty thin ice here, Wilkinson. If I ever catch you with alcohol in my bay again, I'll toss your sorry ass right out of here!"

"Thank you, sir," Larry said meekly. The man turned and stalked off, taking the beer with him into his office.

Still in shock at his father's docility, Nathan and Shiloh cautiously backed away from the door. As Nathan mounted his bike, Shiloh gently placed his paw on his friend's knee.

"I know, boy," Nathan fretted. "I guess I'm not the only one who's getting pushed around here. How I hate this town!"

As he rode home, his brooding transformed into an anger, directed at his father for so risking his job and at the Town of Chino Valley as a whole.

* * * * * *

The next morning, Nathan sat sullenly at the breakfast table, barely speaking to his mother and ignoring his father altogether, the rage still simmering inside him. Larry, having groggily wandered into the kitchen halfway through breakfast, brushed it off as typical teen moodiness, though Sally and Shiloh sensed that something deeper might be at play. After finishing his meal, Nathan scurried from the table, grabbed his backpack, and stalked out the door, not even bothering to say goodbye to his parents.

The classes passed in their customary tedium—history, English, mathematics, science. He ate his lunch alone, ignored Darrian's attempts to engage him in conversation, and brooded through recess and into the afternoon. Finally, the 3:15 bell signaled the end of the school day, and he ran to his bike and peddled home. He dropped his backpack in the living room, got changed in his bedroom, and met Shiloh out in the backyard for his daily workout. As always, Shiloh was full of life and energy, waving the stick in his mouth and daring Nathan to come get it.

Nathan put his pent-up frustration to good use by clearing twenty-nine pull-ups, a new personal best. Then they took off onto the hiking trail, Shiloh setting the pace as usual and Nathan following close behind. The wind blew gently in his face as the bright Arizona afternoon sun glistened in his eyes, and his physical exertion melted away the tension of the previous twenty-four hours. He squinted at the trail ahead as two trekked to the summit where he intended to complete his calisthenics and engage Shiloh in their traditional game of tug-of-war.

He had almost caught up to Shiloh when they entered the summit's clearing. Then the two of them stopped cold at the sound of a reverberating series of blasts.

Standing in the clearing was Tom Manogue, firing a Springfield nine-millimeter semiautomatic handgun at several bottles perched on a nearby tree stump. Startled by the noise behind him, Manogue whirled about to face Nathan and his companion.

"Newbie?" He sneered, lowering his weapon. "What're you doing out here?"

"I'm just going for a run," Nathan said cautiously. Shiloh sensed the tension in Nathan's voice, and glared distrustfully at Manogue.

Manogue gestured toward Shiloh. "This your dog?"

Nathan did not answer. He and Shiloh started toward the trail opening past the summit, but Manogue stepped in front of them. "Where do you think you're going?" he said menacingly.

"Leave us alone," Nathan rumbled, the rage of the last twenty-four hours reigniting inside him. Shiloh let out a low growl and flared his teeth at Manogue.

"Whoa, looks like at least one of you has some guts. What are you looking at, mutt?"

Shiloh growled again, more belligerently. "Easy, boy," Nathan cautioned.

Manogue waved the semiautomatic at them. "This is my dad's nine-millimeter. Sometimes when he's not around I borrow it so I can shoot out here in private." He pointed to the row of bottles. "Usually I just practice on those. But sometimes I look for other things to shoot at."

Then the freckle-faced bully gestured toward Shiloh. "Maybe I just found myself a new target."

"Don't even think about it, Manogue," Nathan snarled.

"Why? What're you gonna do about it? Besides, that mutt's head may look pretty good mounted on my wall."

He stared at Nathan for a moment, then lifted his gun and pointed it at Shiloh.

In an instant, Shiloh leaped at Manogue, his front paws slamming into the boy's chest with the full force of his sixty pounds. Manogue reeled back, dropping the gun and tumbling to the ground.

"Damned dog!" he exclaimed, jumping to his feet and swinging wildly at Shiloh.

Shiloh's selfless courage and Manogue's clumsy attempt to do him harm exploded the rage within Nathan. He propelled himself into Manogue, his right shoulder impacting squarely in his adversary's stomach. The collision drove Manogue backward and again toppled him onto the ground. Before Manogue could react, Nathan curled his fist and punched the bully squarely in the face. Now firmly on top of Manogue, Nathan delivered more wild swings, many missing their target but several connecting. Shiloh moved back, barking loudly at the two.

Stunned by the strength and the fury of Nathan's assault, Manogue could deliver not a single strike; instead he curled into a fetal position as the blows rained down on him.

Nathan raised his fist to strike again but stopped when he felt a tugging at his shirt. Shiloh had firmly clamped his teeth onto the fluttering cloth and gestured at Nathan a single time with his paw, telling him his adversary had had enough.

Nathan lifted himself to his feet. He gazed down at Manogue; blood dripped from the boy's nose, his hair was disheveled, and his shirt was torn in three places. Manogue stood, tears in his eyes, and said not a word as he dashed onto the trail and off toward his home.

For the longest time, Nathan stood silently in the clearing, not quite comprehending what had occurred. His rage had dissipated, and he felt a sensation of pride swelling inside him. He sat down in the dirt next to Shiloh, who stared deeply into his eyes and placed his front paw on Nathan's calf.

"I know boy," Nathan muttered. "I can't believe it either."

Then, he glanced to his right and saw the Springfield nine-millimeter still lying in the dirt. As he reached over to pick it up, Shiloh barked a single time at him.

"Oh, don't give me that. I deserve this, for what that guy put me through."

* * * * * *

Seeing no sign of his parents in his backyard, Nathan approached the toolshed adjacent to the garage, opened the door and peered inside at the aged yard tools and automobile parts his father had been stockpiling to rebuild his 1966 Mustang. Spotting an appropriate hiding place, Nathan concealed the gun behind the rusting wheelbarrow and closed the shed door behind him. As he turned toward the house, he once again observed Shiloh staring pensively at him.

"Will you stop? No one's gonna find it." He waved his hand dismissively at Shiloh and made his way to the house.

"How was your workout?" Sally greeted him as he entered through the screen door.

"Okay, I guess."

"Just okay?" came a voice behind him. Nathan spun around to face his father. Larry eyed him momentarily, noticing the reddened sores on Nathan's hands and knuckles.

"Yeah," Nathan said cautiously. "Why?"

"No reason."

Their eyes meet briefly. Larry remained expressionless but ever so slightly nodded at his son before returning to the living room couch.

* * * * * *

Nathan kept to his routine the next two days, enduring the monotonous class lectures, eating lunch by himself, chatting with Darrian before and after class, heading home for his daily workouts with Shiloh. But he could not help but notice that the general school atmosphere seemed somehow different, less foreboding, more accommodating. And the bullies were nowhere to be found.

At least until the next afternoon when, while riffling through his backpack at his locker, he heard that familiar raspy voice of Travis Roach behind him.

"You got some more Tootsie Rolls for me?"

Slowly Nathan turned around. "No," he responded in a cold but measured tone.

"Well, then maybe you'd better get some, newbie. I'm getting kinda hungry."

Nathan dropped his backpack and took a step toward his pudgy adversary. "My name is Nathan," he snarled.

"I-I'll call you whatever I want," a shocked Travis stammered.

"No, you won't. You won't ever call me that again." Stone-faced, his gaze never deviating from the bully, Nathan took another step toward him, close enough to detect the pungent, smoky odor of the boy's unwashed shirt. But he stopped when he saw a hand clasp Travis's shoulder. Travis pivoted to face Tom Manogue, who sported a cut on his lip and bruises on each side of his face.

"Leave him alone, Travis," Manogue said softly.

"What are you talking about? He's..."

"Don't you have to get to third period?" Manogue snapped.

"Uh, yeah." A befuddled Travis turned away from Nathan and started down the hallway, before stopping momentarily. "Hey, Tom, where you been?"

"I—I fell off my bike near the Exxon station. Hit the pavement face first, so I stayed home the last couple of days."

Travis eyed Manogue's face for a moment. "Must have been a helluva wipeout."

As Travis disappeared toward class, Manogue turned back to the still-defiant Nathan.

"Something you want?" Nathan growled defiantly at him.

"Yeah," Manogue said quietly. "I just wanted to say thanks for not telling anybody about the other day. Most of the other guys here would have told everyone in school."

"No problem." Nathan shrugged, momentarily taken aback by Manogue's honesty.

"You're a lot stronger than I thought you were."

His father's advice from the months past about how to gain the respect of bullies flashed through Nathan's head. "Well, I've been working out a lot."

"I know. I've seen you out on the hiking trail with your dog. What's his name again?"

"Shiloh."

"I also want you to know that I never was gonna shoot him. I was just trying to scare you."

"Thanks for telling me that."

"You know, you're pretty fast. It isn't easy running up and down those trails. I've lived here all my life, and getting up those hills still eats my lunch."

"Yeah, well, it was hard for me at first too, but I think I'm getting used to it."

Manogue glanced down and noticed the Lawrence Taylor sticker affixed to Nathan's notebook. "So, you like football?"

"Yeah. I wish there was an NFL team here in Arizona."

"My dad told me one may be moving to Phoenix soon. You know, I was thinking about trying out for the football team. Why don't you try out too? I bet you'd make it easy. They need receivers, especially someone with your speed and strength."

For a moment, Nathan pondered the ramifications of the suggestion. "Yeah, maybe I will. Thanks for the advice."

"No problem…Nathan."

"Actually, it's just my parents who call me Nathan. My friends back in Arkansas used to call me Nate."

"Sure thing, Nate." Manogue paused as the bell sounded its first alarm. "C'mon. Let's get to third period."

Nathan smiled as he picked up his backpack, and together they headed off through the crowded hallway to their class.

II.2

Mesa, Arizona—October 1990

"Slot right, wing left. We need fourteen yards for the first down. Nate, you're the number one receiver on this play, and I'll be looking for you. Ready? Break!"

The Chino Valley Cougar offense clapped in unison, broke the huddle, and marched to the line of scrimmage. Nathan nodded to his friend and quarterback, junior sensation Darrian Lawrence, and took his position as strong side wide out. He glanced at the scoreboard—forty-five seconds left in the fourth quarter, with the Cougars clinging to a 23–21 lead. One more first down, and they could run out the clock. He lined up across from his adversary, Mesa High's strong safety, who would know from the scouting reports that in this situation Darrian would likely target his most reliable receiver—number eighty-eight, Nathan Wilkinson.

"Set!" Darrian screamed. "Blue forty-eight! Hut, hut!"

The center snapped the ball, and Darrian dropped back into the pocket. Nathan bolted forward, faked a pivot to the sideline and sprinted up field. The all-state six-foot-three-inch two-hundred-pound African American quarterback faded to the right, saw Nathan separate from the cornerback, and fired the ball down field. Nathan snared it as the cornerback buried his shoulder pads into his chest, vaulting him backward into the turf. Nathan heard the whistle, struggled to lift himself up, then proudly showed the ball to the back judge.

"First down, Chino Valley!" the referee cried. Nathan tossed the ball to the ref and trotted back to the forming huddle.

"My man!" Darrian smacked Nathan's helmet. "Mr. Reliable!"

"Way to go, Nate!" shouted the right tackle, Travis Roach. "Now we can run out the clock."

"I'm going to feel that last hit tomorrow."

"Oh, don't be such a wuss," Darrian snickered.

The Mesa defense stood somberly, knowing that they were out of time-outs, while the Chino offense assumed the victory formation and snapped the ball one last time. The rowdy Chino fans counted down the last seconds until the line judge fired his gun, signaling the game's end.

The Chino Valley squad lined up near midfield to shake hands with the opposing players. As Nathan unstrapped his helmet and started toward the sidelines, several teammates approached him, one ahead of all the others.

"Great catch, Nate!" Tom Manogue hollered as he slapped Nathan's back.

"Thanks, Tom. Darrian put it right on the money, as usual. No way was I going to drop it."

"Hey, you!" said a voice behind him. Turning about, he found himself in the embrace of head cheerleader Darlene Tully.

"You were awesome out there!" She embraced him and kissed him firmly on the lips, a speckle of mud from his uniform affixing itself to her outfit.

"Jeez, why don't you two get a room," Tom snorted.

"Later." Darlene giggled. "Right now, you guys need to get over to the team huddle. Coach is calling for you."

In keeping with tradition, the players gathered at the sidelines around the head coach as he gave a brief speech congratulating them on their hard-fought victory. Then, at his direction, they all took a knee for a brief prayer of thanks for the injury-free match. The coach instructed the players to meet at the buses in ten minutes for the ride back to Chino and the awaiting showers.

Tom and Nathan broke from the formation and started across the sparsely lit parking lot toward the buses. Darlene quickly caught up to them, grasping Nathan's hand as they walked together.

"Nathan!" came another voice from the far side of the lot. Nathan turned to see the familiar figures of his parents, Sally taking the lead while Larry lagged, grasping the leash that restrained Nathan's biggest fan. Shiloh whined and tugged against the leash, propelling the two of them forward until Larry finally let go. The shepherd darted across the field and jumped up to his best friend;

Nathan laughed as he tried in vain to curtail the sloppy kisses raining down onto his cheeks.

"Ewww!" Darlene exclaimed, "he should wait until you shower first!"

"Why?" Tom said. "You didn't!"

Hearing Tom's voice, Shiloh momentarily eyed him, a low murmur emanating from his throat. Then the shepherd jumped forward, his paws latching onto Tom's chest as he gave the boy his own kiss on the cheek.

"That's my Shiloh!" Tom laughed as he mussed the shepherd's fur coat.

"Funny how much he loves you now," Nathan remarked.

"That's for sure. We didn't exactly start off on the right foot."

"What does that mean?" Darlene asked.

"Long story," Nathan said, then turned to greet his mother, who had finally caught up to the exuberant Shiloh, while Larry trailed in the background.

"You were great tonight!" Sally beamed as she gave her son a hug. Then she turned to her son's girlfriend. "Darlene, was that a new routine your squad was doing at halftime?"

"Yes, Mrs. Wilkinson. Did you like it?"

"We loved it! I hope you plan on using that at the state competition next month." Then Sally glanced over to see Tom with a look on of anticipation. "Oh, don't worry Tom, I haven't forgotten about your interception!" she said, drawing laughs from the others.

Nathan went over to his father, who stood sullen and forlorn in the background. "Dad, I'm glad you got the time off to come down here for the game. And thanks for bringing Shiloh with you."

"It was a win, at least," Larry muttered. "But you let them stay with you to the end. You should have beaten them by at least two touchdowns."

"C'mon, Dad, a win is a win. What difference does the final score make?"

"And Mesa always plays us tough, Mr. Wilkinson," Tom offered warily. Nathan's friends always seemed more tentative when Larry was around.

"Everyone's going to play you tough. And Nathan, if you hadn't dropped that pass in the third quarter, it wouldn't have been that close."

"You mean that play where Darrian got hit as he threw, and the ball went over Nathan's head?" An annoyed Sally perked up. "He was lucky to even get a hand on it."

"Sounds like an excuse to me. Do better next time."

"Stop being so hard on him."

For a moment, an uncomfortable silence permeated the group; then Larry turned toward the tunnel leading under the stands. "I need to go to the bathroom. Sally, take the dog and meet me at the car. We've got a long drive home."

Sally rolled her eyes as Larry wandered off towards the stands. "Tom, Darlene, give Nathan and me a minute, will you?"

"Sure, Mrs. Wilkinson," Tom said. "Meet you at the bus, Nate."

His father's words still rang in Nathan's ears as he watched Tom and Darlene head off. "Why does he say that stuff to me?"

"He's having a rough time right now. You have to leave him be when he gets in these moods."

"What do you mean, rough time?"

"Well..." Sally paused a moment. "I wasn't sure when I was going to tell you this, but he lost his job this morning."

"He did? What happened?" Nathan sighed in frustration. Shiloh sat down on his hind legs and nuzzled against his friend.

"All the same stuff. He was showing up late, and he kept getting into arguments with his boss and everyone else."

What is this, the third job he's lost since we moved here?"

"That's right."

"So, what are we going to do, Mom?"

"I'm not sure. There are a few body shops in Prescott that your father can apply to, and hopefully they haven't heard about him by now. In the meantime, I've decided that I'm going to look for a job myself."

"Dad's not gonna be happy about that."

"I'm going to talk to him about it when we get home." Sally paused a moment. "I'm sorry I brought this all up. I should have kept my mouth shut. I don't want to spoil your win."

"It's okay. I'm glad you told me. Hey, why don't you let me take Shiloh with me on the bus. You know how much he loves to play with the guys."

"Sure, go ahead. We'll see you when you get home."

Sally hugged Nathan and headed off to the visitor's parking lot. As Nathan made his way toward the bus, he felt a hand on his shoulder.

"Great catch, Nate," Darrian said.

"Thanks, bud. Perfect throw as always. I bet the scouts loved that one."

"Well, you always catch the passes that matter. So, is your alter ego gonna ride with us?" Darrian gestured at Shiloh, who jumped up at him and gave him a kiss under his chin.

"You bet he is."

"Awesome! C'mon Shiloh, I'll race you to the bus!" Darrian took off, with Shiloh close behind, happily yapping and nipping at his heels. Nathan stood for a moment, breathing the crisp autumn air, grinning at the sight, happy for the diversion from his family issues.

* * * * * *

As the team bus trekked north on Interstate 17 toward the Verde Valley, Nathan stretched out in his seat, applying an ice pack to his ribcage. It eased the throbbing pain, though he knew the final shot from Mesa's cornerback would linger for the next few days.

The players were loud and raucous, as they always were when celebrating a victory, especially one over their bitter rivals. They laughed and joked with each other, exchanged high fives, tossed foam footballs back and forth from their seats, and shared bottles of Gatorade to toast their victory.

The players also took turns playing with the team's unofficial mascot. A regular presence on the Chino team bus, Shiloh scampered up and down the center aisle, fetching the foam balls Darrian threw and engaging the players in his favored tug-of-wars and keep-away games. The happy students petted and teased him, some scratching his underside or behind his ear, and Shiloh reveled in the attention.

After the bus arrived at their high school's parking lot, the players retreated to the locker room to shower and change. Still exuberant from the victory, Nathan, Darrian, Tom, and Darlene trekked to the local Dairy Queen to celebrate with Cokes and ice cream. Shiloh sat next to Nathan by the bench seats lining the store's courtyard, eyeing the cone in his hand, ready to intercept the occasional stray drip of melting ice cream. At one point, Nathan held the cone in front of Shiloh, and, transfixed by the proximity of the delicious treat, Shiloh remained frozen as Nathan brushed it against his snout. Darlene giggled in delight as Shiloh frantically lapped the milky substance off his nose.

After finishing their dessert, Darlene whispered in Nathan's ear that she could sneak him into her house and room, as her parents were likely already asleep. Nathan grinned at the thought and of the times before when they had celebrated the team's victory in their own way. But this time he declined; he was tired, and his ribcage still throbbed; he needed to get home to rest. He kissed her goodnight and gave a pat on the shoulder to Tom and a fist bump to Darrian before he and Shiloh set forth for their short walk home.

The full moon lit up the clear sky, illuminating the dusty residential road ahead of them. The temperature had dropped precipitously, and to escape the gathering chill they quickened their pace through the streets of their subdivision. When they arrived home, Nathan made his way around the side toward the back door, but he stopped abruptly near the porch when saw two silhouetted figures through the window inside in the family room facing each other.

"No! And that's final!" he heard his father shout.

"We don't have a choice. We need the money!" his mother retorted. At the sound of the agitated voices, Shiloh glanced pensively at Nathan.

"If you get a job, that tells everyone that I can't provide for my family."

"Don't be ridiculous. Wives work all the time."

"Well, mine doesn't."

Sally sharpened her tone. "Larry, it could be months before you find work again. We can't afford to wait that long. So, I'm not asking for your permission. First thing Monday morning I'm going to start looking for a job."

"The hell you are!"

"You can't tell me what to do! And maybe, just maybe, if you could actually keep a job for more than a few months, I wouldn't have to do this!"

"I-I told you it wasn't my fault I got fired!" Larry stammered. "That idiot foreman always had it out for me."

"There you go again, blaming others for your own problems. Just stop it now. Every time you lose your job, you let all of us down, and you put the whole family at risk. Someone has to take care of this family, and since you obviously can't, it might as well be me. You've been nothing but a failure at everything you've ever done!"

Anger galvanizing from her comments, Larry raised his hand menacingly toward Sally. She stepped back abruptly. For the longest moment, Larry held his hand in the air as if it had been frozen in place.

"Fine," he finally said. "You do whatever you want." He dropped his hand and turned toward the door.

"Where are you going?" she demanded.

"To Murio's, as if you care."

Nathan stepped back toward the toolshed. "Shiloh, come here, boy!" he whispered. The shepherd joined him, and they both crouched behind the shelter.

He peeked through a crack in the siding to see Larry storm out the back door and to the family Oldsmobile. The engine roared to life; Larry slammed it into gear and bolted out of the driveway.

After the car had disappeared, Nathan and Shiloh emerged from behind the shed and made their way to the door. Nathan stepped inside to see his mother sitting on the living room couch.

"I hope you didn't see any of that," she said, dabbing a tissue at her eyes.

Saying nothing, he extended his arms and engaged her in a warm embrace.

* * * * * *

After ensuring that his mother was all right, both physically and emotionally, Nathan finally retired to his bedroom. Exhausted from the game, the long bus ride home, the celebration with his friends and the traumatic events at home, he dropped onto his bed without even taking the time to undress and immediately fell into a deep sleep. Shiloh curled up in his usual spot at the foot of the bed, laid his head down, and drifted off as well.

Shiloh's dreams began as always, set in the open meadow filled with rich smells, fresh water, tasty food, endless hills and the magnificent golden bridge in the distance. The sun shone brightly, a gentle wind swayed the branches of the oak and magnolia trees, and Shiloh could hear the playful yipping from the hundreds of dogs galloping through the rich landscape. He loved returning in his dreams to this paradise, where he would meet up with his friends, the black miniature schnauzer, the Belgian Malinois, and the black and blond Labrador brother and sister; together they would scamper through the meadow on their unending journey of exploration and discovery.

But tonight was different. As he and his friends bounded alongside the meadow's glistening creek, he heard a distinctive bark, soft at first and then louder and more urgent. He stopped and pivoted toward the sound, seeing a statuesque black-and-white border-beagle mix behind him. The border-beagle seemed familiar; its eyes sparkled with a bright-white light, and Shiloh could see neither irises nor pupils. The visitor barked again at him, in a tone of increasing intensity and distress, telling Shiloh he shouldn't be in this dream, that he was needed back in his world.

Shiloh bolted up, shook himself and checked to see if he had disturbed his companion. Lost in his deep slumber, Nathan remained unmoving.

Shiloh glanced about and was startled to see the border-beagle mix from his dream standing in front of the door in the darkened room. He was translucent; a glow illuminated his fur and his eyes continued to sparkle. He was like no other dog Shiloh had ever encountered.

The border beagle barked at him again, a sound that Shiloh somehow knew only he could hear, then scampered out the door and down the hallway. Shiloh leaped off the bed in pursuit, crawled through the dog door into the moonlight-illuminated backyard, and saw the visitor in front of the toolshed, staring intently inside.

Tentatively Shiloh approached the shed, but when he came within a few feet of the visitor, he faded away, leaving Shiloh alone in front of the open door.

Shiloh peered inside the darkened shed, observing a figure sitting at the tool bench, back facing the door. Cautiously the shepherd entered the shed and approached the figure, who, upon hearing the ruffling of paws on the dirt floor, pivoted to face him. The figure reeked from the stench of dried beer and bourbon, and Shiloh whined softly in recognition.

"Shiloh?" Larry said quizzically, his brain foggy from the alcohol. Shiloh yipped in acknowledgment.

"What are you doing here? Nathan, are you there too?" Larry squinted at the doorway but saw no sign of his son. Then he turned back to Shiloh.

"Why don't you go back inside and leave me alone?"

Shiloh returned a stare that informed Larry he wasn't going anywhere.

"Okay." Larry sighed. "Suit yourself. It's not like anyone else around here listens to me either."

Larry lowered his head and kicked at the dirt floor. "A failure," he murmured. "She called me...a failure." A teardrop glistened in his eye.

"She's right. That's what I am. A failure. I can't keep a job, I drink too much, I can't take care of my family, and nobody around here gives a damn about me." The tears began to trickle down his cheeks. "Sally, Nate, even you...all of you are better off without me."

He buried his head in his hands; for the longest time, only his sobs broke the silence of the evening air. Then Larry raised his head and faced Shiloh again. "Now, go on, I mean it, get out of here. I want to be by myself."

Shiloh stared quizzically at him and followed Larry's eyes downward as they both gazed at the object in his right hand, its shiny surface glistening in the moonlight.

It was Tom Manogue's gun.

* * * * * *

Though Shiloh did not comprehend the purpose of the object, he sensed from his memories of the last time he had seen it that it was not benign. The two figures, canine and human, remained fixated, peering silently at each other.

"I said, get lost!" Larry bellowed. Shiloh did not budge. "Why can't you leave me alone? I want to do this—I'll be doing everyone a favor!"

Larry lifted the gun and pointed the barrel toward his head.

Shiloh let out a loud whimper, then stepped forward, raised his front paw and touched Larry on the chest.

"No!" Larry pushed the paw away. "Just let me get this over with!"

Shiloh again caressed Larry's torso with his paw. He whimpered louder, pleading with the older man in his own unique language.

Then Shiloh placed one of his front paws on each of Larry's shoulders, and drew in his head until their noses were within millimeters of each other. He stared into Larry's eyes for a moment, his deep gaze touching the troubled man's soul. Then he gave Larry a kiss on the cheek. Then another. And another after that.

The gesture shocked Larry; it was the first time in his memory the dog had ever shown any affection toward him. As he felt the warm kisses, a sense of contentment enveloped him, a satisfaction felt when a person realizes that his life matters and he is genuinely loved.

Larry dropped the gun onto the dirt floor behind him, then reached over and scratched Shiloh under the chin, the same place he had seen Nathan do so many times before. Shiloh whimpered at the display of affection.

"Thank you, boy," he said softly, tears streaming down his face.

* * * * * *

"Dad?"

Larry glanced up toward the shadowy figure of his son at the entrance to the shed.

"You okay?" Nathan asked.

"Yeah," Larry lifted his arm to conceal the moisture on his cheeks. "I-I just wanted to sit out here for a while. Was by myself, but Shiloh decided to keep me company."

Nathan glanced in puzzlement at Shiloh, who remained nestled against Larry. Then he detected the unmistakable odor on his father's breath and body. "You've been drinking."

"Yes," Larry admitted. "I had a little more than I should have tonight. But I won't do it again. I promise I'm going to get it under control."

"Whatever you say," Nathan said dismissively. "C'mon, let's get you up and into the house." Shiloh hopped up, and Nathan grasped his father around his waist and lifted him to his feet.

"I'm okay," Larry sputtered. "I can make it by myself."

"I don't think so. Let me help." Slowly he guided Larry toward the shed's entrance. Shiloh waited while the two figures made their way into the backyard, and when they were out of sight, the shepherd used his snout to nudge the gun back to its hiding place behind the wheelbarrow. Then he raced out of the shed to catch up with Nathan and Larry.

Ribcage throbbing from the exertion and stomach gurgling from the stench of the dried alcohol, Nathan finally succeeded in steering his father through the back door and into the house. But rather than continuing down the hallway toward his parents' bedroom, he and Shiloh guided him into the living room and set him down onto the couch.

"I don't want you to disturb Mom. Just stay here and sleep it off."

"S-Son..."

Nathan pivoted toward his own bedroom. "Save it, Dad. C'mon, Shiloh, let's go back to bed." The shepherd remained unmoving in the living room.

"I said, let's go!"

Shiloh turned away from him, sat down on his hind legs, and placed his head on Larry's outstretched arm.

"Fine," Nathan snapped. "You want to stay with him, you go right ahead. But I'm tired of his lectures about how I have to do better, how second place isn't good enough, when he can't even stay sober or keep a job. So, you just hang with your pal here. I'm going back to bed." Refusing to acknowledge his father, Nathan turned and, in a huff, marched off to his bedroom.

As the door to the bedroom slammed, a hand caressed Shiloh's head; the shepherd felt the warmth and intensity of the older man's gratitude.

Larry leaned back on the couch, closed his eyes, and within moments was fast asleep. Shiloh lay down at the foot of the couch, nestling himself on a corner of the carpet. He started to close his eyes but bolted upright when he once again saw the border-beagle mix, sitting at the entrance to the living room. Its sparkling eyes shone directly at Shiloh, and after a moment of silence, it yipped a single time, before slowly fading away.

II.3

Chino Valley, Arizona—June 1992

"It feels funny," Nathan mused to his best friend, as he sat in his nearly empty bedroom taping the last cardboard box filled with his possessions. "For the longest time I couldn't wait to get out of Chino Valley. But now that I'm finally going, I think I may actually miss this place." Lying on the bed next to Nathan, Shiloh stirred affectionately and gently swiped his paw at him.

Nathan surveyed the shelves and drawers a final time. He couldn't take all his possessions with him; his dorm room would only provide space for the barest of essentials. Left on the shelves were his favored soldier figurines, his folded letter sweater, and his newly minted high school diploma.

He glanced at the pile of papers spread across the compact wooden desk in the corner. Sitting on top was the letter from the University of New Mexico ROTC program, congratulating him on his admission.

"Tell me I'm doing the right thing, buddy," he said to Shiloh.

"Are you finished yet?" his mother called from the living room.

"Almost—packing the last box now."

Nathan turned to Shiloh, who lingered on the bed staring at him, a pained expression lining his withered face.

"As excited as I am about going off to college, the one thing about this place that I'm going to miss the most is you."

He reached over to Shiloh and scratched the shepherd's favorite spot under his chin. "You've been my best friend since the day we brought you home. I don't know how I would have made it here without having you by my side." He wrapped his arms around Shiloh and inhaled the deep musty smell of the shepherd's fur. Shiloh whined sadly and kissed him on the cheek.

"I promise I'll be back at Christmas, spring break, and summer."

He picked up the box and carried it out to the front door to the driveway, Shiloh following close behind, to Darrian Lawrence's rusty green Oldsmobile. Sally was handing Darrian a bag of snacks while Larry was checking under the hood.

"Oil pressure is fine, and I just changed out a couple of spark plugs," he said to Darrian.

"Thanks, Mr. Wilkinson."

Larry backed away from the hood and turned to face the tall, sturdy, African American teenager. "Darrian, I've been meaning to tell you that we're all proud of you for choosing Arizona State to play football."

"With all the scholarship offers you got," Sally added, "you could have played anywhere you wanted."

"It was a no-brainer," Darrian said. "ASU is a great program, and I wanted to be near my family. And my friends." He reached out and clasped Nathan's shoulder blade. "I'm not playing anywhere without my number one receiver."

"I don't know how to thank you, Darrian," Nathan said. "I wouldn't have gotten my scholarship to ASU without you vouching for me."

"I'm just glad I could help out. And I'm glad you're coming with me, even if it means turning down that ROTC scholarship."

"Well, I certainly think you made the right decision," Larry said.

"You promise you're not disappointed that I'm not going into the army?" Nathan had to ask, once more. Though Larry had been a changed man this past year and a half, Nathan's stomach still fluttered with nerves sometimes, as he feared the return of angry, irrational Larry. But yet again, Larry impressed him.

"If I had the choice between the army and playing for one of the top college teams in the country, I'd choose football too. Like Darrian says, it's a no-brainer. Now you make sure to work your butt off there and make Darrian look good."

"I'll make sure of that." Darrian laughed. Larry strolled off to return his tools to the shed. Sally heard the kitchen phone ringing and dashed inside to answer it.

"Your dad sure seems different now," Darrian mused as the two boys set Nathan's boxes in the car's already cluttered back seat. "I remember how scared of him I used to be."

"He's like a totally different guy," Nathan agreed. "He shows up every day on time to his new job and stays late sometimes, even when he doesn't have to. He told Mom he was proud of her when she got her job at town hall. He's even cut way back on his drinking. I can't even remember the last time I saw him with a beer."

"That's great. I remember seeing him at games after he'd had a few. Wasn't fun to be around."

"You have no idea," Nathan observed. He paused to pet Shiloh, who was still sitting by his side. "I don't know what caused him to change, but I'm sure glad it happened."

A moment later, Sally emerged from the house. "That was Tom Manogue's mother. He left a few minutes ago and will meet you two in Mesa."

Nathan's father reemerged from the shed and shut the hood of Darrian's car. "You guys should be good to go now."

"You'll give us a call as soon as you get to campus, right?" Sally asked, her voice shaking.

"It's only a two-hour drive. We've all made it a hundred times before."

"I don't care. I won't stop worrying until you call me."

"Okay, Mom."

She embraced Nathan first, then Darrian.

"Good luck, son."

Nathan and Darrian took turns grasping Larry's outstretched hand. Shiloh whined softly as he watched the unfolding scene.

"You guys are going to take good care of Shiloh, right?" Nathan asked.

"Of course," Larry assured him.

"I mean it! He needs to be fed twice a day, right after you get up in the morning and just before dinnertime."

"He'll be right here waiting for you when you get home. Don't worry about a thing."

"If you say so."

Nathan kneeled to face Shiloh. "And you," he said. "You're the greatest dog a guy could ever have. I so wish I could take you with me. But you'll always be right here." He pointed to his chest, and Shiloh whimpered again. Nathan embraced the shepherd, a teardrop falling to the asphalt driveway.

A moment later, he reluctantly let go and stood up. Darrian ruffled Shiloh's fur a final time, and the two friends took their seats inside the car. Darrian started the engine and backed out of the driveway. As they pulled away, Nathan saw in the side rearview mirror his beloved shepherd still sitting in the driveway. Then Shiloh leaped to his feet and moved toward the car, only to be restrained by Larry's grip around his collar. Shiloh whined and tugged but could not break free. More tears welled in Nathan's eyes as he looked away from the rearview mirror and focused on the street ahead of him.

As the car disappeared around the corner, a dejected Shiloh sat down on the driveway and whimpered again. Larry leaned over and stroked the top of his head.

"I'm sorry, boy. I know you're going to miss him. We all will. But it'll be okay, I promise."

II.4

Tempe, Arizona—March 1994

College was overwhelming, as challenging as Nathan had anticipated. Unlike some on the football team, he took his classes seriously, striving to attend all lectures and complete his assignments on time. This effort was compounded by the intensity of the commitment required to participate in a Division I football program, not to mention the unfamiliarity of living on his own for the first time.

Nathan struggled to balance the combination of classwork, two-a-day preseason workouts, constant team meetings, daily practices, game day participation, and off-season weight training. While Darrian's influence had secured him a spot on the team, there were far better receivers, and he spent his freshman year on the practice squad. But his hard work and dedication impressed both coaches and fellow players, and in Nathan's sophomore year, the head coach promoted him to the regular squad. Though not yet a starter, he did secure limited playing time in every game, usually as the third receiver on passing downs. And Darrian, who as expected had become the team's star quarterback, always looked Nathan's way during these downs, and usually targeted him when he was open.

In an event Nathan could not have foreseen a few years earlier, he chose to share a dorm room with fellow Chino Valley High School graduate Tom Manogue. Tom was a source of comfort and familiarity, certainly preferable to being randomly assigned a stranger as roommate. He had hung up his cleats after high school, but on those autumn Saturday afternoons, no one cheered louder for Nathan, Darrian, and the rest of the team at Sun Devil Stadium.

Consumed by his new responsibilities, Nathan inevitably began to neglect his old life back home. He tried to maintain his relationship with Darlene, who had remained in Chino Valley. At first, she would drive down to Tempe for the occasional weekend get-together. But he had little time for her, especially during football season, and she increasingly resented his lack of availability. She visited less frequently as the challenges inherent in their long-distance relationship took their toll. The two eventually drifted apart, and by his sophomore year, both had moved on.

Nathan also found little time to journey back to Chino Valley to see his parents. Such visits were out of the question during football season. Unfortunately, in his first two years, the Sun Devils finished with losing records, and with no hope of earning a bowl invitation, the season was over by mid-November. This allowed Nathan to spend Thanksgiving, Christmas, and a few scattered winter weekends with his parents before springtime practice began.

The schoolwork, the football team, the campus social scene...like many college students caught up in the whirlwind of a new life of freedom and responsibility, getting back home to see the family became less of a priority. And he gave less and less thought to the impact it would have on all those who loved and missed him.

* * * * * *

"It's good to hear from you, Nathan. It's been a while!" Sally said into the receiver, her tone reflecting annoyance at not having heard from her son in two months.

"Is Dad around?" an oblivious Nathan responded. "I've got some great news for the both of you!"

"He's out in the backyard. Let me go get him." Sally placed the receiver on the kitchen table and stepped out onto the back porch, shielding her eyes from the bright springtime morning sun. Larry had just heaved the rubber ball, and Shiloh was tearing across the yard in pursuit. He laughed heartily as the shepherd snapped at the bouncing ball with his teeth, striking it with his snout, sending it careering further away. Shiloh growled playfully as he finally secured it and trotted back to Larry, prize in hand.

"There's my guy!" Larry exclaimed. "Never give up—that's the spirit!"

"Larry, Nathan's on the phone!" Sally called out to him. Shiloh's ears perked up at the name; he whined softly at Larry and dropped the ball.

"C'mon, boy!" Larry scurried to the back door, Shiloh flanking him, and once they were inside, Sally pressed the speaker button on the cordless phone as the two sat down at the kitchen table, Shiloh flopping down on the kitchen floor by Larry's feet.

"I've got some great news!" Nathan exclaimed. Shiloh whined again, more excitedly this time, when he heard Nathan's voice.

"After practice today, Coach called me into his office and said he's promoting me to number three receiver on the starting team! It means I'm going to get a lot more reps with Darrian in practice and a lot more playing time this season."

"That's great, honey!" his mother said.

"You should be very proud of yourself," Larry added.

"But it also means that Coach is going to want me to stay in Tempe all summer."

"So, you're not coming home at all?" Sally asked.

"Coach says that first team is a 24-7 commitment. There won't be time for anything else—no vacations, no weekends off, no nothing. I have no idea how I'm going to balance this with my classwork, but at least I don't have to worry about that until this fall."

"It's great that you are going to be starting, but it's…I mean, it's just that…"

"It's what?"

"We would have liked to have seen you, that's all."

"I know, and I'm sorry. But I can't pass up this opportunity. At least you can come to some of our home games."

"Sure, son," Larry chimed in. "We'll definitely be there."

"That's great. Listen, I gotta go. Tom and I are going to go grab a bite to eat to celebrate. But I promise I'll call you every week. Talk to you later, bye!"

Perturbed at the abrupt ending to their call, Sally hung up the phone and turned to her husband. "What do you think?"

"It is a great opportunity," Larry conceded. "But it's hard to believe he won't get at least a little time off, enough to come home for a few days."

"He's twenty years old now. Maybe visiting with his parents isn't what he wants to do."

Larry looked down at Shiloh, who whimpered as he lay sullenly beside them. "I know that, but it's not just his parents who want to see him."

* * * * * *

The team's hard work, long hours and single-minded commitment throughout the summer paid off, as the Sun Devils' 1994 season began with victories over San Diego State, Oregon State, and Utah. As the season progressed, the team piled up more wins, though they did suffer losses to formidable rivals Stanford and Michigan State. But for the first time in many years, they finished the regular season with a winning record.

Though still ranked as the third receiver, Nathan earned more playing time, logging six catches in the first three games. However, Darrian was the true catalyst for the team's fortunes. His precision passing, remarkable proficiency at anticipating defenses, and overall athletic prowess made him the most feared quarterback in the conference, and a sure bet to progress to the National Football League. As good as his word, he searched for Nathan whenever he could on passing downs, though the number one and two receivers were usually more inviting targets.

Sally and Larry attended several of Nathan's home games, thanks to Tom Manogue securing the suddenly in-demand tickets to Sun Devil Stadium. They took great pride in watching their son, and the raucous crowd, giddy at the first winning season in ages, contributed all that much more to the experience. The games ended by late afternoon, sometimes leaving them time to take their son to dinner before leaving for home.

During those game days, Shiloh stayed at home, parked either in his portable bed or on the couch. Yet no matter how late it was in the day, when he heard the car roll into the driveway, he leapt up and barked his greeting. And every time Larry and Sally emerged in the doorway, Shiloh would scan for any sign of his beloved Nathan, only to suffer the inevitable disappointment.

Nathan was always in Shiloh's thoughts, his love for and devotion to his lifelong friend never abating. But as month after month passed by without Nathan coming home to visit, it served only to fuel within the shepherd a cruel combination of sadness, despair, and fear of abandonment. A despair that would make the coming events all that much more difficult to endure.

II.5

Chino Valley, Arizona—January 1995

"Sally!" Larry's voice boomed through the kitchen. "He won't eat again."

Larry stood behind Shiloh, watching the shepherd sniff, then turn away from the half-filled dinner dish.

"C'mon, boy," Larry said, "you need to eat this. It'll be good for you."

Shiloh again momentarily pondered the food dish, glanced up at Larry, and then lay down on the linoleum floor.

"I even put some of that leftover meat loaf into the mix," Larry said to Sally, "but he still won't touch it."

"This has been going on way too long now. I think he's starting to look thinner."

"He is. And the last few times we've been outside playing catch, he hasn't seemed like he's had nearly as much energy."

"Something isn't right. We need to take him to the vet. But I'm working all day tomorrow."

"That's okay. I get off at four. I'll take him."

"Look at you," Sally grinned at her husband, touched by his concern. She reached down to stroke Shiloh under the chin. "Don't you worry about a thing, boy. Grampa will take good care of you."

* * * * * *

"Okay, Larry, I've got some news for you, and it's not very good," Dr.

Grittman began as Larry sat facing him across the veterinarian's office desk. Disinfectant and odor neutralizers emanated from the adjoining examination room, and occasional yips from the boarded canines echoed through the office. Grittman leaned his corpulent body back in his swivel chair, causing it to creak loudly in protest. Shiloh lay obediently at Larry's feet.

"I suspected this from the beginning, with his increasing loss of appetite and his general lethargy," Grittman continued. "The X-rays confirmed it."

"Confirmed what?" Larry asked, his stomach tightening.

"There's a tumor behind Shiloh's left shoulder blade. It's an early form of lymphoma, and it's affecting his prescapular lymph node. It's metastasizing at a pretty alarming rate."

"I'm not sure what all that means, but it sounds pretty bad."

The chair squealed again as Dr. Grittman rose and leaned over Shiloh, using his pen to point to a clump of hair behind the shepherd's left shoulder. "The prescapular lymph node is right about here, and that's where the tumor is. Right now, it's the size of a grape, but, like I said, it's getting bigger every week. For what it's worth, it's a good thing we discovered it now. Had it even been a month later, it might have been too late for us to do anything."

"Is it causing him any pain?"

"Some," Grittman acknowledged as he parked himself again in his desk chair. "It's not that bad yet, probably only a twitch every time he moves. But it's going to get worse the larger the tumor gets."

"So, what can we do?"

"I think I can remove it surgically, but I'll have to put him under a general anesthetic. The procedure will last three to four hours, and I'll need to keep him here in recovery for a couple of days. The best-case outcome is that I get all of the tumor, so he won't need to undergo chemotherapy. But even then, it's going to take Shiloh at least two months to return to good health. That's going to be hard on you as well as him because you are going to have to work with him every day, helping him exercise and making sure he eats and gets his rest."

The veterinarian paused a moment and let out a deep breath. "There's one other thing I need to tell you. I'm afraid that the procedure's going to cost $3,000."

"$3,000?" Larry sputtered.

Dr. Grittman leaned back, the chair squeaking again from the stress of his portly body. "Listen, Larry, we've known each other a long time. So, I'm going to put something out there for you to consider. Shiloh is eleven years old now. He's had a pretty good life, but once shepherds get into the double digits, their bodies start to lose the capacity to cope with such a major procedure.

"I gave you the best-case scenario, but that's not the only potential outcome. I can't guarantee that Shiloh will even survive the surgery or will ever fully recover. In fact, there's even the possibility that his body reacts poorly to the surgery or the cancer returns in some other form. We may go through all of this, and in the end, it doesn't even make much of a difference."

Larry sat silently, still trying to process the stunning news.

"Maybe," the doctor continued, "just maybe, you should think about whether you want to do this."

"What do you mean?"

"Well, maybe he's no longer worth the expense. Three thousand dollars is a lot of money, and I know things are still pretty tight for you and Sally. You probably have a lot of other needs for that money. So maybe instead of paying for an eleven-year-old dog to undergo a risky surgery, you should let me...put him down."

Larry glanced down at Shiloh, who remained at his side, tongue hanging and breathing slightly labored. "Ron, I appreciate your concern about my... situation. I know you mean well, but to you, Shiloh is just another patient.

"He's more than that to me. He's something special. At the lowest point in my life, he was there to save me. He came through for me when I needed him, and I can't say that about many of the people in my life. So, I sure as hell am not going to turn away from him now that he needs me.

"Don't worry about the money; I'll find some way to come up with it. And while I'm grateful that you're being candid with me about the risks, all I know is that I wouldn't be able to live with myself if I didn't at least try to help him."

"Are you sure about this?"

"I've never been more sure about anything in my life."

"Okay, then. It's your decision. I'm going to need you to fill out some paperwork, so we can schedule the surgery." Dr. Grittman reached behind his desk into a metal filing cabinet and grabbed a handful of forms. "By the way," he said as he shuffled through the documents, "how's that son of yours doing these days?"

"He's fine. But he has a lot of responsibilities, between the football program and his classwork. We hardly get to see him anymore, just a few days at Christmas. He's under enough stress right now, so I'm not so sure I want him to know about this."

"I understand, but for what it's worth, I think you ought to tell him. After all, Shiloh is Nathan's dog too."

"Well, he would be if he came home to see him more."

And at the sound of Nathan's name, Shiloh let out a soft, sad whine.

* * * * * *

Shiloh underwent surgery two weeks later, and to everyone's relief, the initial results were encouraging. Dr. Grittman was able to extract the entire tumor, and he found no immediate sign that the cancer had spread. However, the veterinarian expressed concern to Sally and Larry about how Shiloh reacted to the anesthesia, particularly the unusual length of time it took for him to regain consciousness. He also noted that, due to the very nature of lymphatic cancer, it could quickly metastasize in another lymph node. He again warned them that the recovery process from such a stressful surgery would be difficult and dangerous, especially for a dog of Shiloh's advancing years.

Larry spent the next few evenings after work at the clinic, keeping Shiloh company. On the following Monday, they brought him home, leading him into the living room where they set him in his bed and tried to make him as comfortable as possible. But Shiloh did not have much energy, and even his basic movements like climbing onto the couch were slow and tentative.

Each morning Larry took Shiloh for a brief walk around the block, after which he fed him the daily dose of pain medicine, wrapped in a strip of raw bacon. In the evenings, Larry boosted Shiloh onto the couch so they could watch television together, and at night, he covered the shepherd in a blanket as he curled up at the foot of their bed.

It moved Sally to see her husband dedicate himself so tirelessly to their pet.

And his efforts paid off; as spring faded into summer, Shiloh began to rally, regaining his energy and vigor. The outdoor games of catch resumed, and normalcy once again manifested itself over the Wilkinson household.

* * * * * *

But it was a new normalcy, one that incorporated Nathan's continued absence. The successful 1994 season had only elevated ASU's expectations for 1995. The coaches implemented an even more rigorous off-season workout schedule, matched with lengthy team meetings and physically exhaustive springtime workouts. It left Nathan little time for classes and even less for family, though the prospect of playing for a true contender only strengthened his resolve and enthusiasm.

The Sun Devils began the 1995 season with five straight victories, four by decisive margins. Darrian played with his trademark efficiency, throwing eleven touchdown passes, three to Nathan, with only two interceptions. After a heartbreaking loss to Notre Dame, the team won four of their last six games to finish with an impressive 9–3 record.

It should have made for the happiest of times for Larry and Sally, to watch Nathan conclude his senior season on such a successful note. But as is so often the case, fate and providence intervened with plans of their own.

* * * * * *

"How did he do?" Sally asked as Larry stepped inside the house. He closed the door behind him to keep out the chilly early evening autumn air and unbuckled the leash from Shiloh's collar.

"Not so good. He started coughing right about when we reached the Lannings' house, so I had to turn around."

"He only got to the Lannings? Just last week, when I took him out, he made it all the way around the block."

"Yeah, I know." Larry unzipped his coat and brushed his hands over his chest to warm himself up. "Yesterday I tried to get him to chase after his ball, but he wasn't interested in that either. How did he do with his dinner?"

"He didn't touch it."

Larry exhaled and sank dejectedly onto a chair at the kitchen table. Shiloh lay down next to his feet.

"You know what this means, don't you?" Sally asked tentatively.

"Yeah. We always knew the cancer might come back. I—I just hoped it wouldn't be this quick."

"We should take him back to Dr. Grittman."

"What's the point?" Larry bushed his hand against his face; Sally could see the moisture gleaming under his eyelids. She placed her hand tenderly on his shoulder.

"You did what you could. And you gave him another year to be with us."

"It should have been longer." For a moment, they remained silent, as Larry caressed Shiloh's head.

"Let me be the one to tell Nathan," Sally finally said. "It's time he knew everything." Larry pondered the words a moment and then nodded his approval.

She picked up the phone and tapped the number to the Tempe apartment Nathan shared with Tom Manogue.

"Mom!" came the sound of her son's voice in the receiver. "I was just getting ready to call you."

"Then it's good that I called you now. Listen, there's something—"

"You're not going to believe this," Nathan interrupted. "We got word this morning that we've been invited to play Boston College in the Aloha Bowl! It's ASU's first bowl invitation in over a decade!"

"Really?" Sally shot her husband a look.

"Yeah," Nathan stood in his bedroom, holding the phone in one hand while he struggled to button his shirt with the other. "This game could put our program on the map, especially if we can beat a team as good as Boston College. It's going to be televised nationally on Christmas Day."

"Christmas Day?"

"That's right. I just got out of a team meeting, and Coach told us that we're going to have to start ramping up for the game right away. We're the heavy underdogs, and the only way we beat BC is to outwork them. We'll be practicing right through Thanksgiving week, and we're going spend the two weeks before the game in Hawaii getting used to the climate."

"That all sounds great," Sally said hesitantly.

"Is something wrong?"

"I-It's just that your father and I were looking forward to having you home for Thanksgiving and Christmas."

"I know. I'm sorry; I won't have time to come home until after the game. But this is such a great opportunity for us, and also for Darrian. He'll have the whole country watching him, and all the publicity will improve his standing in the draft."

"Well, that's true, but…"

"Aww, no buts, Mom. You know that I'd love to come home and see you and Dad, but I won't be able to until after the game. We can have our Christmas then."

"I understand," she said through clenched teeth as she closed her fists in frustration.

"Thanks. So, why did you call anyway?"

Sally paused a moment. "No reason. We just wanted to hear the sound of your voice."

"Well, thanks for that. Listen, I gotta go. Tell Dad I said hi. Love you, bye!" He hung up the phone, glanced around his bedroom for his trousers, then saw Tom standing in the doorway.

"You even had me convinced you wanted to go home." Tom laughed.

"Are you kidding? I'd rather spend Christmas at the North Pole than back in Chino Valley."

"C'mon, finish getting dressed. We're going to be late."

"What does it matter? All the girls know that the party doesn't start until we get there."

* * * * * *

"So, you heard it all?" Sally asked her husband as she hung up the phone.

Larry nodded as he continued to stroke Shiloh. "Why didn't you tell him?"

"Because I don't want him to be distracted. He needs to focus on the game."

"I bet he wouldn't have been. From what I heard of your conversation, he didn't even bother to ask about Shiloh."

Shiloh gazed at Larry for a moment, then lowered his head, letting out an audible sigh.

"I'm sorry, boy," Larry said, running his hand again across the shepherd's tan-and-black double-coat. In his mind, he added up the days until the game; he felt a twinge of apprehension at the realization that it was six full weeks. "But hang tough; he'll be home soon enough."

II.6

Honolulu, Hawaii—December 1994

"Damn!" Larry shouted at the television as he watched the Boston College running back break away from the ASU defense and gallop twenty-five yards into the end zone. The Aloha Stadium crowd roared, expressing their clear preference for the more popular Eagles over the upstart Sun Devils.

From the outset, the Aloha Bowl had been a raucous offense-based duel, with the lead changing four times over the first three quarters. Darrian was brilliant, throwing three touchdown passes and rushing for another. But the Eagles' offense proved just as formidable, and the latest touchdown gave Boston College a four-point lead as the seconds ticked away in the final quarter.

Larry sat riveted on his couch as the ABC broadcast flickered on the aging solid-state television. He tenderly stroked the dozing Shiloh, who lay at his side, his breathing noticeably labored.

It was Christmas evening in Chino Valley, a day the Wilkinsons had spent in eager anticipation for the upcoming bowl matchup. Larry burst with pride when he saw his son, number eighty-eight, take the field as the third receiver on passing downs. But most of Darrian's passes had been to his running back or to the number one and two receivers; thus far, Nathan had only been targeted twice.

"Only a minute and a half left..." Sally muttered. She was perched on the chair flanking the couch next to the decorated Christmas tree, her arms folded over her legs to cope with the stress.

"There's still time for one last drive, but it's not going to be easy," Larry said. "Darrian and the offense have to come through."

"I wish we could be there."

"Me too." Larry sighed. He knew his wife wasn't complaining, but her unrealized desire still stung. He hated that they couldn't afford plane tickets to Hawaii or a hotel room, the cost at even the rattiest of places jacked to three hundred bucks because of the demand. He knew. He'd checked. He again caressed the lethargic Shiloh's coat; the shepherd whined and struggled to lift his head.

"You don't have to say it," Sally said.

"Say what?"

"That you wouldn't have wanted to go anyway, because we would have had to board Shiloh. It's okay, I feel the same way. Especially after the last few weeks, I wouldn't board him either."

Larry nodded to his wife, grateful for her understanding and support, both for Shiloh and for himself. Support he hadn't deserved, given his past, but would try to continue to be worthy.

* * * * * *

He was fatigued, his hip was sore from the hit he had taken the previous quarter, and the late-afternoon Hawaiian heat steadily drained his energy. But none of that mattered; Nathan and the rest of the two-minute offense huddled with single-minded determination as Darrian barked out the next play.

"Okay, guys, third and nine, thirty-four seconds left!" Darrian hollered. "Wideouts, get past the first-down marker on all routes. Six-eight-six Dayton F-stop on two! Ready, break!" The offense approached the ball, aware that they had to make something happen, and quickly.

The players set, Darrian shouted out his cadence, and the center snapped the ball. Darrian faded back, checked down all the receivers, and hurled the ball into the middle of the field. The ball whizzed past Nathan, who was shadowed by the free safety, and into the hands of the number one receiver, who was immediately taken to the ground. Darrian excitedly called time-out. Twenty-five seconds left, with the ball at the Boston College forty.

* * * * * *

"Yes!" Larry hollered. Though disappointed that his son had not been the target, Larry saw that the number one receiver was both open and farther down field. Darrian had made the right choice.

Shiloh struggled to his feet, jumped off the couch, and slowly shuffled to the back door. "He needs to go out again?" Larry asked.

"Yeah," Sally responded. "Fourth time in the last two hours." Grateful that play had been halted due to the time-out, Larry dashed into the kitchen to open the back door, and Shiloh started to make his way to the outside. Then he stopped, turned, and stared at Larry for a long moment. He kissed Larry's hand, whined at him, then slowly turned and gingerly made his way down the steps and into the backyard.

"He's been restless all evening," Larry said as he returned to the living room. "He keeps going outside. Last time I watched him for a few minutes; it was like he was looking for something."

"Yeah, I've noticed that too."

"I'm going to leave him outside for a while, let him get whatever's bugging him out of his system."

Sally cuddled up to him in the spot vacated by Shiloh. "I'm awfully proud of the way you've been taking care of him. From the morning walks to making sure he takes his medicine, you've gone out of your way for him. I know he appreciates it."

"No one deserves it more than he does... Okay, here we go! C'mon ASU!"

* * * * * *

"Good catch, Artie!" Darrian shouted inside the huddle over the deafening crowd noise. "Listen up, guys. We're forty yards out, and we have one time-out left. So, wideouts, whatever you do, once you make the catch, get out of bounds."

"Look for me, Darrian!" Nathan exclaimed. "I can shake that safety!"

"I will. Four-five-two, Hampshire G-still, on three. Ready, break!"

The center snapped the ball, and Darrian faded into the pocket. He checked for Nathan, but once again the safety had him covered. He hurled the ball toward the number two receiver, who made the catch and dashed out of bounds at the thirteen-yard line, stopping the clock after a twenty-seven-yard gain. Fourteen seconds left.

* * * * * *

Shiloh wandered through the backyard, sniffing urgently for a special spot, feeling the darkness consuming him. His breathing became more tortuous, and he felt a searing pain pulsating through his chest. He used what little remaining energy he possessed to rearrange the dirt and grass into a resting place. He turned back toward the house and with a marked sadness gazed at it and the silhouetted figures inside for what he knew to be the last time. The world began to spin; he lay down on the small makeshift spot he had fashioned for himself and closed his eyes.

* * * * * *

Darrian again set himself in the pocket and checked off his receivers downfield. Nathan cut sharply to the right, broke away from the safety, and sprinted into the open toward the end zone. Darrian's heart skipped a beat—he cocked his arm to launch the sure to win pass.

At that moment, the blitzing blindside linebacker laid a punishing hit to his back. The ball popped out of Darrian's hand and bounced onto the turf; in a microsecond, a half-dozen players lunged toward it. But the Sun Devils' running back somehow managed to squirm to the bottom of the scrum and snag it. While the alert play had enabled ASU to maintain possession, they lost six yards, it ran precious seconds off the clock, and the Sun Devils were forced to burn their last time-out.

* * * * * *

"Shiloh's been outside a long time," Larry said. "Maybe I should check on him."

"Are you kidding? There's six seconds left, and we're on the nineteen-yard line!"

Larry was on his feet. "It won't even take me until the end of the time-out."

* * * * * *

"This is it, guys!" Darrian barked in the huddle. "Last play, one more chance. We are nineteen yards from a bowl championship! Now, listen; don't bother with any routes; everyone just get to the end zone, and the guy who's open gets the ball. Seven-eight-three, Carolina F-stop shotgun on two. Let's do it!"

The team scurried to the line of scrimmage, and Darrian took the shotgun position five yards behind the center. The linemen could barely hear his cadence over the screams of the raucous crowd. Darrian lifted his right leg as a signal, and the center snapped the ball back to him.

* * * * * *

It was a distinctive bark, in a tone that Shiloh understood was directed at him. With the last of his energy, he lifted his head to see the black-and-white border-beagle mix, the same one from those many years earlier, once again facing him. The sparkling glow still ebbed from the visitor's eyes, piercing the surrounding darkness. The border beagle gestured to him, and Shiloh felt engulfed in a warm, comforting familiarity.

It's time to return to the Meadow.

Shiloh again laid down his head, and a moment later, he found himself gazing downward at his unmoving body. For a moment, he and the visitor faced each other as they hovered in the darkness. Then the border beagle began to float away toward a bright light in the distance, beckoning for Shiloh to follow. Shiloh understood, took one last look at his body, and moved with his guardian toward the light.

Then he stopped. He yipped at the border beagle and, in their unspoken language, explained that there remained a last bit of urgent, unfinished business. The visitor nodded, and they swung about and proceeded in a new direction.

* * * * * *

Nathan, the two other receivers, and the running back sprinted simultaneously toward the end zone as Darrian's pocket collapsed, and he found himself under pursuit from the linebacker who had sacked him on the previous play. But this time Darrian anticipated the linebacker's blitz, which gave him enough time to scramble toward the sideline.

Tailed by the free safety, Nathan hitched abruptly to his right at the three-yard line and opened a one-step gap with the defender as he entered the end zone. Darrian saw Nathan's move and realized that this was his chance. They were on opposite sides of the field, which would make the throw difficult. Relying on the considerable strength of his right arm, Darrian launched the desperate cross-field pass as the final gun sounded.

The spiraling ball hurled through the air toward Nathan; he extended his arms to haul it in. The winning catch was within a yard of him when the strong safety's shot to Nathan's ribcage sent him crashing to the turf. He slammed the back of his head on the hard surface as the ball passed him by and bounced out of bounds.

The impact left him dazed, barely able to perceive the chaotic events around him. The heated shouting from his teammates at the back judge, who had inexplicably failed to flag the strong safety for pass interference. The boos and jeers erupting from the ASU fans, directed at the same official. The Boston College players celebrating their defensive stop and victory.

His mind still foggy, Nathan rolled over, shook his head and saw two four-legged figures standing on the sideline near the back of the end zone a few feet from him. He did not recognize the one dog with the bright sparkling eyes, some sort of mixed-breed border beagle, though it seemed strangely familiar. But the other, a black-and-tan shepherd, he did know.

"Shiloh?" he mumbled. The shepherd stared at him with forlorn eyes and let out a single, soft yip.

Then Nathan felt himself being lifted to his feet by two teammates. "You okay?" one of them shouted.

Nathan shook his head to purge the cobwebs. Then he glanced again at the back of the end zone, but the two canines had disappeared.

"Nate!" the other said firmly. "Are you all right?"

"Yeah, I think so." Still dazed, he tentatively pivoted about and, guided by his two teammates, made his way to the sideline.

* * * * * *

"I can't believe this!" Sally screamed. "That was pass interference! How could they not call that?" Her words echoed those of the announcers, who were just as incredulous at the no-call. For a moment, she tempered her anger as she watched a close-up of her son being helped to his feet. She saw Nathan shake his head, glance at the sideline as if looking for something, and then start to make his way to the ASU sideline.

"Don't worry, Larry, he's going to be fine..." Sally realized that she had been so absorbed in the action on the screen that she had failed to notice that Larry had not returned to the living room. Astonished that he had missed the critical, final play, she hurried to the back door and stepped outside, only to see Larry bent over an unmoving Shiloh, his sobs echoing into the nighttime sky.

II.7

Chino Valley, Arizona—December 1994

It was a somber late-night flight back to Phoenix, devoid of the levity that often-accompanied team excursions. Though ASU had been a heavy underdog that they had come so close to victory served only to intensify the disappointment and frustration. And worst of all was the near-unanimous sentiment that their upset win had been snatched away by the officials' failure to flag an obvious pass interference call.

Darrian and the rest of Nathan's teammates were supportive, assuring him that he bore no responsibility for the loss. After all, Darrian noted, it was hard to catch a pass while lying on the ground because of an early and illegal hit.

When they reached Sky Harbor Airport early the morning after the game, they all exchanged hugs and high fives and departed to their homes for a few long-overdue days of rest. Nathan was tired, his mood still dark, he made the drive home to Chino Valley. He looked forward to seeing his parents, and to seeing Shiloh, whom he couldn't get out of his mind since the odd, dreamlike vision of him at game's end.

Two hours later, he pulled his car into the driveway of his parents' home. It had been months since his last visit; the house seemed even smaller than before, so unassuming, so nondescript. Sighing, he rolled out of the car, grabbed his duffel bag from the back seat, and slammed the door shut.

"Nathan!" Larry called from the front door. That surprised Nathan—his father never was the first to greet him. Larry approached Nathan and extended his hand, a solemn expression etched across his face.

"It's good to see you, son." His hand moved from Nathan's to the back of his son's neck, almost as though he was going to pull him in for a hug. "Your head okay? You could drive here okay?"

"Yeah, just bad in the moment. Team doctors checked me out and cleared me." Nathan smiled tiredly, and his father withdrew his hand. "And I got some sleep on the flight. The drive was pretty uneventful too; very little traffic this time of day."

"That's good. I'm sorry about the loss. Your mother and I watched the whole game, and we really thought you were going to pull it out."

"Yeah, we did too." Nathan paused and glanced around. "Hey, where's Shiloh?"

Larry's stomach tightened. "There's something I have to tell you."

It was the way he said it that made Nathan's blood run cold. "What is it?"

"Last night, we let him out like we always do. But he didn't come back right away, so I went outside to look for him, and...I found him lying on his side in the backyard. He had died a few minutes earlier."

His legs growing wobbly, Nathan dropped his duffel bag on the ground. "Shiloh's dead?"

"I'm sorry, son."

"But he was fine the last time I saw him!"

Larry's gaze met and held Nathan's. "You haven't been home since spring break. The truth is, Shiloh's health took a turn for the worse this past year."

Nathan's shock turned to anger. "And who's fault is that? Didn't I ask you to take care of him?"

"I did what I could..."

"I know I shouldn't have trusted you to take care of him!" Nathan shouted. "You screwed that up just like you screw up everything! You let him die!" Nathan abruptly bolted past Larry and into the house, angrily slamming his bedroom door behind him.

* * * * * *

They only seemed to fuel the heartache; the memories within his bedroom walls. In the corner lay the old stick with which the two of them would engage in their epic tug-of-war duels. Stray hairs from Shiloh's double-coat were visible on Nathan's bedspread, and a photo of a young Nathan hugging Shiloh was taped to the dresser mirror. Nathan kneeled to caress the stick, then pulled the photograph off the mirror. He gazed at the image for several moments, the happy memories of their neighborhood adventures flooding back into his consciousness. Then he sat down on the bed and began to weep softly, until he was jolted by a knock at the door.

"Leave me alone!" he shouted. His mother opened the door and stepped inside.

"I said I didn't want to talk!"

"I heard what you said to your father outside. You were kind of tough on him, don't you think?"

"Why shouldn't I be? It's his fault that Shiloh's gone!"

"And you haven't even said hello to me."

Nathan scowled, as petulant as the little boy in the photo he held could be.

Sally sat beside her son. "Shiloh was getting old, and his health was failing," she said softly.

"What do you mean? He was only twelve. Dogs live longer than that!"

"I know. But about a year ago, Shiloh was diagnosed with cancer. There was a tumor near his shoulder that was causing him a lot of pain. We took him to Dr. Grittman, who said we should put him down."

"What?"

"But your father wouldn't hear of it. That's right—your father. He dedicated himself to doing everything he could to help Shiloh. Dr. Grittman warned us that trying to get rid of the cancer through surgery might not be successful, but your father insisted on doing it anyway. He told me he wouldn't be able to look at himself in the mirror if he didn't at least try to help him. And he did. Thanks to your father, Shiloh had another year to be with us."

Nathan remained silent for a moment as he tried to process his mother's words. "Dad did all that?" he finally asked.

"He did. You would have known that if you had been around here more.

"And one other thing. The operation to remove the tumor cost $3,000, and your dad paid for it."

Nathan paused, but his expression didn't change. "Where did he get the money?"

Sally gestured toward the window. "Take a look outside."

Puzzled, Nathan gazed outside at the familiar landscape of the backyard. The toolshed sat in its usual place, and the garage door was open.

"You see the 1966 Mustang your father was refurbishing? You know, the one he kept calling his pride and joy?"

Nathan squinted at the garage. "No. Where is it?"

"It's gone. He sold it to pay for the procedure."

A shocked Nathan sat back down on the bed. "I-I don't know what to say."

"Your father and Shiloh formed some kind of bond these last couple of years. I don't know what caused it, but it changed him. He really loved that dog, and he took his death pretty hard. I think you should know that too."

* * * * * *

Larry's hands were shaking from the numbness and despair that flowed through his body. He had dreaded the moment he would have to tell Nathan, and it had gone even worse than he feared. He felt the urge returning to him, that impulse that so often had surfaced in the past, to submerge unbearable feelings in a familiar comfort.

Larry stalked into the kitchen, opened the refrigerator door, and reached for a can of Budweiser. He stared intently at it as the conflict played out inside him. It would be so good, so comforting, and it would make the pain go away. But…he couldn't let down his family, not again. And Shiloh deserved better from him. He took a deep breath and dropped the cold can into the trash.

As he closed the refrigerator door, he felt a hand on his shoulder. He turned to face his son. For the longest moment the two stared at each other. Then, without speaking, tears filling his eyes, Nathan wrapped his arms around his father, and the two entered into a warm and lasting embrace.

III.

LINDSAY

III.1

Goodyear, Arizona—March 1999

Charles Fletcher sat back in his office desk and scratched his chin, contemplating his handsome, sandy-haired twenty-five-year-old employee as the young man wrapped up his presentation. It was a persuasive argument, compellingly researched and documented, and the wealthy franchise owner had long ago learned to carefully evaluate any proposal Nathan Wilkinson brought to him.

"It's an ideal location, Mr. Fletcher," Nathan was saying. "The strip center is being built right off Highway 60, for easy access, and the developers want to make us the anchor store. Sure, there's not much out there right now; Queen Creek doesn't even have a McDonald's yet. But I know of at least four developers looking at building subdivisions there, and those future homeowners are going to need our store's hardware and home supplies. We can't miss at this location."

"I'll agree that the area has a lot of potential," Fletcher admitted. "But you know the definition of potential—it means that it hasn't happened yet. What if the growth doesn't come?"

"Sure, it's possible the subdivisions won't be built. But Arizona is the fastest growing state in the country, and much of that growth is right here in Maricopa County. Queen Creek is close enough to Phoenix for people to be able to commute, and the homes there are much cheaper than Scottsdale and other suburbs. All the stars are aligned to make this town the next big growth area."

"So, if this area is so great, why hasn't Home Depot or Lowes already put a store there?"

"Because they don't have someone in charge as visionary as Charles Fletcher."

"Stroking my ego won't sell this for you." Fletcher chuckled good-naturedly. "Of course, it never hurts either."

Nathan stood up and ran his hand through his sandy hair. He leaned his taut, commanding, six-foot-three-inch frame across the desk toward Fletcher. "Seriously, Mr. Fletcher, Lowes and Home Depot are both bigger and better known than Handy Hardware and Supplies. So, the only way we are going to hold our own is to outmaneuver them and establish ourselves in places where they aren't."

"I don't know. This all sounds good, but I'm a little out of my area of expertise here. Most of my other franchises are fast food or personal service. You're asking me to sink a lot of capital into a business I don't know that much about. Are you sure your numbers are solid?"

"Absolutely, sir."

"Okay." Fletcher sighed. "You've got me interested. Set up a meeting with the strip center's reps. And tomorrow, let's you and I take a drive out to Queen Creek and so I can see the location for myself."

* * * * * *

"And to Mr. Charles Fletcher and Fletcher Holdings, we present this certificate of appreciation, as well as our personal thanks, for making Handy Hardware a part of the Queen Creek community."

The mayor handed the framed certificate to Fletcher as the cameras clicked and the small crowd applauded in front of the newly finished store.

"Thank you," Fletcher said, shaking the mayor's hand. "We hope to be serving your needs here in Queen Creek for many years to come."

Standing behind Fletcher, Nathan grinned and enthusiastically joined in the applause. Eighteen months had passed since their first discussion about Queen Creek, and all their long hours of analysis, meetings, and construction supervision had culminated in this opening ceremony. The store's employees, dressed in their bright-orange vests, took their positions in front of the entrance. The mayor offered a few more canned remarks, making sure to provide the local media maximum opportunity to snap more photos. As the ceremony drew to its conclusion, the politician sauntered over to the employees and shook each of their hands.

"Great job organizing this, Nathan," Fletcher said. "Everything went flawlessly, and it's going to get the new store plenty of free publicity. I think you're going to be pretty happy with your year-end bonus."

"Thank you, sir. I really appreciate it."

"Now, along with the money, I'd like to give you a little advice."

"Advice?"

"Yes. Take some time off. Stop working all those crazy hours. You don't have to do that to impress me. I'm already happy with your work. You're young and full of energy, but from what I can see you don't have much of a personal life. Don't wake up one morning when you're forty and ask yourself what the hell happened to your life."

"Maybe you're right. It has been a pretty intense year."

"Of course I'm right. Being right all the time is one of the perks that comes from having my name on the business."

"That's for sure." Nathan chuckled. "But some day I'd like to have my own business. Be my own boss, make all my own decisions."

"I have no doubt you will. But remember something important. In order to truly be a success in life, you have to do more than just run a business. You have to have a family. A wife. Children. That's what makes life worth living.

"I think I've done pretty well in my career. But my greatest success has been having a wife and three beautiful daughters who love me," Fletcher said. "They make all of the stress, all of the late nights, all of the struggles worthwhile. I think it was Ronald Reagan who once said, 'There is no greater happiness for a man than approaching a door at the end of a day knowing that someone on the other side of that door is waiting for the sound of his footsteps.'

"That's what I want for you, Nathan. That's what will make you happy. And you're not going to find it if you stay holed up in your office every hour of every day. Now, go ahead and take the next week off, starting tomorrow. Don't check your messages, don't make any phone calls, don't worry about anything. Just relax and try to restart your personal life."

"Charles." The mayor had finished his meet-and-greet with the store's employees and was next to Fletcher and Nathan again. "I want you to know that I really do appreciate your bringing Handy Hardware to Queen Creek. This is a big deal for us, and it is going to help put us on the map."

"Thank you, Mayor," Fletcher said, gesturing toward Nathan. "But the person you should thank is my lead analyst, Nathan Wilkinson. He's the one who convinced me this was the perfect town for us." The mayor smiled warmly and grasped Nathan's hand.

"Nathan, why don't you take the mayor and the town manager on a tour of the store?" Fletcher said. "And don't forget what I told you."

"Sure, Mr. Fletcher," Nathan said, grateful as always for his boss's kindness and generosity.

"Oh, and Nathan?" Fletcher said to him as he departed with the mayor. "I think it's time you started calling me Charles."

III.2

Chino Valley, Arizona—October 2000

"Okay, let me see if I have this straight," Tom Manogue said to Nathan as he set his Coors Light back on the table. "You've been working your butt off the last two years because you think it will impress your boss. But instead he tells you to work less hard and take more time off?"

"Yeah, pretty much."

"Then tell him to call my boss tomorrow and offer up some of his employee management tips." Nathan chuckled as the two friends picked through the plate of chicken wings that they always ordered whenever they visited Murio's, Chino Valley's most popular tavern.

"So, what are you going to do with your newfound free time?" Tom asked.

Nathan pondered his friend a moment. Freckles less prominent yet still speckled across his face, Tom had gained a few pounds since college but remained as recognizable as ever. It seemed a lifetime ago when they began as adversaries, in the hallways of middle school and the hiking trail summit...

"I dunno. Coming up here to see Mom and Dad was my first stop. Other than that, I'm pretty open."

"Miranda and I are heading up to Sedona for the weekend. Why don't you come along, and bring that babe you've been hooking up with—the flight attendant, what's her name?"

"Barbara, and I'm not seeing her anymore."

"Why the hell not? Dude, she's an eleven on a scale of one to ten."

"Yeah, I know, she's gorgeous. But she doesn't have any—I'm not sure what to call it—substance to her."

"Like that matters?"

"Yeah, yeah, at first that's all I cared about too. But after a while, you want a little more out of a relationship." Nathan leaned back in his chair, beer dangling by its neck from his fingers.

"Let me tell you about something that happened last week. We're out to dinner, and she's telling me about a flight she worked from Albuquerque to LAX. She said she was in the cockpit about twenty minutes after takeoff, and she looked out the window and saw this big crater next to the highway."

"You mean the one near Winslow?"

"Yeah, the Barringer Crater. So, she tells me she asked the pilot how the crater got there, and the pilot told her that it was caused by a meteor the size of a house that hit something like fifty thousand years ago. Then, swear to God, she says to me, 'I told the pilot that it was a good thing that meteor didn't hit the highway.'"

"No way!"

Nathan rolled his eyes. "Right then and there, I knew that it wasn't going to work."

Tom snickered as he lifted his beer again. "Okay she's not going to win any Nobel prizes. But is that any reason to dump her?"

"It's just that Barb knows she's hot, and she can have any guy she wants. She's not ambitious, and she doesn't care about anybody but herself. Her looks are all she has to offer. It's been great being with her these last few months, but a relationship has to be more than just sex a few times a week."

"Could have fooled me. No, you know I'm kidding, buddy. And I don't blame you. I'm lucky I have Miranda, someone who actually puts up with me."

"Yeah, she's going to heaven, that's for sure."

"You got that right. But don't worry. Dating sucks at times, but some day you'll find someone, the right one for you. Probably when you least expect it."

"Yeah, that's what my mom and dad say."

"How are they doing, by the way?"

"Surprisingly well. Dad's now lead mechanic at the Chevy dealership, and he and Mom just got back from a vacation at Yosemite."

"That's great to hear. I remember how rough it used to be for you back in in the day, how they used to always be at each other's throats."

"Funny how relationships change over time, huh?" Nathan said dryly, and the two friends smiled warmly at each other. "Oh, that reminds me, Mom said to tell you to come on over sometime when I'm visiting, and she'll make the both of us dinner."

"Well, I'm free tonight. What are we waiting for?"

* * * * * *

Time off is overrated, Nathan thought as he jogged through the park adjacent to his apartment complex the morning after returning from Chino Valley. Clad in a tank top, running shorts, and a Diamondbacks baseball cap, he followed his usual four-mile route from Litchfield Road through the park toward the city water-treatment plant. It felt good to be running again, breathing the crisp morning air, feeling the sunlight radiating against his body; his busy work and travel schedule had allowed for only intermittent exercise these past several months. Running was also a means to kill a couple of morning hours, after which he planned to drive to the mall and catch that movie about Tom Hanks getting stranded on a desert island with nothing to do. *I can relate to that!*

The park's jogging path snaked through a foliated trail adjacent to a creek. Nathan picked up his pace as he navigated through the greenery toward the busy street in the distance. Sweat glistened from his brow, and his wiry leg muscles strained from the exertion.

Then he stopped abruptly at the sound of a soft whimper emanating from the thick brush near the creek. The sound intrigued him; it wasn't normal and did not belong among the quiet chirping of the park's natural wildlife. He carefully approached the brush, and saw its branches rustling from some sort of movement inside. He kneeled, parted two of the branches, and peered inside.

Barely visible was a young black miniature schnauzer, gazing out from a makeshift nest inside the brush. It was small, not more than fifteen pounds, and covered in dried mud. Ticks infested its unkempt fur. It whimpered when it saw Nathan and retreated to the back of the nest, out of his reach.

"Hey there, little fella," Nathan said in a reassuring tone. "What are you doing out here all by yourself?"

The schnauzer whimpered again and turned away from Nathan.

"Come on out. Don't be scared. I promise I won't hurt you."

Nathan cautiously stretched out his hand. The dog reached forward to sniff it, peering up at Nathan. Then it whined again, abruptly pivoted, and burrowed under the brush at the back of the nest. In an instant it was gone.

"Damn," Nathan muttered. He lifted himself up and checked behind the brush; he could see no more than a foot. Locating such a small dog inside the dense foliage would be impossible, especially if it did not want to be found.

Reluctantly Nathan retreated to the trail and resumed his morning jog. But the frightened and anxious expression on the little schnauzer remained etched in his memory.

* * * * * *

Listening carefully for any of the telltale sounds from the previous morning, Nathan wiped the sweat from his forehead as he approached the same brush patch near the creek. Hearing nothing, he first scanned the area, then crouched down and parted the brush to expose the makeshift nest.

To his relief, the schnauzer was back, startled at encountering Nathan once again. It whined and again pivoted toward its emergency exit at the back of its nest.

"Not so fast!" Nathan blurted. He pulled out a napkin from the mini pocket in his running shorts and unwrapped it to reveal four freshly cooked bacon strips. "Maybe you'd like some of this first?"

The schnauzer stopped abruptly. It glared first at him and then at the bacon, mouth opening slightly.

"Go ahead," Nathan said, dangling a strip. "I know you're hungry." The dog cautiously sniffed the bacon and then bit off a portion of the strip. Nathan smirked as the bacon's intoxicating aroma sent a memory flashing through his head, of his surreptitious smuggling of strips under the breakfast table to Shiloh while his mother's attention was diverted.

Nathan let the schnauzer chew and swallow before offering the remaining fragment, which the dog devoured more urgently.

"I was hoping I'd run into you again this morning. Here, you want some more?" Nathan backed away from the brush and offered another piece of bacon.

Inhaling the tantalizing odor, the schnauzer tentatively crawled out from the brush. It remained in a crouched position, still peering warily at Nathan.

Now that it was in the open, Nathan was able to get a better look at the dog. He did not appear to be injured, and unlike many schnauzers, its ears and tail were not clipped. It wore a light-blue collar embroidered with silver bone symbols.

As he fed it another piece of bacon, Nathan reached around the schnauzer and grasped its midsection. The dog backed up a step, then stopped and relented. It shivered as Nathan picked him up and held it against his chest.

"Don't be afraid, little guy," he reassured the schnauzer as he eyed the tag attached to the collar.

LINDSAY
Ana Trevino 602-555-4965

"Or should I say...girl. Your name is Lindsay?" The dog yelped softly at the sound of her name. "I'm sorry you got yourself lost. Tell you what, sweet girl. I'm going to take you back to my apartment, get you cleaned up, give you some more to eat, and call your owner. With any luck, you'll be back in your own home by tonight." He smiled affectionately at her, a feeling of contentment overcoming him at the realization that it was the first time in several years he had held a dog.

Though she couldn't understand the stranger's words, they seemed soothing to Lindsay. She swallowed the last piece of bacon and leaned her head against Nathan's shoulder, allowing him to cradle her against his body. His warmth provided her a reassuring comfort.

She lifted her head again and gazed at her companion of the last few days, who was standing by the brush, asking in her own way if it would be okay to go with the strange man. The black-and-white border-beagle mix with the sparkling eyes nodded; Lindsay whined as Nathan turned back to his apartment.

* * * * * *

"You clean up pretty well, little girl."

Crouched in his sink, Lindsay shivered as Nathan sprayed lukewarm water over her fur to cleanse the encased dirt from her body. After drying her off, he combed the still-damp fur with one of his own brushes, taking pains to remove the remaining ticks clinging to her body.

Then he lifted her out of the sink and placed her on the kitchen floor. He retrieved a leftover boneless pork chop from his refrigerator, chopped it into pieces, placed it into a bowl, and set it in front of the schnauzer, who vigorously delved into it.

"Look at you go. It's been a while since you've had a real meal, huh?"

As he watched the schnauzer hungrily devour the remnants of the pork chop, a brief feeling of sadness overcame Nathan. It had been so many years since he'd enjoyed the companionship of a dog. But given his work and travel, caring for one was out of the question now. He sighed, then entered the number from Lindsay's tag into his flip phone. It rang twice before a female voice answered.

"Hi, can I speak to Ana Trevino?"

"This is she," the voice on the other end responded warily.

"I think I found your dog."

"What? You have Lindsay?" Her tone changed immediately.

"Yes, a black schnauzer, about fifteen pounds? My name is Nathan Wilkinson, and I live at the Stonebrook Apartments near Litchfield Drive in Goodyear. I was jogging through the park earlier today, and I found her hiding in the brush near the creek."

"Oh my God. Is she okay?"

"She's fine. A little dirty and a little hungry. I have her in my apartment now. I gave her a bite to eat and got her all cleaned up."

"Oh, that is so wonderful!" the woman exclaimed, her voice shaking with emotion. "She got out of my backyard five days ago, and I've been looking for her everywhere. Can I come over and pick her up?"

"Of course. She'll be right here, and I bet she'll be just as glad to see you."

* * * * * *

Thirty minutes later, Nathan heard the knock at his front door. Holding Lindsay in his arms, he strode to the entrance and opened the door.

Ana was striking. The twenty-four-year-old stood at just over five and a half feet tall, with flowing, black hair and pristine auburn skin; she was clad in tight jeans, a flowery blouse, and high heels. A touch of makeup around sensual dark eyes that were fighting back tears.

Lindsay whimpered at the sight of Ana and squirmed to free herself from Nathan's grip.

"Lindsay, my beautiful little girl!" Ana exclaimed.

Nathan handed the writhing schnauzer over to Ana, who hugged her fervently, letting the kisses rain down on her face. "I think someone is happy to see you," he smiled.

"I missed you so much!"

Lindsay delivered several more kisses before Ana finally set her down on the hardwood flooring. She scampered excitedly through the living room, still whimpering, then circled back to jump at Ana's leg.

"I can't thank you enough—Nathan, is it?" He nodded. "I'm Ana."

"Think nothing of it. The minute I saw Lindsay in the brush by the creek, I could tell she was lost."

"I live about two miles from here. Every Thursday a crew comes over to my house to mow my lawn while I'm at work. Last week they must have left my back fence open after they finished. When I got home that night, I let Lindsay out as I always do. About ten minutes later, I noticed that she hadn't come back, so I went outside and saw that the fence was open and she was gone. I've spent the last five days looking for her every morning before I go to work and every night after I get home. I haven't been able to eat or sleep, I've been so worried."

Lindsay returned to Ana and again jumped up to attract her attention. Ana reached down and picked her up, receiving another kiss on the cheek as a reward.

"And now I have you back," she declared, rubbing her nose against Lindsay's underside. "I promise I'm never going to let you out again without checking that fence first!" Then she turned back to Nathan. "I can't tell you how much I appreciate what you've done for us. Let me give you a reward or something. It's the least I can do."

"Oh, that's not necessary."

"Are you sure?"

"Of course. I'm just glad I was able to help."

"Okay then." Her voice betrayed a hint of disappointment. "I guess in that case we ought to get going."

As she started toward the door, Lindsay again squirmed, her paws gesturing in Nathan's direction as she gazed wistfully at him.

"Wow," Ana said, "she's really taken with you. That's odd; she usually doesn't care much for strangers."

Ana lowered Lindsay to the ground, and she ran to Nathan, jumping at his leg, whimpering excitedly. Ana giggled as she strained to attach a leash to the schnauzer's collar. "Though I can see why she'd like you. You saved her. You're her knight in shining armor."

"Please, no need to get all Hallmark on me!"

"Really, thanks again for everything."

Nathan held the door open; she glanced at him again and, after a slight hesitation, stepped into the corridor, Lindsay trailing on the leash behind her.

As Nathan watched them, a feeling came over him—one of urgency, importance, consequence—as if he was experiencing a defining moment that would set a course for his life, but only if he acted, and acted now.

"Ana?" She turned back to him. "Maybe instead of a reward, we could, you know, do something else."

Her eyes narrowed. "Something else?"

"Oh, man, that didn't come out right, did it?" The two stared at each other for a moment, then together burst into laughter.

"So, Nathan, what did you have in mind?"

* * * * * *

"Would you like some more wine?"

Ana nodded, and Nathan poured the Chardonnay into her crystal glass. They sat in the corner of the half-full, rustic Italian restaurant, the candle burning in the center bathing their darkened table in a soft glow. A pianist seated in the center of the serving area played a soft melody that echoed through the bistro.

"This is wonderful," she said, taking another sip. She looked stunning in her short, black dress, her hair flowing over her bare shoulders, a crucifix draped at her neck sparkling in the candlelight.

"Cakebread Cellars, Napa Valley. I discovered it a while back during a business trip to California. I don't drink very often, but when I do, it's either this or a cold beer."

"You're very disciplined."

"Well, that's one reason."

Ana hesitated a moment, sensing it was topic about which he did not wish to elaborate. "So, you travel a lot on business?"

"Yes, just about every week. Mostly here in Arizona and in California, sizing up potential locations for my company's new franchises. Long hours, but it gets me a lot of perks, like hotel points. It's a growing company with a lot of opportunity, and I have a great boss. I enjoy working there, even if it isn't what I originally envisioned I would be doing with my life."

"What did you think you'd be doing?" He started to answer before she abruptly interrupted him. "I'm sorry. I hope I'm not being too nosy with all my questions."

"I don't mind, about this, at least. I originally thought I would go into the army. My father and uncle both served in Vietnam, and I used to love to play soldier when I was a kid. I was offered an ROTC college scholarship when I was eighteen, but I turned it down to play football at ASU. I don't regret that decision, and this may sound a little corny, but I sometimes I wish that I could have done more to serve our country."

"I don't think it sounds corny at all," Ana said. "I admire you for feeling that way. Most of the guys I know have no interest in serving; they're too busy playing video games or smoking weed.

"So, Nathan Wilkinson,"—Ana leaned in toward him—"did you ever get the chance to play in the NFL?"

"Nah." Nathan shrugged. "I wasn't a bad wide receiver, but I didn't have what it took to make it in the pros."

"Well, only about 5 percent of college players ever make it to the NFL."

"You know your football stats, don't you?"

"Been watching both college and NFL with my brothers since I was a kid. I've been to a few ASU games, and I'm a big fan of Darrian Lawrence."

Nathan grinned. "Darrian's a great guy...and a long-time friend of mine."

"Wow!" Ana's eyes sparkled. "So, I probably saw you play too!"

Nathan blushed a little under his smile. "I was only his number three receiver. But he did try to target me whenever I got on the field. So…" Nathan held her gaze. "Maybe you did see me." He took a sip of wine. "I was really happy to see the Cardinals draft him. He always wanted to play for his hometown team."

"I think he'll win a Super Bowl someday."

"He probably will."

The conversation paused as the server brought the main courses. He placed the chicken marsala before Ana and the four-cheese ravioli in front of Nathan.

"So, what about you, Ana Trevino?" Nathan asked.

"What about me what?"

"You've heard all about me, my family, my aborted military and football careers, my job and my travel. What's your story?"

"There's not much to say." She shrugged and brushed back her hair. "I grew up in Avondale and went to the University of New Mexico. Majored in psychology. But I didn't want to go into that field directly, like, as a therapist or something, so I went to work for Van and Laurin Engineers in their HR department. I'm now deputy HR manager."

"That probably makes some use of your psych degree."

Ana laughed her agreement.

"I've heard of Van and Laurin. They're pretty huge; they do a lot of work for the cities I am setting up franchises in. To be the number two HR person there after just a few years out of college is pretty impressive."

"Thanks. And, of course, you know I also live in Goodyear. By myself." Ana smiled, and Nathan appreciated her dropping the confirming hint. *No boyfriend, no roommate.* "Well, by myself except for Lindsay, of course."

"How is Lindsay? She back to normal?"

"Yes, pretty much. She ate two full servings of her food after I got her home…and then slept for about two days straight. But now she acts like nothing ever happened."

"Hopefully the next time she sees an open gate, she'll realize that your side of it is a lot better than what's on the other side."

"I can only hope. You know, Nathan, you did a great job taking care of her. You're a natural with dogs. Do you have any of your own?"

"Not now." Nathan stroked his chin. "I had one when I was a kid. He was my best friend, and for a long time after my family moved to Chino Valley, he was pretty much my only friend. But when I got older, I started getting involved in football and other things, and I guess I decided that I had more important things to do than spend time with him. I didn't realize that while I had other friends and other priorities, he only had me.

"It wasn't until after he died that I found out he had been sick. I wasn't there for him when he needed me, which still makes me feel guilty. This may sound crazy to you, but sometimes I wish I could have one more chance to tell him how sorry I am and how much he meant to me."

"I don't think that sounds crazy at all," Ana said softly. "What was his name?"

"Shiloh."

"Is Shiloh the only dog you've ever had?"

"Well, when I was really young, my family apparently had another dog."

"Apparently?"

"I have a vague memory of a dog running around our house when I couldn't have been more than two or three. One time I brought it up to my mother, but I got the distinct feeling she didn't want to talk about it. So, I didn't ask again."

"Do you have any idea what happened to him?"

"No, but based on the way my mom reacted, it must have been pretty bad. I think for the time being, I'm going to stay away from dogs. Being a dog owner doesn't seem to end well for me. Besides, I couldn't take care of a dog now even if I wanted one, with all my travel."

"Well, I can't imagine ever not having a dog. My family has had dogs my whole life."

"So, Lindsay is the latest?"

"That's right. I got her when she was a puppy, just after I bought my house. You know, if you ever have an urge to spend time with a dog, Lindsay is always available."

"Maybe I'll take you up on that." Nathan grinned. "I could be her godparent, or something like that."

"Yes, you could. But being a godparent means having a lot of responsibility. You'd have to see her pretty frequently—her birthday, holidays, you know, all the important occasions. And, of course, you'd have to bring her presents for every occasion. Would you be willing to do that?"

His mind flashed with the unspoken rule of first dates: *don't come on too strong, don't show interest too early.* It was a rule Nathan had always followed, until this moment, when he found himself drawn toward this beautiful, lively, intelligent, and alluring woman. He summoned his courage, inhaled deeply, and braced himself. "Of course I would," he said. "That is, if I'm invited."

For the longest time, they sat unspeaking, gazing at each other, the flickering candle illuminating their faces, before Ana finally broke the silence.

"Yes. You're invited."

III.3

Goodyear, Arizona—September 2001

Shielding his eyes from the bright morning sun shining through the partially open window, Nathan switched off the alarm's shrill buzz, then stretched and rolled over on his side. His stirrings vibrated through the bed, alerting his slumbering companion. She came to life instantly, hurling her body on top of his, nuzzling her face against his chin.

"Mmmm." Nathan sighed, eyes still closed, feeling the warmth of her tongue on his cheek. "Nice way to start the day."

"Yes, and it would be even better if it were me."

"What? That's not you?" Nathan chuckled, earning from Ana a playful slap on his shoulder. Remaining perched on top of him, Lindsay squirmed and whined excitedly as she continued to rain kisses upon him.

Nathan smiled warmly as Ana reached over and wrenched a protesting Lindsay off him. "C'mon, girl, that's enough love for now. It's time for your breakfast." Lindsay's ears perked up at the last word; she wiggled out of Ana's grip, jumped to the floor, and scampered off to the kitchen.

"I've had her since she was eight weeks old, you've known her not quite a year, and sometimes I think she loves you more than she loves me."

"Well, the two of you have something in common: you both know a quality male when you see one."

Ana snorted and began to withdraw from the bed.

"Don't you roll your eyes at me, woman!" Nathan shouted playfully, grabbing her waist and pulling her on top of him.

"Nathan! I have to feed Lindsay!"

"She won't starve if you're delayed a few minutes."

"I can't take that chance." She laughed, freeing herself from his embrace. She made her way to the door, then glanced back at him. "But you know how quickly she eats…"

* * * * * *

"You all packed?" Nathan called to Ana from her living room.

"Almost." A moment later she appeared from her bedroom, toting a thirty-inch suitcase behind her; its wheels clacked loudly against the wooden floor.

"My God," Nathan exclaimed, "we're only going to be at my parents' house for a couple of days. How much stuff are you taking with you?"

"You guys can live for a month out of a duffel bag. I can't."

"It is one of the great benefits of being male. That and peeing standing up." Then he hesitated, his expression turning serious. "Don't be nervous. It'll all be fine."

"Honey, of course I'm nervous. I'm meeting your parents for the first time."

"What's to be nervous about? My dad's a recovering alcoholic, and my mom thinks no woman will ever be good enough for me. Other than that, no problem." He smiled warmly at her, charmed by her anxiety, her desire to make a good impression on his parents.

"You're not making things better."

"Just be yourself. You'll be great. I'm just glad we were both able to take a few days off for this trip. I'm looking forward to showing you where I grew up."

"Me too. Maybe I'll learn a little more about what it is that made you into you."

"And really, don't worry about my parents. They're going to love you as much as I do."

Ana blushed; then, alerted by the scratching at her leg, she reached over to pick up the ever-enthusiastic Lindsay.

"Well, if they don't love me, I bet they'll settle for this little girl."

* * * * * *

"Ana, would you like some more scalloped potatoes?" Sally asked.

~ 100 ~

"No, thank you," Ana replied as she sat next to Nathan at the Wilkinson dinner table. "I have more than enough already."

"So, how do you like Chino Valley so far?" Sally inquired.

"It's really pretty. Even though I grew up here in Arizona, I never got the chance to come to this part of the state. I love the fact that you can see the mountains from your front porch. And it's not nearly as hot as it is in the valley."

"It gets plenty hot here, but now that we're into September, it'll be a lot cooler, especially in the evenings."

Nathan glanced at his father as he took another bite of his roast beef. Never much for small talk, Larry sat silently, sipping an iced tea while Ana and Sally dominated the conversation. Then Nathan noticed Larry taking a small piece of his roast beef and lowering it under the table.

"Larry!" Sally scolded. "You shouldn't feed Ana's dog table scraps."

"She'll be fine," Larry said dismissively. He turned to Ana. "It's kind of nice having a dog around the house again. So, let me get this straight—Lindsay is the reason you two met?"

"That's right," Nathan replied. "I kidnapped her and told Ana I wouldn't give her back unless she went out with me."

"Nathan!" she exclaimed.

"Well, whatever it takes." Larry chuckled, then sat back in his chair to let Lindsay vault into his lap. "I'm sorry you got yourself lost, little girl, but I'm glad you ended up here with us."

As the conversation meandered through the rest of dinner and into dessert, Ana felt her nerves easing. She was appreciative of the elder Wilkinsons' friendliness and welcoming hospitality. For a while, Lindsay remained perched on Larry's lap, but before long, she hopped off and found her way back to Nathan, scratching at his thigh to inform him it was now his turn to pay attention to her. Nathan chuckled as she jumped onto him and made herself comfortable between his legs.

"Don't take it personally, Mr. Wilkinson." Ana laughed as she sipped her wine. "She always seems to end up with Nathan. I'm always competing with her for his attention."

"I guess I'm just irresistible to all the Trevino women," Nathan remarked as Lindsay rolled over to allow him to stroke her belly.

After dinner, Ana and Sally remained in the kitchen to chat over coffee while Nathan and Larry retired to the living room. Larry parked himself on the worn couch and took another swig from his iced tea. "She's a quality woman," he remarked to his son. "I can already tell that."

"Thanks. She just sort of came crashing into my life."

"Funny how things work out that way. You know, when you least expect it. For what it's worth, I like her a lot more than that girl you used to be with. And I can tell your mother approves of her too."

Nathan smiled at his dad remembering back to his first girlfriend; it was true that Ana was the first woman he'd brought around since Darlene. "That's important to me, because you may be seeing a lot more of her in the future."

"Does that mean what I think it does?"

Nathan pulled a small square box out of his pocket and opened it to show Larry a one-carat diamond ring. "Tomorrow night I'm taking her to dinner in Prescott, and I'm going to pop the question."

"Son, I'm very proud of you." The emotion was audible in Larry's voice. "She'll be good for you. I'm glad you brought her here to meet us."

Nathan paused a moment. "You know, Dad, I'm sorry I haven't come up here to visit you and Mom more often. It's just that I've been so busy with my job, I haven't had time."

"That's okay. But I'm glad you're here now, because I have something I've been meaning to give you." Larry got up, went over to the bookcase in the corner of the living room, pulled a small, shiny object from the middle shelf, and handed it to Nathan. It was a shiny silver container with a wooden base, on which was carved a solitary name:

SHILOH

"Dad, is this…?" Nathan stammered.

"Yes, it is. I never told you this, but after he died, I had him cremated. I've been keeping him here at the house, but I figured it was time for him to be with you."

"I—I don't know what to say."

"You don't have to say anything. He was a good dog, and a special friend. And now he can be with you again."

Nathan's eyes moistened as he embraced his father. "I can't tell you how much I appreciate your being with him in his last years."

"I'm glad I did. He ended up giving as much to me as I gave to him."

At that moment, Lindsay scampered back into the living room and jumped against Nathan's leg.

"Besides, it looks like you've got another one to take care of now." Larry grinned.

"I don't think this one will ever let me neglect her."

* * * * * *

By the time he woke up the next morning, Nathan could already feel the butterflies forming in his stomach. Lying in bed, he went over the plans for this Tuesday. During the daytime, a drive to see the sights around Chino Valley, followed by a stroll up the hiking trails behind his house to the summits where he and Shiloh had embarked on their adventures. Then off to dinner at Chantilly's, a cozy Italian restaurant near the Prescott town square with an atmosphere reminiscent of his and Ana's first date. That would be followed by a motorcycle ride to the Grandfather Juniper, the famous one-thousand-year-old tree off the Rim country walking trail. He would lead her underneath the juniper's magnificent, protruding branches, and then fulfill the tradition of countless other men at that very spot, dropping to his knee and asking his love to become his wife.

As he stood in the bathroom shaving, he reflected on the awkwardness of sharing his childhood bedroom with his girlfriend. Amazingly enough, his parents didn't seem to mind. But then, he was twenty-six now. Besides, it saved him the cost of a hotel room, and his parents enjoyed their company at the house. The trip was going well, and as he had hoped, his parents had taken a liking both to Ana and to the ever-present Lindsay.

He glanced at his watch: 6:10 a.m. He wiped his face with a towel, grabbed the ring box, stuffed it into his pocket, then stepped out into his bedroom, expecting to find Ana still lying in bed. Surprisingly, she was not there.

"Ana?" No answer. He shrugged, grabbed a shirt from the closet, and headed out to the living room. Still fumbling with the buttons, he stopped suddenly when he saw Ana, Sally, and Larry all standing in front of the television, staring intently at the screen. Lindsay sat behind them, uncharacteristically subdued.

Repeatedly, and in slow motion, the television showed a 767-passenger plane flying through Manhattan and crashing into the South Tower of the World Trade Center.

His legs wobbly, Nathan placed his hand on Ana's shoulder; she pivoted and hugged him tightly. He caressed her hair and kissed her softly on the cheek to comfort her, knowing at that moment that none of his plans, hopes, and dreams for this day would come to pass.

IV.

THE GENERAL

IV.1

Sadr City, Iraq—April 2004

"Take cover! Now!"

At the platoon leader's command, two of the patrol's Bradley Fighting Vehicles veered off the dense urban street and onto the right sidewalk behind the hulking wreckage of several automobiles. Two other Bradleys retreated to the left side of the street and formed a defensive position alongside three Humvees. Soldiers from Bravo Company Second Platoon scrambled out and formed positions across the street from each other, using the natural barrier of the wrecked cars to their advantage. Despite the fortifications, they remained dangerously vulnerable to sniper fire from the multistory buildings lining the block.

A pickup truck emerged from behind the rubble of a burned-out building fifty meters down the road. It pulled into the center of the street, and an insurgent wearing a New York Yankees baseball cap began firing the DShK machine gun mounted on the truck. The shells exploded into the barrier, spraying the clustered soldiers with metal shards from the wrecked automobiles.

"Freaking murder holes!" 1st Lieutenant Nathan Wilkinson swore as more bullets from insurgent AK-47s pinged against the sides of the fighting vehicles. He pivoted to the soldier crouched next to him. "Diesel, listen up. Airmail and I are going to lay down suppressive fire to distract that gunner. When he stops firing, get to the turret in the lead Humvee and blow him to hell!"

"Yes, sir!" snapped Private Donnie "Diesel" Maurizio.

Nathan gestured to Private Ryan "Airmail" Hoff, and in unison, the two fired their M4s at the enemy vehicle. Two insurgents jumped out of the truck to escape the hail of bullets and fled into an adjoining building, while the insurgent manning the DShK stopped firing and ducked for cover behind the mount.

Maurizio saw his opportunity; brushing dust from the perpetually day-old stubble on his face, he took position behind the .50 cal on the Humvee and opened fire on the pickup truck. The insurgent hurdled himself off the bed as the .50 cal's bullets ripped into the chassis. Several shells hit the gas tank, and the pickup exploded into flames.

"First rate, Diesel!" Nathan shouted, giving a thumbs-up to the young, black-haired soldier.

But the celebration was cut short when Nathan spotted a pointed metallic cone emerging from a second-story window of the building to which the insurgents had retreated. "RPG!" he screamed.

Maurizio leaped from the Humvee as the insurgent fired. The RPG whistled through the smoke-filled haze and struck the Humvee in the center of the driver's-side door. The explosion was deafening; the shockwave sent Maurizio tumbling to the ground, where he lay dazed and exposed in the center of the street. The Bradley burst into flames that shot high into the afternoon sky, sending the pungent smell of burning metal and fuel through the landscape.

"Covering fire—now!" Nathan ordered. The soldiers opened up at the decimated building housing the insurgents, who once again retreated below the windows.

To Nathan's left scurried First Sergeant Enrique "Shiv" Silva. "Lieutenant!" the muscular, six-foot second-in-command shouted to Nathan, pointing at Maurizio. "Diesel may have caught some shrapnel!"

"Copy!" Nathan turned to another private beside him. "J-Run, get ready. We're going to lay out some more suppressant, and when we do, you go get Diesel. But keep your damned head down!"

"Aye, sir!" Private James "J-Run" McCollom said.

"What the hell do you mean 'aye'? This isn't the damned navy!"

McCollom smirked at Nathan before returning to the business at hand. Nathan gestured again to the platoon's soldiers, and all of them sprayed their M4s at the building housing the insurgents. As the bullets flew over him, the lanky, curly-haired McCollom crawled on his stomach into the open street toward Maurizio. Dust and smoked seared through his lungs as he gasped for air.

"Diesel!" he cried out. "You okay, man?"

Maurizio muttered something unintelligible; with some effort, McCollom turned the stocky private over, scanned for blood and open wounds, then gripped onto his Desert Camouflage Uniform and started to drag him back to the makeshift barricade. Two insurgents emerged from the third-story rooftop of their sanctuary and fired several shots at the exposed soldiers; the shells kicked up dust as they impacted the dirt road inches from them.

"You're gonna owe me big time, buddy," McCollom said to the dazed Maurizio as they neared the protective Bradley-enforced barricade. "At the very least, your sister's phone number."

Several agonizing moments later, the two reached the first Bradley. Silva reached out and pulled the two of them behind the barricade as more shots pinged behind them.

Silva ran his hands over Maurizio's body, reaching behind the armor plates in his uniform and across his lower back. "I checked him too, and I didn't find any shrapnel wounds," McCollom said.

Silva turned Maurizio over and shook his head. "You okay, soldier?"

Maurizio gave him a dazed look and nodded. "Yeah, I think so. I was a little too close to that RPG explosion. I think I just got my bell rung."

"Okay, give yourself a minute to clear your head. The rest of you, stop firing and let the lieutenant and me assess the situation."

Maurizio glanced back at McCollom. "Thanks for pulling my chestnuts out of the fire back there. But forget about my sister—she's still too good for you."

* * * * * *

"Shiv, give me a report," Nathan commanded.

"There's about a half dozen of them, best we can tell," Silva responded, pointing through the smoky haze at the structure in front of them. "They're all still holed up in that three-story building."

"Okay. I see the main entrance, near what's left of their pickup truck. Can you spot any other entries?"

"There's a side door at the south wing."

It didn't take Nathan long to complete his assessment. "They don't have enough men to engage us and to cover both entrances simultaneously. So, here's what we're going to do. You take three men and move up behind the lead Humvee on the right. Light them up, throw some frag grenades, and make them think you're the main line of attack. I'm going to take the rest of the squad and breach the side entrance."

"Aye, Captain."

"Now don't you start!"

While the brawny second-in-command snaked back to the lead Humvee, Nathan pivoted to the men behind him. "Where's Herrington?" he demanded as the men prepped their M4s for the assault.

"Here, sir!" came a voice from behind the rear Bradley.

"You're up here with me!"

Careful to remain beneath the barricade in order to prevent a clear shot from the snipers still holed up in the building, Private Brian "Breeder" Herrington made his way toward his commanding officer. As usual, the blond-haired, baby-faced private wasn't alone; by his side strutted his companion, a stout, muscular, fifty-five-pound tan Belgian Malinois. The dog sported a flat-topped head with a sharp muzzle, black nose, and triangle-shaped pointed ears. Its dark brown eyes bore an alert and intelligent expression, and its muscles were taut, exuding a quiet but formidable resolve. Herrington gripped the vest strapped to his canine companion's body as he crouched in front of Nathan.

Nathan placed his hand on Herrington's shoulder. "Breeder, when Shiv starts the diversion, you and I are going to lead the assault on the south side entrance. There could be IEDs all along our path. Keep Georgie at the front; if he picks up any IED scents, you let me know stat."

"Yes, sir!"

Nathan turned to the Malinois. "You ready, Georgie?"

The dog bestowed upon Nathan a cold and intense stare, an expression conveying that it was all business and all about protecting his comrades.

Nathan gestured again at Silva, who commenced with a barrage of fire, shattering what was left of the building's windows and pocking the gray concrete walls. One insurgent tried to return fire while the others cowered beneath the windows.

"Let's go!" Nathan commanded. The soldiers dashed toward the building's south entrance. Supporting fire from the .50 cal mounted on the parked Humvee provided critical cover for the risky assault.

Georgie kept in front of the team, maintaining his position next to his handler as bullets flew past them. As they approached an open stormwater drain, a favorite hiding place for IEDs, Nathan looked to Georgie for a signal; the dog made no gesture. Nathan sighed in relief and pride at the Malinois' effectiveness and efficiency, and without a second thought, the squad passed the drain and approached the doorway. Nathan grabbed the door handle; unsurprisingly, it did not budge.

"Sir!" called a voice behind him. Nathan stood aside as a fellow soldier heaved a portable battering ram against the door, shattering the wood frame.

Light shone through the broken door and windows, illuminating an open entryway. Splintered furniture lay throughout the large foyer, covered by dust that rained down from the torn ceiling tiles. A musty smell permeated the structure. To the right was a staircase to the upper floors. There was no sign of any insurgents.

"Herrington! Sweep the room now!"

Nathan held his breath as Herrington led Georgie through the foyer. Another favored tactic of the budding insurgency was to lure troops into a deserted building, then detonate IEDs strewn in the walls to maximize casualties. Georgie scanned the room and glanced back at his handler—again, no gestures.

"Clear!" Herrington shouted.

Then Georgie let out a loud yelp. Nathan pivoted toward a doorway on the right to face an insurgent emerging from behind, AK-47 in hand. Instantly Nathan fired his M4; hit multiple times in the chest, the insurgent vaulted backward and crashed to the ground.

"Good job, Georgie!" Nathan hollered. "Fire teams, clear this building now!"

The riflemen and grenadiers moved forward in rhythm, stacking outside the entry point to each room on the ground floor. Herrington and Georgie remained in front, clearing each room of IEDs before the soldiers entered.

Within minutes the team had secured the entire first floor. Then they moved up the staircase to the second floor, surprising two more insurgents who had been firing out the windows at Silva's team. The troops fired in unison, and both insurgents dropped to the ground. A third insurgent fumbled with a hand grenade; two riflemen fired point-blank, and he propelled backward, crashing through the window and impacting the street with a dull thud.

An eerie silence set forth in the decimated, smoke-drenched building as Nathan made his way onto the second-floor landing. "Report!"

"Secure, sir! Six Muj casualties."

"Sir!" called out a female private near a rear window. "Take a look at this!"

Nathan dashed over to the window and glanced downward. A matted-haired insurgent dressed in a plaid shirt was frantically wriggling through a first-floor window into a back alley.

"How the hell did we miss him?" Nathan snarled. There was no time to get down the stairs and out the door before the insurgent could free himself, make his way down the alley, and melt into the crowd. Nathan unleashed a string of expletives aimed as much at himself as at his troops.

"Sir!" Herrington called out. "I think we can get him!" he shouted.

Herrington led Georgie to the window and pointed at the insurgent, who had freed his torso and was now wiggling his lower legs through the opening.

"Georgie, seek!"

In an instant the dog was down the stairs and out the door; Nathan, Herrington, and two other soldiers followed behind.

The insurgent was now through the narrow window. As he started toward the alley, he witnessed the flash of an American military war dog tearing out the south entrance of the shattered building and toward him. The Malinois lunged at the fleeing combatant, his body slamming into the enemy's back and sending him tumbling to the dusty street. Georgie locked his jaw around the insurgent's bicep; the enemy howled in pain and flailed about in a hopeless effort to free himself.

Within moments Nathan and Herrington were upon them. Nathan jammed the nozzle of his M4 against the side of the insurgent's head.

"Georgie! Release!" Herrington shouted. Somewhat reluctantly, the Malinois relinquished his iron grip on the insurgent's arm. Blood dripped from several open punctures, staining the man's ripped sleeve.

"On the ground!" Nathan shouted. "Face down!" The insurgent meekly lay

~ 111 ~

down; the female soldier thrust her knee into the man's back, pulled out zip-tie handcuffs, and bound his hands.

"That was amazing!" Nathan exclaimed to Herrington. "I thought Georgie was just a bomb sniffer!"

"He is. But he's also a soldier."

* * * * * *

As late afternoon progressed into evening, the convoy rolled into Camp War Eagle, a central seat of coalition operations located on the site of a pre-war Iraqi army base at the northeast corner of Sadr City. The vehicles ground to a halt near the flagpole in the compound's center, and Nathan hopped out of the lead Humvee, removed his Kevlar helmet and sunglasses, and fumbled with his body armor. Despite the lateness of the day, the heat remained oppressive and stifling. Silva jumped out behind Nathan and rubbed the sweat from his forehead as he unbuckled his vest and dropped it to the ground. Both men could smell the pungent spices from the meals cooking in the nearby homes as the call to prayers reverberated from the loudspeakers mounted on the local mosque's minaret.

"Must be 120 degrees right now," Nathan muttered to Silva. "I may be from Arizona, but even to me that's still damned hot."

The remaining soldiers disembarked from their vehicles, and Nathan observed two of his men leading the handcuffed and blindfolded insurgent toward the base's holding area.

"I see you got one, at least," came a voice behind him. Nathan turned to face his battalion commander, Colonel Isaiah Richardson. The imposing six-foot-four-inch African American was accompanied by a younger captain whom Nathan did not recognize.

"Yes, sorry, sir. It was a bit of a crap show we got ourselves into. We wanted to take a few more alive, but they wouldn't cooperate."

"I'm not gonna cry any real tears over that. I know HQ wants to question more of al-Sadr's guys, to find out where they're from. But I think we already know the answer. Most aren't even Iraqi, probably coming from Saudi Arabia or Chechnya to take on the Great Satan."

"Well, the Great Satan fought back today, sir. Six confirmed kills, no casualties on our side except for Maurizio, who got a little too close to an RPG. He'll be okay; he'll just be seeing stars for a while."

"Have the meds check him out and send the rest of your guys to the DFAC for a bite to eat. But you and Silva stay with me, and tell Herrington to get over here too."

Nathan passed the order to find Herrington on to McCollom, and then he and Silva turned back toward their colonel.

"Gentlemen," Richardson said, "I want to introduce you to Capt. Robert Fornier. He's an aide to the Joint Chiefs, and he's just arrived from the Pentagon."

"Welcome to hell, sir," Silva said.

"That's a pretty apt description, from what I can see," Fornier replied. "As you guys are well aware, this insurgency is really heating up, and a lot of the bad guys are holed up right here in Sadr City. Despite what they're telling us in Washington, we're starting to think that this is going to go on for a while. It'll be mostly low level, but in dense urban areas like here, it's likely to get ugly. The insurgents' objective is mass casualties—they think that if they can kill and wound enough US troops, we'll get fed up with all this and pull out."

"Like Vietnam," the colonel added.

"The Pentagon is planning for the long haul," Fornier continued. "You guys have already seen that the insurgents' weapon of choice is the IED. We're working on several different countermeasures, but there are a lot of people in Washington who are hoping that MWDs, or Military Working Dogs, may be one of the key solutions.

"We're starting to assemble war dog teams at the Proving Ground in Yuma, Arizona. We've set up an advanced skills K-9 course out there, and we're training thirty teams of dogs and their handlers. But before we go full scale into the program, we want to see how well they perform under real combat situations. That's why we assigned the first unit to your platoon. A pilot case, if you will."

"If the other MWDs are anything like Georgie, I think they'll be a helluva asset," Nathan responded.

"That's good to hear, Lieutenant. I'll be spending some time here on the base conducting a full assessment of your MWD. The Pentagon expects a report by early May."

At that moment, Herrington, still dressed in full battle gear, with Georgie, ever dutiful at his side, arrived and saluted the colonel.

"Ah, speak of the devil," Nathan said and then introduced Herrington, who saluted the captain. "And," he continued, "Captain, this is Georgie, which is short for General George S. Patton." Georgie, still in combat-ready mode, warily sized up the captain before concluding that the man was a friendly.

"That's quite a namesake to live up to."

"Sir," Nathan said, "I think you'll find that Georgie is every bit as fearless and cocky as Old Blood and Guts himself. And if he continues to perform like he did today, he may end up getting promoted to general for real."

* * * * * *

"Man, that shower felt good," Nathan mumbled to himself, wrapping a towel around himself as he walked into the portable trailer that served as officers' quarters. Relieved that the coarse, fetid odors of combat no longer clung to his body, he stepped into his private quarters to find Enrique Silva sitting on the desk chair next to the bed.

"What brings you here, First Sergeant?"

"Sam wanted to pay you a visit." Silva handed Nathan a cold bottle of Samuel Adams Boston Lager.

"Well, I'm not gonna say no to Sam, that's for sure." Nathan twisted off the cap.

"I know you're not much of a drinker, Lieutenant, but I figured we could both use one after today."

"You got that right." Nathan set the beer down while he let go of his towel and pulled on his pants. "When we deployed here, they told us that it could get pretty hairy at times. And somehow I think we're in for a lot more days like today before we pacify Sadr City."

Silva took a drink from his own bottle. "Kinda makes you question why you signed up, doesn't it?"

"Sometimes. But then I think about 9/11, and it all gets pretty clear again."

"I hear you."

Nathan paused as he picked at the label of his Sam Adams. "When I was younger, I thought about making the army my career. But I decided to go to

ASU to play football instead. I was only thinking about myself, my own wants and needs, and I never considered the fact that one day my country might need me.

"I was at my parents' home when I saw the 767 hit the South Tower that morning. For the rest of the day, I just sat glued to the TV. Like we all did, huh?"

Silva nodded.

"We saw horrible things, didn't we... The people leaping out of the Twin Towers to avoid being burned alive.... The firefighters running in, probably knowing it was a one-way trip...

"I think a lot about those people on Flight 93 who didn't even know each other when the plane took off but who came together and stopped that day from being even worse," Silva said.

It was Nathan's turn to nod. "They were just the latest group of Americans who sacrificed themselves to keep us free. Heroes, every one of them. And they made me realize that I couldn't just sit on the sidelines and let other people make all the sacrifices so that I could enjoy the freedoms they gave me. I owed it to them, to my family, and to my country to join the fight.

"So, a few days after 9/11, I decided to enlist. I drove to Phoenix and went to the army recruitment center there. And because I had a college degree, right away they pegged me for Officer Candidate School."

"That's a tense time to join the military," Silva said. "How did your family react?"

"To put it mildly, not well. My mother got hysterical, and my girlfriend cried. Even my girlfriend's dog seemed to know I was going away. After I signed up, she wouldn't come near me for two days. I swear she was mad at me.

"The only person who seemed to understand was my father. And I wouldn't have thought that, given that he never talks about his experiences in Vietnam, so I always assumed it didn't go well for him. Regardless," Nathan said, his expression turning to one of relief, "all of them have been incredibly supportive of me ever since."

"That's great," Silva responded. "My mom and my three sisters have supported me as well. Before 9/11, I was thinking about getting out, but once I saw the Towers fall, I knew I'd be in for the duration. And I have no regrets at all." Silva met his commander's gaze. "What about you—do you have any regrets?"

Nathan pressed his fingertips against the base of the back of his head, easing a tension point. "After days like today, maybe a few. But for the most part, no. One of the things I think we've both learned, in Afghanistan and here, is that there are a lot of bad people in the world. To them, America and everything it stands for have to be extinguished. Well, I'm going to do my part to make sure that doesn't happen."

"We all are."

The men clinked their beers.

As they took their next sips, the conversation was interrupted by a scratching sound at the partially open door. Nathan and Silva looked over to see Georgie wandering in. The Malinois momentarily eyed the two of them, then moved to Nathan's cot and flopped down onto it.

"Hey!" Nathan barked in full pretend-fury. "Soldier, that's an officer's bunk! You will remove yourself right now!"

Georgie stared at Nathan for a moment, yawned, and laid his head down on the pillow.

"Oh, insubordinate too, are we? Well, you know the penalty for that!"

Nathan rolled Georgie over onto his back and began scratching the Malinois' belly. Georgie sighed, closed his eyes, and grunted happily. His look of contentment brought to Nathan, ever so briefly, a poignant memory of Shiloh.

A moment later there was a knock on the door.

"Sorry, sir," Private Herrington said as he peered inside. "I let him run loose to work off a little of his adrenaline, and he made a beeline for right over here."

"That's okay. He's always welcome. He may be all business out in the field, but it's nice to see that here on base he has time to be a dog."

IV.2

Camp War Eagle, Iraq—October 2004

It was as the command at Camp War Eagle had feared. The hostilities in Sadr City continued for the next several weeks, with Bravo Company engaging in almost daily firefights with the insurgents. Often the fighting was house to house, the most dangerous form of combat.

After engaging in brief exchanges with coalition troops, the nonuniformed enemy often faded into the populated centers, making capture by coalition forces all but impossible. Enemy combatants used ambulances, school buses, and other civilian vehicles to mask their attacks and sometimes even used families and children as shields. IEDs were becoming more pervasive, and deadlier, and US casualties began to mount.

During the spring and summer months, Nathan led his platoon on thirty missions into Sadr City, aiding the marine contingents and Army Rangers. Many were combat missions, to weed out and defeat the insurgent militia. But others involved more humanitarian goals, including restoring water supplies, guarding hospitals from looters, and assisting the remnants of the local police in maintaining order.

The two-pronged strategy of engagement and pacification started to show results by early summer, as the fiercest fighting came to an end, though the sporadic insurgent attacks continued.

Despite the intensity of the engagements, Nathan's platoon suffered no major casualties, other than a flesh wound to Private Hoff's left arm and a rather embarrassing shrapnel puncture to Private McCollom's right buttock. Both men were patched up and returned to duty; McCollom was especially eager to repay the insurgents for the good-natured ribbing over his wound that he received from his comrades.

But the primary reason for Second Platoon's lack of casualties lay in the remarkable efforts by the General and his handler, Private Herrington. Employing a sense of smell a thousand times greater than that of a human, Georgie could identify from a distance an IED's central ingredients: TNT, potassium chlorate, C-4 plastic explosive, and ammonium nitrate. He could even detect the scent of a detonating chord from several feet away.

The routine was well-established. Herrington and Georgie would be stationed with the patrol leaders at the head of the squadron, Georgie fixing his head low to the ground as he sampled the smells. When he detected something, he would stop suddenly and either sit or lie down. Herrington was keenly aware of all of Georgie's mannerisms and alerted the squadron the moment Georgie uncovered a threat.

Georgie skillfully exposed dozens of unexploded IEDs, which in the urban sector of Sadr City could have caused significant casualties to civilians as well as the military contingents. On several other occasions, he detected the smell of C-4 from specific buildings and residences, which led to raids that broke up the bomb-assembly factories housed inside. Georgie could even identify the scent of bomb-making ingredients on individuals, resulting in the arrest of more than fifty insurgents.

The Malinois became ever more noticeable as he marched through the city with his handler and the rest of the squadron on their frequent patrols. Iraqi civilians would stop and stare, some pointing at Georgie. On more than one occasion, Herrington was approached by groups of children who reached out to Georgie and excitedly said one of the few English words they knew: "General!"

A resourceful and faithful warrior, Georgie remained devoted to Herrington, rarely leaving his side during the patrols and firefights. The bond between the two proved unbreakable, both knowing that they were guardians of the other's life.

While Georgie was all business during missions, back at Camp War Eagle, he often let his playful side emerge. He enjoyed engaging with the other soldiers, running up to them with Frisbees or rubber balls, egging them into playing chase and seek games. The soldiers relished it as well, not just because they respected Georgie for his service and dedication. The playtime also served to remind them of the lives that awaited them back in America.

Nathan in particular enjoyed throwing a nerf football to Georgie in the camp's central grounds. Georgie would leap into the air and snag it with his mouth, then trot up to Nathan and dare him to take it back. For Nathan, it brought fond memories of his long-ago games with Shiloh, and of home, during more peaceful times.

"He's a helluva receiver," Silva pointed out to Nathan during one of their interludes. "Good thing he wasn't at ASU; you'd have ended up spending even more time warming the bench."

At night, when the troops got together to watch movies or play cards, Georgie always accompanied them. The men of Second Platoon appreciated his company, but more importantly, they respected him as a fellow comrade-in-arms who had more than earned the right to be with them.

* * * * * *

"Okay, listen up!" Nathan addressed his platoon as he entered the containerized barracks. It was a typically-stifling July evening; most of the men and women were lying on their bunks reading, surfing the internet on laptop computers, or listening to music on their iPods, recovering from another exhausting day of operations in the oppressive heat. The smell of dried sweat permeated the air-conditioned quarters as many, in various stages of undress, awaited their turn in the showers.

"I have some news I want to share with you. Colonel Richardson wants you to know how pleased he was with our support during First Calvary's assault on the Mahdi Army's stronghold in the abandoned police station. With that group's surrender, HQ thinks a turning point in Sadr City has been reached. Muqtada al-Sadr's envoys have reached out to discuss an accommodation."

"Accommodation?" Maurizio said, incredulous. He waved his M4 in front of Nathan. "I'll give those guys an accommodation, right between their eyes."

"I feel you, Diesel, but it's time to let the diplomats see if they can work things out."

"Yeah, what could go wrong with that?" Hoff muttered.

~ 119 ~

Nathan made his way over to Herrington's bunk; as always, Georgie was perched next to his handler and best friend. "I also spoke with Captain Fornier today. He told me that he's been very impressed with Georgie's performance. He said he is going to recommend that the Pentagon go forward with a full military war dog program for all divisions."

The men erupted in hoots and hollers. "Way to go, General!" Silva called out. Herrington remained characteristically silent, but the pride he felt at his dog's service and dedication was visible to all.

"The army is going to establish a comprehensive inter-service advanced skills K-9 course at the Yuma Proving Ground," Nathan continued. "It's going to be tough, both for the dogs and their handlers, and those who make it through will be assigned to forward operations units here and in Afghanistan.

"But there is one other thing the captain shared with me, something all you guys need to know about." The serious tone in Nathan's voice quickly dimmed the celebratory atmosphere. "Eagle Company Third Platoon was on a routine patrol in the northwest quadrant of Sadr City today, and they came across this." Nathan pulled a scrap of paper out of his back pocket, unfolded it, and waved it at the soldiers. "They found several of these flyers posted on telephone poles, mailboxes, and the sides of buildings."

He handed it to Maurizio, who turned pale as he read it. Maurizio handed it to Hoff, who, after a similar reaction, passed it to the rest of the soldiers.

It was a crudely fashioned leaflet, featuring a grainy photo of Georgie taken at a distance. The wording on the flyer in both Arabic and broken English was laced with venom about Georgie being a devil dog from the pits of hell. It promised a reward of US$100 for a successful hit on Georgie, and it ended with the vow that they would feed his carcass to the coyotes that roamed the outskirts of the city.

"It looks like our comrade has gotten the bad guys' attention," Nathan said. "They know he's hurt them, and they want him taken out."

Herrington stepped forward; Nathan sensed the visceral anger building up inside the young private. "Lieutenant," he growled, abandoning any reserve, "those bastards who want to kill Georgie are going to have to crawl over my cold, dead body to do it."

Maurizio stood up. "And mine too," he declared.

One by one the rest of the soldiers rose to their feet. Flashes of rage burned in their eyes at the threat against their comrade. Sensing the atmosphere in the barracks, Georgie stood up and resolutely strode over to face Nathan.

"Georgie, you are a member of Bravo Company Second Platoon," Nathan said to the Malinois. "That makes you one of us. We will fight together, we will protect each other, and if it comes to that, we will die together. But every one of us will be at your side, now and to the end!"

With that, the soldiers closed around Georgie, and whooping and hollering again, they took turns stroking his short, tan fur.

* * * * * *

"I still can't get over how amazing this is!" Ana exclaimed. Her image was grainy and slightly off-color, and a nominal lag caused her words to not quite match her lip movement on the Dell computer's screen. "We can see each other even though you are halfway across the world!"

The software Skype had been released a few months earlier, and the army immediately set it up on the computers in the rec hall. All the guys, including Nathan, were enjoying seeing their loved ones in addition to hearing them.

"I wish the picture quality was a little better," Ana continued.

"Don't worry, I'm still the same handsome guy you fell so madly in love with."

"Of course you are!" She laughed. Then she backed away and pivoted the screen toward Nathan's parents, who were sitting next to her. Larry and Sally waved at the tiny camera mounted on top of the monitor.

"Are you getting enough to eat, honey?" Sally asked him.

"Now that's the motherliest thing you could possibly ask me. Yes, I'm eating well."

"Seriously, though, you doing okay?" Larry chimed in. "I keep reading stories about how bad it's been getting around Baghdad."

Repressing in his mind the ugly things he'd seen, Nathan said instead, "The media's blowing it all out of proportion, as usual. Sure, we get the occasional gunfire from the random insurgent, but it's nothing my platoon can't handle. Please don't worry about me."

"If you say so," Larry responded, not quite convinced.

"We're very proud of you, Nathan," Sally added.

"Thanks. And thanks for coming down from Chino to sit in on this call. We don't have the luxury of separate calls to everyone."

"Do you want us to leave now so you can talk to Ana alone?"

Nathan smiled. "I only have a few more minutes anyway. The others are waiting for their turn."

Larry swiveled the monitor back toward Ana. "Before we go," Ana said, "there's someone else here who wants to say hi to you."

Ana reached down and lifted a wriggling black miniature schnauzer to the monitor's camera.

"There's my other favorite girl!" Nathan exclaimed. At the sound of his voice, Lindsay stopped and glared at the screen, a puzzled look on her bushy black face.

"Lindsay, sweet girl, here I am!"

Lindsay yelped again at the sound of his voice. She peered at Nathan's image on the monitor and sniffed at it.

"Now you've got her all confused!" Ana said.

"I know, not very nice of me, huh?"

"Well, she misses you terribly. She still sleeps on your side of the bed every night."

"Uh, honey, maybe you shouldn't be talking about what side of the bed I sleep on with my parents sitting next to you."

"Oh!" Ana's face turned bright red. "Sorry!"

"Yeah, like we had no idea." Larry snickered. "We all miss you, son."

"I miss you guys just as much. In fact, I have something important to tell you. I'm due to roll out of Iraq in two months, and I've decided I'm not going to re-up."

"Does that mean...?"

"Yes, that's what it means. I've been serving for three years now, both in Afghanistan and in Iraq. It's time for me to come home."

"That's wonderful news!" Ana exclaimed. "We can't wait to see you!"

"Me too. I think I've done as much as I can, and it's time for me to be with my family again."

"We'll take good care of this girl until you get home," Larry assured his son as he extended his arm around Ana's shoulder. Just then Lindsay jumped into Larry's lap and whined again at Nathan's grainy image on the screen. "I mean, both of these girls, of course! Now, you stay safe, hear?"

"Sure, Dad. Don't you guys worry about a thing. I'll be fine."

* * * * * *

"You wanted to see me, sir?" Nathan asked as he entered Colonel Richardson's office.

"Yes, sit down, Lieutenant." The colonel motioned to an empty chair. Captain Fornier stood in the foreground as Nathan took the seat facing the colonel. The air conditioner in the window strained to temper the always-oppressive heat.

"You are aware of the deteriorating situation in Fallujah, correct?" the colonel asked.

"Yes, sir."

"Last spring the marines cleaned out the city and offed most of the bad guys. But as usual, we won the war and lost the peace. The CIA estimates that in the last few months as many as five thousand insurgents have regrouped in Fallujah. They've started launching almost daily attacks against us, and they've taken to kidnapping and beheading Western civilians."

"Damn," Nathan grunted.

"So, command has decided to launch another attack on Fallujah. This one's code-named Operation Phantom Fury. And no screwing around, either. We're going in big-time, and we're going to get rid of those bastards once and for all."

"How many men are you sending?"

"Fifteen thousand. Mostly marines, but they're going to need our support."

"How so?" Nathan asked tentatively.

Richardson unfurled a map on his desk and pointed to one of several highlighted villages. "We're going to use our brigades to secure the area surrounding Fallujah. See this village? It's called Nasifah, and it's about ten miles to the east of central Fallujah. We want you to lock it down and make sure Johnny Jihad can't use it for support or supplies."

"Shouldn't be that difficult, Lieutenant," Fornier added. "There haven't been any reports of insurgent activity there in over a month. Normal population is about two hundred, and many of the civilians are going to leave once the fighting gets hot."

"The village is about fifty miles from Camp War Eagle. We're going to chopper your team in. You will be assisted by Alpha Company, who will take the land route. They'll meet up with you at the designated staging area outside the village. While there aren't any insurgents there now, we want your two teams to secure the place before they change their minds and go back in."

"Sounds good, Major," Nathan said, feeling a twinge of guilt over the relief at the low-intensity assignment. "When do we go?"

"Tonight. Have your guys ready by twenty-one hundred hours. And take the General with you. Just because the insurgents are gone doesn't mean they haven't left any IEDs behind."

"Yes, sir. If there are any there, Georgie will find them. He always does." Nathan stood up and saluted.

"So, Lieutenant, you disappointed you'll be missing the real action in Fallujah?"

"No, sir. I think I've been shot at enough. Time to give the jarheads a turn."

IV.3

Nasifah, Iraq—October 2004

"You know, I've always hated flying," Silva muttered, his jaws rattling from the vibrations of the Chinook's powerful engines as the chopper roared through the nighttime desert sky.

"C'mon, Shiv, enough with the clichés." Nathan laughed. "Everyone who ever goes anywhere in one of these buckets says he hates flying."

"Yeah, well, you blame me? I swear, that pilot must be aiming for every air pocket between here and the landing site."

The two men were seated beside each other clad in full combat gear, metal plates inserted in their bulky vests, sidearms strapped to their legs, night goggles fastened to their Kevlar helmets. Nathan cradled his M4 against his waist as he took the measure of his platoon. The two rows of combatants sat silently, strapped to their seats on the periphery of the chopper, facing each other across an open passageway. A few had closed their eyes, others gazed down at the floor, lost in thought and introspection.

Seated across from Nathan and Silva, Herrington spread his legs wide to allow Georgie to nestle himself. He clasped his M4 with his right hand while his left gripped Georgie's protective vest.

"You two ready?" Nathan asked Herrington.

"Always, sir."

"Good. We need Georgie's A game tonight."

Georgie sat motionless, eyes burning with intensity. The playfulness and relaxation of the previous days at Camp War Eagle had vanished. Combat operations were approaching, and once again it was time for business.

"Make us proud, Georgie," Nathan said to the Malinois.

Ten minutes later, the Chinook touched down at the staging area on the village outskirts. "Second Bravo, get ready to dismount!" Nathan shouted over the idling engine's reverberations. The crew lowered the cargo door while the soldiers unstrapped themselves and gathered their equipment. The door's underside hit the rocky terrain with a thud, and the men and women piled out into the desert evening.

They observed a cluster of buildings adorning the desolate landscape three hundred meters down a two-lane dirt road. As in most Iraqi villages, the buildings were one- and two-story crude stone-and-concrete fabrications. Intermittent beams of light shone through the boarded windows from the kerosene lamps inside.

"A dozen crappy buildings in the middle of nowhere," Maurizio muttered. "It looks pretty deserted, sir."

"Copy that. But proceed cautiously. Those lights mean that there are civilians huddled inside some of these homes."

As Second Bravo's soldiers regrouped into assigned teams, four Humvees rolled up to the Helos and screeched to a halt. Their leader jumped out and saluted Nathan.

"First Sergeant James Ferguson, Alpha Company, Third Platoon. We're here to support your team."

"Good to have you here, Sergeant." Nathan snapped his night vision goggles into place, then peered toward the desolate settlement. "Don't see any activity yet. No civilians in the town center."

"We were told that the jihadi boys abandoned this place a month ago," Ferguson said. "Probably headed into Fallujah to join their buddies."

"Yeah, we were told that too."

"I don't blame them for ditching this town. But now we end up watching over a bunch of empty buildings while the marines are getting to have all the fun in Fallujah. I'd rather be sticking it to the muj over there than sitting here in this dumpy town."

"Noted, Sergeant," Nathan said dismissively—*Bet you haven't seen much combat, hero!*—then turned to address his squadron. "Everyone, listen up! Our orders are to secure this town and confirm there are no enemy fighters here. We are also to search for any IED or WMD storehouses.

"When we get to the town center, I want teams going through the residences one by one. Maintain squadron integrity at all times. The civilians are going to be scared and jumpy, and some of them may be armed. Watch your back and don't shoot unless shot at first.

"Ferguson, you and your team stay in the Humvees and flank us. Have gunners at the ready in each of the turrets."

Ferguson jumped back into his Humvee and slid behind the steering wheel. The Humvee roared to life, and the platoons moved forward in unison, Bravo soldiers in the center of the street, safeguarded by the vehicles' protective armor. Herrington maintained his grasp on Georgie's vest as two took the lead, the Malinois scouting and sniffing. They passed the empty stores and boarded-up buildings lining the outskirts to the village. Then, boots crunching the gravelly road, the soldiers scouted the village through their night vision goggles, detecting no signs of any activity, insurgent or civilian.

Moments later the unit rolled into the town square. A crumbling statue of Saddam Hussein was surrounded by a three-foot-high stone fence. To the left were several commercial buildings with derelict automobiles parked in front. To the right sat a row of residences bordered with similar stone fences. A four-foot-high pile of hay was stacked in front of one of the residences. A deserted petrol station lay in the northwest corner of the town center, adjacent to one of three roads leading out of the town center. It was dark and desolate, unnaturally quiet.

"I know it's nighttime and we're in the middle of nowhere," Silva said, "but there still should be some activity here. Instead, nothing, not even any stray animals. I don't like this."

"Agreed," Nathan responded. "Doesn't feel right. Stay alert." He called out to Herrington, who remained in front of him. "Breeder?"

"Georgie hasn't picked up anything yet, sir."

Ferguson steered his Humvee over to one of the residences and hopped out. A torn curtain covered its window, and pockmarks from stray bullets riddled the concrete walls.

"This looks like as good a place as any to start," he said, motioning for the other soldiers to disembark. The team surrounded the entryway; Ferguson approached the door and pounded on it. After a moment, it cracked open; the team could see only the outline of a figure standing in the hallway shadows.

"Get your hands up now!" Ferguson shouted, his M4 locked and ready. The figure stood motionless for a moment, then moved forward, revealing himself to be a child not more than ten years old, clad in baggy pants and a gray frock that hung over his waist, bearing an expression of genuine fear.

"It's just a kid!" the gunner hollered from the Humvee's turret.

"Come closer; let me have a look at you," Ferguson commanded. The child stared blankly at him.

"Speak English?" No answer. Ferguson gestured with his hand, and the boy stepped forward.

Ferguson eyed him carefully. "You look harmless enough. You got family in there?"

"He doesn't understand you," Nathan called out from his vantage point a few meters behind the team. "Just pat him down."

"All right," Ferguson responded, "but he looks too young to be a jihadi." He pointed at the residence's wall, next to the open doorway. "Okay, kid, assume the position." The boy remained motionless.

"I said, get up against that wall!" Ferguson grabbed the child by the arm and shoved him forward. Distracted, he did not see a second figure emerge from the shadows into the open doorway. The figure hurled a plastic bag filled with liquid into Ferguson's side; it burst open, covering his thigh and leg with a warm liquid. Immediately Ferguson recognized the foul smell of urine.

He swore loudly as he whirled about toward the open doorway. Another child, a few years older than the first, scurried from the entryway toward the main road leading out of the town center. The Humvee's gunner whirled about toward the child, .50 cal at the ready.

"No!" Nathan barked. "Do not fire!"

Ferguson took off after the child, who was now fifteen meters ahead of him. Despite carrying fifty pounds of equipment, Ferguson rapidly closed the gap; the youth diverted past the stacked hay and headed toward the petrol station.

"LT!" Herrington shouted. Nathan pivoted to see Georgie squatting and bowing his head as the child passed the haystack.

Nathan spun back to Ferguson. "IED!" he screamed, too late. As Ferguson passed the haystack, it exploded, the blast vaulting him backward, his body riddled by nails and ball bearings. He tumbled to the ground, shrieking in agony.

Two soldiers jumped from the Humvee and started toward Ferguson. A flurry of gunfire erupted from three different locations in the square as eight insurgent shooters emerged from behind the buildings. The soldiers dove behind the cover of the Humvees, scrambling to return fire.

Herrington, Silva, and Nathan crouched behind the left rear Humvee. Bullets pinged all around them, one just missing Silva's head.

"Shots are coming from all corners!" Nathan shouted.

"Abandoned village, no insurgents—great freaking intelligence we got there."

"LT!" one of the Alpha Company soldiers hollered from his position behind the adjoining Humvee. "We've got to get Ferguson!"

"No can do! Fire's too intense!"

Ferguson lay on his back, screaming in pain, a pool of blood forming underneath him. The soldiers watched helplessly as more shots rang out; dust from the bullets' impact puffed all around the stricken first sergeant. In rapid succession, four shots found their mark; Ferguson's body twitched from the impacts, and he fell silent.

Nathan grunted through clenched teeth at the horrific sight. "Where did those last shots come from?"

"Rooftop—gray two-story ten meters northwest!" Silva fired a volley of shots at the targets, sending two shadowy figures diving for cover.

"They've still got the elevation on us!"

Through his night vision goggles, Nathan saw another insurgent fling a grenade from the rooftop right at them. He dove forward, caught it with his right hand, and in a continuous motion hurled it back toward the roof. It exploded as it landed, and the rooftop gunfire stopped.

"Just damn!" Silva said as Nathan crouched back behind the Humvee. "Hands like those and you were still third receiver?"

"Darrian always said that I caught the passes that mattered."

Despite the intensity of their situation, Silva managed a chuckle.

"Shiv, there are at least three more hostiles in that hut behind the fuel station. Take Diesel and Airmail and approach it from the left flank. Breeder, go with them and take Georgie. There's probably more IEDs between us and that station."

Nathan laid out covering fire as Maurizio, Hoff, and Herrington dashed toward the cover of the abandoned cars near the petrol station. Herrington led the way, and the soldiers all followed as Georgie cleared the cars for any explosives. It had to be done quickly, given the volleys streaking past them, but Georgie remained calm and efficient, unfazed by the bedlam.

After the group took their positions behind the cars, Nathan signaled the Humvee's gunner, who pivoted toward the petrol station and opened fire. The .50 cal rounds tore into the hut, sending the two insurgents fleeing into the open, where Diesel and Airmail took out both with a barrage of M4 fire.

They had no time for congratulations, as more fire erupted from another residence east of the team. Several insurgents mounting a battered SUV emerged from behind one of the houses. Four leaped from the cab, raised their AR-15s, and fired indiscriminately at the Americans.

"Lieutenant, there's too many of them!" McCollom cried out. "We're going to have to withdraw!"

"Call in air support now!"

McCollom fumbled with the transmitter strapped to his chest as Nathan engaged the aggressors from his position. Additional insurgent teams spread out from the buildings, attempting to flank the trapped soldiers. Bullets flew at them from all sides, pinging the Humvee behind which Nathan was stranded.

A moment later McCollom gave Nathan the thumbs-up. "Apaches inbound! Four minutes!"

"All right, get over to Diesel, Airmail, and Breeder and tell them to get back here now, before the Apaches light this place up!"

McCollom sprinted over the thirty-meter open area in the town square to where the other soldiers hunkered behind the abandoned cars. Bullets traced his pathway, hitting the ground behind his feet. Nathan pivoted to the source of the fire, an AR-15 extending from a hole in the boarded-up window of the residence from which the first boy had emerged. He fired several more times, and the barrel withdrew back into the house.

"All teams, fall back now!" Nathan barked into his transmitter. Three of the Humvees threw into reverse and backed up; the gunners continued to fire as they began their withdrawal. Nathan remained behind the unmanned Humvee.

"Behind you!" Herrington screamed at Nathan, pointing at the residence. Nathan pivoted and saw a cylindrical cone emerge from the hole in the boarded-up window. He jumped up as the RPGs fiery launch shattered the remains of the window, but he could only manage to cover a few meters before the aerial grenade slammed into the Humvee. The explosion rocked the town center, spraying deadly shrapnel from the stricken vehicle. The force of the detonation knocked Nathan to the ground in the middle of the street twenty meters from his comrades.

Dazed from the violent blast, he was only vaguely aware of the searing pain emanating from his left leg. He felt a cold dread stream through his body, of vulnerability, of fright, and of panic. The pain intensified as consciousness began to slip away.

Maurizio, Hoff, and Herrington watched in horror as more rounds struck the dirt within centimeters of the incapacitated lieutenant. Georgie whined in distress and helplessness from his position aside Herrington. Then the Malinois heard something unusual, a sound that did not belong in the chaos.

A bark.

Georgie pivoted and saw behind him a border beagle mix. Transparent, unseen by anyone else, the four-legged visitor started intently at him through its sparkling eyes, its message unmistakable.

He needs you!

In a flash, the General sprinted into the open toward Nathan, bullets whizzing past him from the insurgents' redirected fire.

"Georgie!" Herrington shouted.

"What the hell!" Maurizio exclaimed.

Reaching Nathan, Georgie lowered his snout and pressed it against his stricken comrade's cheek. The gesture jarred Nathan out of his semi consciousness.

"G-Georgie?" Nathan mumbled, and the Malinois yipped in response. Then Georgie saw that Nathan's pant leg was torn and soaked with blood, several large shrapnel fragments embedded in his lower calf. Abruptly he pivoted, gripped Nathan's loosened vest with his teeth, and used all his might to try to drag him through the street. But the weight of Nathan's body, plus the additional fifty pounds of equipment, was too much for the Malinois. A bullet struck the ground less than a centimeter from Georgie's front left paw.

"I though you trained him not to do anything stupid!" Maurizio bellowed, then turned to see Herrington lurching into the street toward his lieutenant and his best friend. "I can't believe this!" he moaned.

More bullets sailing past him, Herrington reached the clustered pair and kneeled in front of Nathan. "Can you walk?"

"Don't think so."

Letting go of Nathan's vest, Georgie grunted loudly at Herrington.

"Okay," he said to the Malinois, "we'll do it your way!"

Herrington rolled Nathan onto his back and grabbed him by the arms. Georgie sank his teeth deeper into the right side of Nathan's vest and, in sync with Herrington, pulled with all his might. As they dragged Nathan across the dirt, Maurizio and Hoff fired volleys to impede the insurgents from acquiring a clear shot at their exposed comrades. Nathan howled from the pain that engulfed his leg as it chafed against the terrain.

After several agonizing seconds, the trio came within reach of the protective cover of the cars. Maurizio reached out from the barricade and grabbed Nathan's shoulders while Herrington pushed against the lieutenant's waist.

Georgie let go and leaped behind the barricade. He glanced about for the mysterious visitor, but it was gone.

"Good job, Georgie!" Maurizio said as the two dragged Nathan's torso behind the barricade.

"Hey, what about me?" Herrington grinned as he positioned himself in front of the car to push Nathan's right leg forward behind the barricade.

"Yeah, well, your dog's always been your better half, but you—" Maurizio stopped at the sound of a thud against Herrington's back. Nathan, still dazed and in great pain, saw Herrington's face whiten, a glassy look envelop his eyes. He bolted up just in time to catch the slumping private.

As Herrington fell forward, an insurgent dressed in a plaid shirt and blue jeans stepped into view in the open fifteen meters behind him, a whiff of smoke emitting from his AR-15. The insurgent jerked the trigger again, but this time his weapon did not fire. He cursed in Arabic and fumbled with the empty magazine.

"Bastard!" Hoff roared and fired at the insurgent, who scrambled for cover behind the crumbling Saddam statue.

Despite the agonizing pain in his leg, Nathan summoned the strength to sit up and roll Herrington onto the ground behind the barricade. He tore off Herrington's vest; the private's chest was drenched with blood, and he heard a sucking sound from the exit wound in the chest cavity.

"Breeder! Stay with me, buddy!"

Georgie whined and grimaced in a tone that combined abject fear and denial. Herrington gasped and coughed, spattering blood onto Nathan. He gave Georgie a final look of recognition in the enveloping fog before his head fell to the ground.

"Oh Jesus, Breeder!" Nathan moaned. Georgie's look conveyed a silent pleading for Nathan to do something, anything to save his friend. But Nathan's return glance told the General everything.

Then Georgie's expression changed. His eyes narrowed, and he growled menacingly, flashing his teeth, a cold rage brewing in his eyes.

In the distance, the insurgent who had gunned down Herrington was fleeing toward the road leading out of the town center. Georgie launched himself from behind the barricade, into a full gallop across the center toward the retreating combatant.

"Georgie! No!" Nathan cried out. But for the Malinois, all the months of training and discipline had vanished; he was now propelled by pure instinct, hatred, and a quest for vengeance.

Then the soldiers heard in the distance the churning rumble of approaching Apaches. A moment later the first Hellfire missile streaked toward its target, its whistling sound burning through the air. It slammed into the two-story building where several insurgents were holed up, the thundering explosion blowing a cloud of dust through the square. Still fixated on his pursuit, Georgie bolted straight ahead toward the petrol station and disappeared into the dust cloud.

The second Apache fired two more missiles, and a residence and the petrol station erupted in flames and debris. The dust blanketing the town center thickened to the point that Nathan could barely see ahead of him.

Pain from his severely damaged leg pulsated through his body, causing him to drift into and out of consciousness. It all became a haze: missile explosions, soldiers screaming a cacophony of directives, the clatter of automatic weapons. Then darkness.

He briefly came to again to find himself on a stretcher, a tourniquet wrapped tightly over his left leg.

"LT, you with me?" Through the haze he heard Silva's voice. "Medivac chopper is here; we're going to evac you to Baghdad!"

"No…I need to stay here!"

"No can do," Silva declared as they arrived at the chopper. "You need help, right away. I'm taking charge of Bravo."

"Georgie…"

"He went after the SOB who hit Herrington. I've got Diesel and Airmail looking for him now, but it's pretty chaotic out there."

"Find him…" Nathan mumbled. But once again consciousness streamed away from him; the explosions, the choppers, the medics, and finally Silva faded from view, the first sergeant's voice the last thing he heard floating through the chaos until it too vanished into darkness.

IV.4

Phoenix, Arizona—January 2005

"She just won't leave you alone, will she, Lieutenant?"

The young, brunette nurse laughed at the sight as she placed Nathan's lunch tray beside his bed. Nathan sat upright, propped in place by the foldable mattress while Lindsay had snuggled herself underneath his shoulder, her head resting on his forearm. Her fifteen-pound body stretched down to his leg, her back paws dangling near the still heavily bandaged stump below his left knee.

"She sure won't," Ana said. She sat on the couch across from Nathan in the private room at the North Phoenix Hayden VA Medical Facility. The room was decorated with photos and cards from Nathan's friends and family and assorted other well-wishers. Prominently displayed on the bed was a football signed by Cardinals star quarterback Darrian Lawrence, urging his long-time friend to get better soon. A now-empty cookie basket attached to deflating balloons was perched on the dresser.

"The first time I brought her here and she saw her Nathan, she parked herself right by him, and I haven't been able to move her since," Ana explained to the nurse. Nathan smiled weakly and stroked the top of Lindsay's head. Lindsay stirred momentarily before closing her eyes and resuming her nap.

"It's really nice to see such devotion," the nurse said.

"She worships her Nate. We really appreciate the staff letting her stay here with him."

"That's no problem. We all love Lindsay. Don't we, little girl?" The nurse

~ 135 ~

rubbed Lindsay on the belly. Lindsay opened her eyes and gave Nathan a kiss on the cheek.

"See?" Ana said. "You scratch her; she kisses Nate. She's all about him." She stood up and ran her fingers through Nathan's hair. "C'mon, honey, eat your lunch."

"Maybe later. Not hungry right now."

"You've got to eat. You need the energy for rehab this afternoon."

"I said later."

"Okay, then." She shrugged off his snippy tone. "Do you need anything from the store? Any books or magazines? How about a mocha from Starbucks?"

"No, thanks." Nathan sighed, his mood easing a bit. "Don't trouble yourself."

"If you need anything, just call." Ana leaned over and kissed him on the forehead, and he smiled weakly at her. Her jaw visibly tight, she gave Lindsay a pat on the head and departed along with the nurse.

"I don't mean to get involved in your relationship with your boyfriend," the nurse said to her in the corridor, "but he just needs a little more time to process all of this. I've seen my share of these cases since the Iraq war started. He's suffered a very traumatic injury that's going to change his life. He's going through a lot right now, both emotionally and physically."

"I know. I'm trying hard to give him his space."

"He's taking it better than most of the men and women who have been here. There are some who have never been able to come to terms with their wounds. But Nathan is strong, I can tell. And he has a lot of support, from you and from his parents. And even from his little dog."

"What can I do to help him?"

"Keep doing what you've been doing. Be there for him. Look the other way if he pops off at you. And love him with all your heart."

* * * * * *

The latest episode of *Lost* blared from the TV mounted in the corner of Nathan's room, though he was only half-heartedly paying attention to it when he heard the knock on the door.

"Ana said you might be stopping by today," Nathan said as his father emerged through the doorway.

Larry closed the door behind him. Lindsay bolted up at the sound, crawled across Nathan's chest and sniffed at the older man.

"Hey there, girl!" Larry scratched her behind the ears. "You taking good care of my boy?"

"She's been great. All the nurses love her; they keep coming by and bringing her treats. Hopefully she won't put on too much weight before I get out of here. Is Mom here too?"

"No. I told her not to come."

"Why not?"

Larry slid one of the metal folding chairs over to the side of Nathan's bed and sat down. Lindsay crawled over to the side of the bed and jumped into Larry's lap. "I thought that you and I could spend a little time alone together. Well, almost alone, that is." He laughed as he scratched Lindsay on her shoulder. "I thought we could talk."

"About what?"

"You know what. About what happened to you in Nasifah."

"You want to know everything about what happened to me in Nasifah?" Nathan said in a tone combining anger and self-pity, then pointed to his amputated left leg. "Just look right there."

"I know, son, and I'm sorry about that, believe me."

"Yeah, well a lot of good being sorry does me." He clenched his fists in frustration. "I was a Division One wide receiver, and I could still run a six-minute mile. Now I'm going to spend the rest of my life as a cripple."

"Comments like that are why I came here to talk to you. Yes, of course I know all about what happened that night. After we got that call from your commanding officer, all of us, your mom, Ana, and me, took turns crying through the night."

"Even you?"

"Damned right. You're my only son, and it still pains me to watch you lie here day after day in this damned hospital bed."

Nathan felt something sour grow from his stomach up into his mouth. *I'm so sorry my injury is so hard on you all.*

"But your injury isn't the reason I'm worried about you. You are one tough guy, and I know you'll get past your physical injuries. What I care about right now are the injuries to your spirit. Those are the injuries that, if you let them, will eat away at you until there's nothing left."

Nathan refused to say anything for a moment; then he loosened his tight jaw and said quietly, "The army counselors told me the same thing. But it's not the easiest thing in the world to talk about."

"I understand." Larry sat back in his chair as Lindsay, comfortable now in his lap, yawned and closed her eyes. "You know, I've never talked to you that much about what I went through when I was in Vietnam. Just like you, I had trouble discussing it with people who weren't there. But I saw some things, and I did some things, that still impact me, thirty-five years later."

"Like what?"

"The details don't matter. But like you, I was a soldier, and I did my duty. I had friends and comrades who I fought with and who I saw get wounded, and who I saw get killed. That kind of experience changes you. It can make you angry and bitter, and it can consume your life if you let it.

"I spent years trying to get my head back on straight. You want to know why I couldn't hold a job when you were younger? That had something to do with it.

"Between the drinking and the anger, I was letting my life spiral out of control. It all could have ended badly for me. But it was your mother's love, your love, and"—Larry smiled weakly—"Shiloh's love, that made me realize that the life I had was worth living.

"One night that was made very clear to me," he said so quietly that Nathan almost didn't catch it.

"How?"

"Again, doesn't matter. But once I realized all that, I pulled myself together and tried to make myself worthy of all of you.

"You know, when I got that call from your commander, I knew that what happened would change you. I worried that your life would become my life. But that's the thing. My life isn't yours. You're not me, and you aren't going to make the mistakes I made. I'm proud of you for serving, because country sometimes needs to be bigger than all of us."

"I appreciate your telling me that," Nathan murmured, moved by his father's willingness to open up. "You've come a long way since I was younger."

"You've been a great role model for me."

"Some role model I am. I let my guys down."

"No, you didn't! You were specifically told that there weren't any insurgents in that village. You're not the first platoon to get ambushed, especially by an enemy who doesn't fight by the rules. None of that is your fault. I've talked to your superiors; they all said you saved your platoon."

"I didn't save all of them."

"Are you talking about Private Herrington?"

"Yes." Nathan paused a moment. He knew his father was aware of the casualty, but he doubted he understood the extra reasons it weighed so heavily on him. He needed to tell someone. "When I was lying in the middle of the street, I remember thinking that if I were lucky I'd only lose my leg. But Herrington and Georgie, his military war dog, teamed up and dragged me to safety right during the worst of the firefight. No sooner had they secured me behind cover than Herrington got shot right in the back. He fell on top of me and died in my arms."

Larry stayed quiet, letting his son unburden himself.

"And if that wasn't bad enough, Georgie took off after the insurgent who killed Herrington at the same time the Apaches lit up most of the settlement. My first sergeant later told me that they never found Georgie; he must have been killed by one of the blasts. There isn't much left of that village, so there's no way he could have survived."

"Georgie must have been quite a dog."

"He was devoted to his handler, but he also used to hang out in my quarters back at Camp War Eagle." Now Nathan's words were coming fast and warm. "I enjoyed having him around, and when he was off duty, he loved to play, like any other dog. He reminded me of all the good times I had with Shiloh. But he was every bit as much a soldier as any of the others in my platoon."

"Both Herrington and Georgie were heroes," Larry said firmly. "To honor their sacrifice, you owe it to them to be the best you can be for the rest of your life."

Nathan took a deep breath. "I know that, Dad. I will never forget either of them."

"And that means you have to pick yourself up, put your life together, and make the most of what you've been given."

Nathan nodded in a manner that made Larry realize that his words had their intended impact.

"We parents tend to get smarter when you get a little older, don't we? Now, son, there is one other thing you need to do."

"What's that?"

"You need to marry Ana. And I mean now. She's the best thing that will ever happen to you, and she loves you more than life itself. I saw how she worried about you, first when you deployed to Afghanistan and then when you went to Iraq. And when you got wounded, I thought she would fall apart.

"You may think that I never appreciated how your mother was willing to put up with me. Believe me, I do. I don't know how I would have made it without her love and support, even though I often didn't deserve it. And that's what you have with Ana. The kind of love and devotion Ana shows for you comes only once in a lifetime."

Nathan nodded. "Dad," he said, "do me a favor and open up the top dresser drawer."

Puzzlement on his face, Larry reached over and opened the drawer. Inside was the small black box, which he had first seen those years before, when Nathan has shown it to him in the living room of his house. The night before the day that changed the nation forever. Larry smiled warmly as he handed the black box to Nathan.

"I think I've already figured that out."

IV.5

Fallujah, Iraq—February 2005

"Take it out, Diesel! Don't let them get to that compound!"

"I'm trying!" Maurizio snapped. But the jolts ripping through the Humvee as it bounded over the unpaved road prevented him from locking onto his target, and his .50 cal's shots kept missing their mark. The commandeered turbo-charged ambulance swerved back and forth across the pockmarked thoroughfare as bandana-clad insurgents leaned out the windows and fired their AK-47s at the pursuing Humvees.

The chase continued eastward until both parties came into sight of one of the many isolated compounds strewn across the barren landscape. The three-acre compound contained a main residence, an outhouse, a barn, and a tool shack, surrounded by a six-foot rusty chain-link fence with a partially open gate.

"Don't let them get inside!" Silva shouted as the ambulance swerved toward the entrance. Maurizio fired more shots, missing again.

"J-Run! Give it all you've got!"

McCollom floored the accelerator; the Humvee's engine roared, and the vehicle began to close the gap. It wasn't enough, and the ambulance remained well ahead of the pursuers as it neared the settlement.

"Sir!" Hoff radioed Silva from the adjoining Humvee. "Let me try something!"

"Like what?"

"You'll see!" Hoff tapped his driver on the shoulder and motioned to the left. The Humvee veered off the road onto the sandy terrain, slanting away from the fleeing ambulance.

"What the hell?" Silva shouted, seeing the second Humvee banking sharply to open up an angle from the ambulance. Hoff leaned out the passenger-side door and fired another volley; several bullets hit the side of the ambulance. One found the left rear tire; it exploded, and the ambulance shuddered and kicked up dust as it snaked off the road.

Hoff fired more shots, and this time took out the left front tire. The ambulance spun counterclockwise and screeched to a halt, ten meters from the compound's fence. Three insurgents leaped out of the car and sprinted toward the entrance. Hoff, still leaning precariously out of the careening Humvee, fired into the path of their flight; all three dropped to the ground.

"Diesel, compound!" Silva commanded. Maurizio swiveled his gun and fired a dozen shots at the main residence. There was no return fire. Silva signaled again, and the Humvee's gunner joined Maurizio in spraying the compound with a second volley. Again, no response.

The Humvees rolled to a stop in front of the compound, and half a dozen soldiers spilled out. Silva cautiously approached the insurgents lying on the ground; he quickly checked them out, then turned back to Hoff, who had exited the vehicle with the other members of the squadron.

"Mighty fine shooting there, my man," Silva said. Hoff turned pale as he stared at the unmoving bodies.

"Listen up!" Silva addressed his platoon. "Everyone stay on alert! We're going to sweep each of these shacks and make sure these stiffs don't have any buddies inside!"

Maurizio joined Silva, and two squads formed to probe the desolated compound's buildings. It was dangerous work, searching the barren, manure-laced structures in the darkness, knowing that at a moment's notice any one of them could come face-to-face with the barrel of a loaded AK47. Tension-filled minutes ticked away while the squads meticulously combed through each of the crumbling edifices.

"Looks deserted, sir," Maurizio finally said. "If there was anyone in there, our guys would have come across them by now."

"Yeah, maybe. But I remember the last time we walked into one of these crapholes thinking it was deserted."

"Copy that, sir. Actually, we aren't too far away from Nasifah right now. It's about ten miles to the east of us."

"That so? Is there anything even left of that place? I thought the Apaches took care of it."

"Yeah, good riddance to that dump."

"Sir!" Hoff shouted from inside the compound. "You need to check this out now!" Alarmed at the urgency of the private's tone, Silva dashed inside the compound, M4 at the ready, toward a group of four soldiers who were poised near the barn.

"House and toolshed are clear, sir," Hoff reported. "But there's something rooting around inside the barn. We're not sure if it's human or animal."

"Okay, Diesel, you're with me. Airmail, you and J-Run approach from the back entrance. If you feel threatened in any way, take it out, whatever it is."

M4s locked and loaded, the soldiers spread out and took positions on each side of the barn. Silva and Maurizio cautiously approached the front entrance. He gave the *ready* hand signal to his squad, then kicked the barn door open. It was pitch-black inside, and none of the troops could see more than a few feet ahead of them.

"Hands up now!" Silva shouted, M4 at the ready. He heard a rustling sound from the corner of the darkened barn. "Light!" he commanded, and Maurizio shone his high-powered flashlight toward the source.

The beam illuminated a pair of eyes from a figure cowering in the corner of the barn. Then Silva heard a whine conveying both distress and fear, and the figure emerged into the light.

"I'll be damned!" Silva bellowed.

IV.6

Phoenix, Arizona—April 2005

"You know I hate going out in public like this," Nathan grumbled as Ana maneuvered the minivan into a handicapped parking space adjacent to the Barry Goldwater terminal at Sky Harbor Airport.

"So, you'd rather not welcome your army buddies home?"

"I didn't say that."

After placing the car into park, Ana took a deep breath, turned to her boyfriend, and put a gentle hand on his left leg. "When you get your prosthetic leg, I think you'll start feeling better."

"You're right, as usual."

"Of course I am. Now be quiet and let us do all the work."

Nathan turned to his parents, who were sitting in the back seat. "Dad, am I supposed to let her talk to me like that?"

"Of course you are. Just accept it, and it'll make your life a lot less complicated."

Ana opened the driver's-side door, and Larry and Sally hopped out. Larry pulled a silver-and-black wheelchair from the back, then unfurled and positioned it on the pavement next to the front passenger door. Nathan swung himself to the side, allowing Larry to guide him down from his seat into the chair. Sally set a blanket over his waist to conceal his missing lower left leg.

As usual for an April afternoon in Phoenix, it was ninety degrees and sunny. Nathan was dressed in fatigues and a green army T-shirt, feeling proud that he was once again wearing his colors for this special occasion. Larry took position behind the wheelchair and pushed Nathan toward the entrance to terminal four.

"It's great that they are all going to be stopping here in Phoenix for a couple of days," Sally remarked.

"Yeah. I would have thought that they'd want to get right home to their families. But Enrique said they all really wanted to see me."

"That's nice of them," Ana said and glanced at Sally, who smiled back at her.

Tom Manogue and his wife, Miranda, greeted them as they entered the terminal. Tom slapped Nathan on the back, and Miranda gave him a kiss on the forehead.

"Thanks for meeting us here," Nathan said.

"Wouldn't have missed it for the world," Tom replied, flashing a mischievous smile at Nathan.

After dismounting the elevator on the second floor, they proceeded toward the TSA security checkpoint, only to have the agents open up the security line and wave them through. The breach in security protocol struck Nathan, but he shrugged it off as they entered the concourse. Ever since he'd come home a disabled veteran, he'd been experiencing all sorts of accommodations, little and big. He wondered if it'd always be this way. He wondered if he'd ever get used to it.

As they approached the gate where the military charter jet was due to arrive, Nathan spotted a throng of people milling about, many with signs welcoming their loved ones home. The crowd was larger than expected, filled with excited family members of all ages. Crews from each of the local television stations positioned themselves across from the crowds, their cameras already recording.

"There's my main man!"

Nathan pivoted to see Darrian Lawrence, clad in his Cardinals jersey, amid the crowd. Darrian finished inscribing his name and jersey number on a football for an appreciative fan and recapped his Sharpie as he strode over to Nathan.

"Darrian!" Nathan exclaimed. "What are you doing here?"

Darrian bent his hulking frame over to give his friend a hug. "So happy to finally see you again, man." Straightening back up, he shook Tom and Larry's

~ 145 ~

hands and gave Sally, Miranda, and Ana hugs. "I'm here to help welcome all these troops home and support my number one receiver."

"C'mon now, I wasn't even your number one receiver when I had both of my legs."

"Now, what have I always told you, Nate? There's more to being a teammate than running fast and catching balls. Being a true team player requires heart, courage, commitment, and character. You have all of that and then some."

Nathan smiled, feeling full-on happiness blossom in his chest. "Well, I was wondering why so many people were here, until I saw you. You draw a crowd wherever you go."

"Yes," Darrian sighed. "But I don't want it to be about me today."

"Darrian!" As if on cue, a young reporter holding a microphone called to him, a camera crew behind her. "What would you like to say to the soldiers who are arriving home from Iraq today?"

"Like everyone else here," Darrian said pointedly, sweeping his hand to encourage the camera to focus around him, not at him, "I want to say to them, welcome home and thank you for your service."

"Do you think it will mean a lot to them to have you here for them?"

"Maybe, but it means a lot more to me to be here. You know, I often read about how people consider me to be a role model, and I try to be, both on and off the field. But all I do is throw footballs a few Sundays each year. It's these men and women, the ones who are about to get off that plane, who are the true heroes. They are the ones willing to put their lives on the line to protect you, me, our families, our country, and our way of life. And I want each and every one of them to know how grateful I am and that I will always be here to support them."

"That guy has always had a gift for working the media," Tom whispered to Nathan.

"That's because he means every word of it."

They glanced out the terminal's windows to see the 757 charter jet touch down on the north runway, veer left, and rumble toward its designated gate. The crowd parted to allow Larry to push Nathan's wheelchair to the front, across from the color guard by the entrance to the jet bridge. The jet came to a halt; the gate crew swiftly affixed the jet bridge and opened the door, through which soldiers began deplaning to the thunderous applause of the crowd. A few soldiers tearfully embraced their spouses. A young child, recognizing his mother, ran forward and jumped into her arms. The videos rolled; dozens of cameras clicked in unison.

A moment later, Nathan saw the familiar stubbled face of Private Donnie Maurizio and the chiseled jaw of First Sergeant Enrique Silva as they emerged from the jet bridge, like the rest of the troops still clad in their desert fatigues. A memory of Enrique's tortured face over his as he was led away on the stretcher flashed through Nathan's mind, but he pushed it away, focusing on the grin now emanating from his friend.

"Shiv! Diesel!"

The two soldiers hurried over to Nathan, who leaned forward in his chair to embrace them both.

"It's great to see you guys!"

"You too, LT," Silva beamed. "And it's great to be back on American soil, let me tell you."

"Guys, I'd like to introduce you to my family. This is my mother and father, and my friend Tom Manogue and his wife, Miranda."

"Pleased to meet you." The two soldiers shook each of their hands.

"And this is my girlfriend, Ana Trevino."

"I've heard a lot about you guys."

"Us too," Silva rejoined. "And right away I can tell that he doesn't deserve you."

"Sure he does. He deserves the best."

Silva turned back to Nathan. "This one's a keeper, let me tell you."

"And, guys, this is my friend Darrian Lawrence."

"Great to finally meet you," Maurizio said. "The lieutenant used to talk about you a lot. I'm a big fan of yours."

"Not as big a fan as I am of you." Darrian smiled as he grasped both of their hands. "Thank you for your service, and for watching my friend's back. Y'all are great Americans."

"So, where are the other guys?" Nathan asked.

"They're right behind us," Silva said, pausing a moment. "And ... there's something they want you to see."

Nathan glanced back at the jet bridge to see standing in the entranceway among the deplaning soldiers Privates Hoff and McCollom. Between them, affixed to a leash held by McCollom, proudly stood a tan Belgian Malinois.

* * * * * *

"*Georgie!*" Nathan gasped, his heart skipping a beat.

McCollom dropped the leash, and the General dashed forward to Nathan, jumped into his lap, and showered him with kisses.

"Oh my God!" Tears streamed down Nathan's cheeks. "It's really you!" He wrapped his arms around the writhing dog, noticing that Georgie had lost a great deal of muscle mass.

Silva stroked Georgie's head as the Malinois continued to squirm in Nathan's lap. "We found him about two months ago."

"You survived Nasifah?" Nathan exclaimed to his pal.

"Incredible, isn't it," Silva said. "Since we were choppered in, after he got separated from us he didn't know how to get back to Camp War Eagle. So, we figure he must have spent his time wandering through the countryside scavenging for food. We found him in an abandoned compound about ten miles west of Nasifah that he had turned into a makeshift shelter."

"I can't believe he didn't get shot by an insurgent trying to get that reward," Nathan sputtered. "Or by any Iraqi who just wanted the menace of a street dog gone." That had been one of the hardest day-to-day parts of his service, watching the way dogs were treated in Iraq.

"It's nothing short of a miracle that he survived," Hoff agreed.

Georgie hopped off Nathan's lap and, still delirious with excitement, took turns jumping on Maurizio and Silva.

"He had lost a third of his body weight and was near starvation," Hoff continued. "He also had a couple of festering wounds, from catching some shrapnel in the firefight. We got him back to camp, and he spent a month getting rehab. He's relatively healthy now, but not what he used to be, and he's likely to have some lingering health problems in the coming years. Command says his MWD days are over."

Georgie yelped, and Nathan embraced him again. Other soldiers who had shared the long plane ride with the Malinois patted and embraced him as they shuffled past, to pay their respects and to say goodbye.

"Since he's being discharged, and since Herrington was KIA, we thought you might want to take him home with you," Silva said.

Nathan glanced at Ana, who wiped tears from her eyes as she nodded her approval. "Of course we'll take him."

He heard behind him the same young reporter who had talked with Darrian now speaking into her microphone in front of her camera crew. "It's been a joyful reunion here at Sky Harbor for these military families, who are welcoming their loved ones home from Iraq," she was saying. "But it is particularly joyful for one soldier: Nathan Wilkinson, who was injured and lost part of his leg, and who has been reunited with the military dog with whom he served. The dog had been thought killed in action but is now not only very much alive but also going home with him."

"How did she know all that?" a puzzled Nathan asked.

"Well…" Darrian said sheepishly, "your buddies contacted me a couple of weeks ago and told me all about how they found your dog. They thought the media would be interested in the story and asked me to help set this up for them. One of the perks of my job is that I can get media access whenever I want it."

Nathan turned to Ana. "Were you in on this too?"

"You're not mad, are you?"

Nathan turned back to Georgie, who again jumped into his lap, his excitement for the moment unabated. "How could I be mad? You helped bring my friend back to me. I couldn't be happier!"

"Now, keep something in mind," Silva cautioned. "Georgie's been through an awful lot the last few months. The vets say he's been pretty traumatized by his experience. He may not be the same as last time you saw him."

Nathan looked into Georgie's eyes. "That makes two of us. We'll heal together, won't we, boy?"

As Nathan hugged him again, Georgie saw standing at the front of the crowd the border-beagle mix with the sparkling eyes. The mix conveyed a single wordless expression to Georgie.

Take care of him.

Georgie yipped his acknowledgment, and his gratitude for all his companion had done for him those last months, and the border beagle acknowledged it with a single nod, before slowly fading away.

IV.7

Goodyear, Arizona—April 2005

"Well, this ought to be interesting," Larry said as Ana steered the van into her driveway.

"She'll be fine," Ana insisted.

"Honey," Nathan said, "Lindsay has been the queen of your house for six years. She's not going to be happy about having a new housemate, especially one bigger and hairier than her."

"Why? I was able to get used to you, wasn't I?"

"Ouch," Larry snorted.

Nathan gripped Georgie's head and shook it affectionately. "Not to worry, big guy," he said. "It'll all go fine. Of course, that's what I said about Nasifah."

Larry chuckled, oddly relieved that his son could joke about that subject.

"What time are we meeting your friends for dinner?" Sally asked as she guided Nathan into his wheelchair.

"Six. Darrian's taking us all out to III Forks." Darrian had told him the best steaks in Phoenix were the least he could do for Nathan, his family, and the people he'd served with.

"That's awfully generous of him," Larry said as he fastened a leash onto Georgie before leading him out of the van. "So, what's the plan?"

"Bring him inside, and let's see what happens," Nathan replied.

Stretched out in her bed in the master bedroom, Lindsay perked up at the sound of the front door opening. Ana stepped inside and opened the bedroom door; Lindsay jumped onto her leg, whimpering with excitement, as if she had not seen her in months rather than hours. She yelped when she spotted Nathan in the foyer, then pivoted and galloped toward her hero, halting in shock when she saw Georgie standing next to him. Larry tightened his grip on Georgie's leash, prepared to reassert control if the introduction went poorly.

For the longest moment, the recovering war veteran and the energetic schnauzer glowered at each other; Georgie stoic and reserved, Lindsay suspicious and defensive. Then Lindsay took a tentative step forward, a low growl emanating from her throat. Georgie remained motionless. Lindsay yipped a single time, took another step forward, and sniffed intensely. Again, no reaction.

The standstill persisted for another long moment, the two canines from such vastly divergent backgrounds cautiously taking the measure of each other. Lindsay closed in on Georgie and gazed deep into his eyes, sensing for the first time the weariness and melancholy tormenting the larger dog. That snuffed out the territorial instinct of which schnauzers are so renowned, and in her own gaze, she conveyed to him a subtle yet visible empathy. She moved in again and brushed her face lightly against his cheek; Georgie whined softly, and together they glanced at Nathan, their common bond.

Then Lindsay withdrew and trotted off into the kitchen, returning with her favorite stuffed toy clenched between her teeth. She waved it in front of Georgie, who tentatively nipped at it. Lindsay dangled the toy at him again; Georgie latched onto the opposite end, and the two commenced an introductory game of tug-of-war. Lindsay wagged furiously as the contest continued; a moment later, Georgie did so as well.

Sensing a budding familiarity between the two dogs, Larry took a deep breath and unhooked Georgie's leash. Lindsay released her grip on the stuffed toy and gestured for Georgie to follow her; tails still wagging, they darted outdoors for a tour of his new dwellings.

"Amazing," Sally said.

"That went great!" Nathan added. "No growling, or marking, or flashing of teeth. How in the world did that happen?"

"I think we all know the answer," Larry offered.

* * * * * *

~ 151 ~

From that day on, the two dogs ate together, played both inside the house and outside in the fenced-in yard, and rarely spent time apart. At first Georgie found it unsettling; like most MWDs, his had been the life of a loner, more accustomed to the companionship of humans than fellow canines. But the combination of Lindsay's acceptance and the love and encouragement of his humans proved invaluable to Georgie in his difficult transition from wartime to civilian life. Together the two canines forged a special spot in the corner of the backyard, where they would take the steak bones given to them after the family barbeque dinners and happily lie side by side on their stomachs as they gnawed for every last piece of meat.

Each morning on her way to work, Ana dropped off Georgie and Lindsay at Hayden to spend the day with Nathan. The two dogs accompanied Nathan to his strenuous physical therapy sessions, barking their encouragement as he struggled to rebuild his upper and lower body muscle mass and to learn basic motor skills with the new state-of-the-art prosthetic leg attached below his left knee.

Fully aware of the General's heroism, the facility's staff granted him free rein to wander the hallways visiting other recovering soldiers. Georgie's new stepsister often scampered alongside him as he marched through the corridors, nipping at his heels and playfully trying to distract him, to the delight of the patients and staff.

The television news story featuring Georgie's reunion with Nathan proved popular among the public. Soon the *Arizona Republic* learned that Georgie and Lindsay had become Hayden VA's unofficial morale officers and dispatched a reporter to chronicle their activities. The reporter's subsequent story graced the front page of the Sunday edition, which further amplified public interest in the sacrifices Georgie and other MWDs made for their country.

After Nathan was finally discharged from Hayden, he promptly set up residence with Ana and the two dogs in her Goodyear home. As part of his continuing therapy, he embarked upon daily walks around the block with Lindsay and Georgie. The dogs' enthusiasm during the outings motivated Nathan to further press himself with longer distances, and it brought back poignant memories of the similar role Shiloh had played in his youth.

Eventually Nathan became accustomed to the prosthetic limb, and was able to walk with only a barely noticeable hitch. He also began driving again, after which he resolved to take Georgie and Lindsay back to Hayden on a weekly basis so that they could continue their roles as morale officers.

But despite the boost in spirits Georgie bestowed upon his wounded comrades, and the supportive home to which he had been placed, the Malinois continued to struggle with the lingering effects of post-traumatic stress disorder. Occasionally at night, after a particularly vivid dream, he would crawl shaking and whimpering into Nathan and Ana's bed, where they would take turns embracing and him and caressing his shiny fur. Lindsay joined in as well, snuggling beside him, her head against his chest, conveying that she was there for him too.

Georgie abhorred loud noises and sudden movements, and had particular difficulty with thunderstorms. The evening of the Fourth of July proved particularly trying; after a group of youths set off a string of firecrackers near their house, Georgie darted into Nathan's arms and shook and wailed for a full hour as Nathan stroked his back in an effort to calm the General's tattered nerves.

Worse yet, the lingering trauma of his wounds and near starvation conveyed an accelerating toll on his body. Though the army offered its own veterinarians, the family insisted on taking him to Dr. Grittman, who prescribed a special diet and a series of medications to ease the effects. But the vet warned that the combined aftereffects would increasingly impact Georgie's health, potentially taking years off his life. The distressing news only inspired with Nathan and Ana a resolve to make the most of the time their beloved Georgie had remaining.

* * * * * *

As Nathan's recovery neared completion, he decided to take the next, and long overdue, step in his life. He finally took Ana to that dinner at Chantilly's in Prescott town square, and afterward, in the crisp evening air, they rode his motorcycle to the famous thousand-year-old Grandfather Juniper on the outskirts of town. He guided her to the tree, where he flashed the engagement ring and dropped to his knee, a feat that for him required considerable effort. He asked her if she would bestow upon him the honor of becoming his wife; her tears of joy wordlessly conveyed her answer.

A few months later they were married in what had been planned as a simple ceremony at St. Elizabeth Ann Seton Catholic Church outside Goodyear. Nathan stood at the altar in his dress uniform, his best man, Tom Manogue, at his side. His two groomsmen were First Sergeant Enrique Silva and Darrian Lawrence, while Privates Maurizio, McCollom, and Hoff attended as honored guests. Ana looked stunning in her designer ivory wedding gown as she walked down the aisle, arm in arm with her beaming father.

Though they intended the ceremony to be low-key, they recognized that Darrian's presence might draw unwanted media attention. Darrian offered to withdraw from the ceremony to preserve the couple's privacy, but Nathan and Ana would have none of it. He was their friend, and they were proud to have him stand up for them, even if it meant dealing with the paparazzi.

The media van parked across the street from the church verified their hunch. But the story of the day turned out not to be about the participation of the Arizona Cardinals' star quarterback at his wounded veteran friend's wedding. Instead, it was about the ring bearer.

The guests all watched with delight as the veteran war dog, full name General George S. Patton, proudly marched down the aisle, the rings affixed to a drape over his back, his sister Lindsay at his side. The camera crew seized on the heartwarming story of the MWD supporting his friend, comrade, and master, once again splashing Georgie across the local airwaves, in a segment that proved so popular that it was picked up by the national networks.

IV.8

Goodyear, Arizona—June 2007

"You wanted to see me, Charles?"

"Yes, Nathan, come on in." Nathan strolled over to the plush mahogany chair facing Charles Fletcher's desk and sat down, gently repositioning his prosthetic left leg.

"I know things have been hectic around here, and I haven't had a chance to spend much time with you these past several weeks," the older man said, brushing back his flowing silver hair. "But I just wanted to take the opportunity to tell you how great it's been having you back here at Fletcher Holdings. I always thought that after you got home from Iraq you would go on to bigger and better things."

"Not a chance. After all you did for my family while I was serving, I wouldn't think of going anywhere else."

"A lot of employees wouldn't have given up a promising career to get shot at in Afghanistan and Iraq defending our country. It's the least I could do for you. And it doesn't hurt that you are one helluva analyst."

"I've always appreciated the confidence you've had in me."

"Well, I think I may be able to make it mean even more to you."

"How so?"

"I've come across a new franchise opportunity that I want to pursue. It's called SportsWorld, and it's a warehouse-type sporting goods outlet. I had a meeting with the founder yesterday, and he wants us to form a separate company for the purpose of finding, building, and owning SportsWorld franchise outlets in the southwest."

"I read an article about them online. Seems like it's just another sporting goods store."

"What makes this chain unique is that the founder has somehow managed to secure very favorable distribution agreements with all the major suppliers. I don't know how he got such great terms from these companies, but SportsWorld's selection is going to be incredible, and its prices are going to be cut-rate. And most importantly, it's going to target the small-to-midsize markets, cities with populations of five to twenty-five thousand. The big chains haven't touched those markets, but with the margins we'll be getting from our distribution agreements, we think we can get in there and make a sizable profit.

"The key to SportsWorld's success is going to be picking the right locations. And I can't think of anyone better at finding those locations than you. But here's the deal. I'm getting a little too old to be venturing out into new opportunities like this. So, what I want to do is set you up to roll this one out yourself."

"Seriously?"

"Absolutely. We'll establish the new holding company under your ownership. I'll help you with the initial seed capital. Once the stores get rolling, your holding company will be able to fund all future expansion on its own."

"Charles, this is incredibly generous of you."

"Glad you think so, but you'll be doing all the work and taking all of the risk. I'll just be sitting here in my chair and taking a percentage of your profits."

"Fair enough. But this is a great opportunity for me, and for my family."

"I'm sure you'll make the most of it. That reminds me; how is that wonderful wife of yours doing these days?"

"Ana couldn't be better. She's four months along now and pretty much over the morning sickness. But we haven't decided whether we want to find out in advance if it's a boy or girl."

"I suggest that you do it the old-fashioned way and let yourself be surprised. It's good to hear that she's feeling better. And how about those dogs of yours?"

"They're getting along great. Funny enough, Georgie has fifty pounds on Lindsay, but Lindsay thinks she's the alpha dog."

"Not surprising. That's how my own dogs are. It's always the little ones who have all the attitude."

* * * * * *

Using the seed money provided by his mentor, Nathan plunged into his new opportunity, forming a holding company that he christened Natana Enterprises. He quickly identified the first location in Arizona, in the town of Gilbert to the east of Phoenix. He acquired ten acres on the city's outskirts and secured both an engineer to design the facility and a contractor to oversee construction.

SportsWorld's first Arizona outlet opened to considerable fanfare in 2008. Cars jammed the parking lot, and customers reacted positively to the new store's selection and pricing. Of course, Darrian's well-publicized attendance at the opening ceremony only fueled interest among his countless fans across the valley.

While encouraged by the initial customer traffic, Nathan quickly discovered that the store's cash demands were far higher than forecast. The chain's advertising boasted that it stocked everything any reasonable sports fan would want or need. Fulfilling this promise required a huge investment in inventory, which immediately began to strain cash flow.

At the three-month mark, Nathan sat down with Charles Fletcher to assess the initial store results. They agreed on a plan to increase sales and cash flow through aggressive expansion. Nathan had already identified second and third location sites, one in neighboring Apache Junction and the other in the town of Florence, south of Phoenix. He would be gambling by investing in these new locations, as it would require him to commit of all his fledging company's cash reserves. If the new stores underperformed, or he encountered any unexpected expenses, he would not have sufficient cash to stave off bankruptcy. Despite his concerns, he took the advice of his mentor and implemented the plan.

"I know this expansion is risky," Fletcher told him, "but you can't let the threat of failure stop you. If you want to build a real company, then you have to be willing to take risks.

"It always aggravates me that so many people seem to think businesses sprout up out of the ground on their own, as if by some kind of magic. They

~ 157 ~

don't. A business becomes a success because people like you take risks and bet everything you have on your abilities and your vision. And your sweat.

"So be that guy who is willing to put everything on the line to make his business a success. Bet on yourself. Give it everything you've got. Then, no matter the outcome, you will know that you did the best you could."

* * * * * *

In August 2008, the Apache Junction SportsWorld opened to the same fanfare and high customer volume as the first store. Word of mouth about the exceptional choice and bargains had spread throughout the valley; Nathan was relieved and encouraged to see the lines of customers waiting to enter the store on opening day, knowing their patronage would translate to badly needed cash flow. But he still had to bring forth the other component—the Florence location—and quickly, for the expansion financing plan to be successful.

When he found time away from his duties as CEO of Natana, which was not very often, Nathan enthusiastically embraced his other major new responsibility: Justin Lawrence Wilkinson. In the evenings, he took charge of bottle-feeding his infant son and changing his diapers, relieving his sleep-deprived wife of those inevitable yet mundane chores. And after those tasks were complete, he enjoyed nothing more than relaxing on his couch watching TV while cradling the boy in his arms as Ana lay beside them.

That was, when Lindsay would allow Nathan to devote attention to Justin. The two dogs had exhibited markedly different reactions to the newborn when the proud parents brought him home. Ana set the portable carrier on the floor so that Lindsay and Georgie could partake in their first sight and scent of the family's newest member. Georgie reluctantly approached the sleeping child, and after a perfunctory once-over, he yawned and shuffled off to his bed, satisfied that the baby was neither a threat to his family nor a responsibility of his.

Lindsay, however, sniffed energetically; she gazed up at Ana and down again at Justin, realizing that whatever this was, it wasn't going away, and now there was going to be yet another competitor for Nathan's attention. Every time Nathan picked up Justin and sat with him on the couch, Lindsay would leap up and snuggle beside them, sometimes laying her head on Nathan's thigh just to ensure that he was aware of her presence. Nathan's feeding or changing Justin always seemed to trigger in Lindsay a sudden desire to play ball or tug-of-war. Her fervent desire to ensure that she was still loved always amused Nathan, and he would reward her with an energetic scratch to the belly.

* * * * * *

While the two locations in Gilbert and Apache Junction hummed along, the Florence site development remained riddled with complications. In the meantime, the profits from the second store improved cash flow, but not sufficient to cover the combined costs of operating the two stores and constructing the Florence location. His cash reserves soon depleted to less than thirty days of operating expenses.

And then, to further complicate matters, the sudden and severe 2008 national recession brought the Arizona economy to a screeching halt. Overnight, new home construction flatlined across the state, and layoffs in the construction and other growth-dependent industries meant that families would have less disposable income. In the final quarter of 2008, sales dropped precipitously in both stores despite the onset of the Christmas season.

Nathan's fledging operation found itself confronting the financial equivalent of a perfect storm: economic recession, lower sales in the existing stores, higher-than-anticipated expenses, and construction delays in the critical third location. It was too late to back out of the Florence site, as he had already purchased the land. He needed the cash flow from the new store, so he had no choice but to move forward, despite the perilous economic environment. But events had to turn in his favor, and quickly, or his dream of building Natana would be over before it had barely begun.

IV.9

Florence, Arizona—February 2009

"As if I didn't have enough to worry about," Nathan muttered as he steered his Ford F150 eastbound on Highway 87, "now I have to deal with this. At least I've got you to keep me company for a change."

He reached over and patted Georgie, who sat in the passenger seat with his hear thrust out the partially open window, his army-insignia-embroidered collar flapping in the wind.

"That's my guy. Nothing like the morning breeze to rally your spirits and make you forget your problems. Someday soon I'm going to start bringing Justin along so the three of us can enjoy some real guy time."

Nathan's mind flashed back to the previous week's visit to Dr. Grittman and their collective struggle to combat Georgie's mounting health challenges. Now they were on their way to a meeting called at the last minute by some guy in the Town of Florence's Public Works Department. Unexpected and last minute were never a good combination.

Soon Nathan arrived in the historic downtown section of Florence, Arizona. An aging water tower loomed over the landscape; the county courthouse gleaned in the ever-present Arizona sunlight. To the east lay the state and federal prisons for which the town was known.

Nathan steered down a side street, passing several residential subdivisions shuttered by the recession. He turned onto an empty lot by a sign with bold script announcing SportsWorld's imminent arrival. A stocky man in his forties with a bushy beard, clad in jeans and a sports shirt, stood in the lot leafing through papers on a clipboard as he leaned against a Town of Florence Public Works truck.

Nathan parked his truck and motioned to the General. "C'mon, Georgie. I know you're not feeling well, and you could use a little fresh air. Why don't you wait for me in the bed?" Georgie gazed mournfully at him, then hopped out of the truck; Nathan curled his arm around the Malinois' waist and lifted him into the bed, knowing that the combination of worsening health and wartime injuries prevented Georgie from making the jump on his own.

"You stay here, boy. I'll be right back." Georgie lay down on a section of carpet in the bed's corner while Nathan approached the man holding the clipboard.

"Mr. Wilkinson?" the man said. "I'm Harry Schroeder, director of public works for the town. We spoke on the phone yesterday. Thanks for coming out to see me."

"What can I do for you, Mr. Schroeder?"

"First, let me say that I really like SportsWorld. My wife and I went to the one in Apache Junction a couple of weeks ago to pick up some new camping gear. Great selection, and the prices were incredible."

What does this guy want to talk about? Nathan shifted his weight from foot to foot but forced himself to be polite. "Thank you very much."

"I'll get right to the point, Mr. Wilkinson."

Nathan smiled to himself. *Right.*

"The town has run into a complication regarding your proposed development here."

"What kind of complication?"

"Our outside engineers have completed an assessment of your store's water demand, like we do for all new development. We were planning to use the six-inch water main adjacent to the road to service the store."

Nathan heard the but coming, and tried desperately to head it off. "We just sell sporting goods. We won't require that much water."

"That is true. But it's a large store, almost one hundred thousand square feet. It's going to need fire protection, and this line doesn't have sufficient pressure to meet the town's fire code. We are going to have to replace this line with a larger size that has sufficient capacity."

"That sounds like a town issue. What does it have to do with me?"

"The town has a very strict policy that new growth has to pay all the costs associated with that growth. The idea is that people who are already living here shouldn't have higher water rates or taxes to support new development. Your store will have to pay for the cost of the new line."

"How much is that going to cost?" Nathan asked warily.

"For the one mile of line that we will have to replace, we estimate the cost at $2 million."

Nathan turned white as he grasped the implications. "I can't believe this! How am I just finding out about this now?"

"Originally we thought the existing line would be sufficient to meet fire code. But I wasn't sure, so I had the engineers re-run the town's water capacity model. The new analysis shows that there won't be enough capacity without a larger line."

Nathan's stomach knotted. "Mr. Schroeder, I'm a very small operation. I need the cash flow from this store just to make ends meet. I sure as hell don't have $2 million to pay for a new water line."

"I'm sorry to hear that, Mr. Wilkinson."

Nathan inhaled deeply. "I'm taking a huge risk coming to a smaller town like Florence. I'll be giving your citizens real options and choice, not to mention the fact that it will create more than a hundred new jobs. Doesn't that count for anything?"

"I'm afraid it doesn't. The town's ordinance is very clear on this matter."

"This could put me out of business!"

"I wish I could do something to help, but my hands are tied."

"I—I don't believe this," Nathan stammered, stepping back and rubbing his forehead as he contemplated what could be the final nail in his financial coffin.

Then Nathan heard the straining motor of a battered, aging van rolling down the street behind him. Its rear window was shattered, and smoke belched from the rear exhaust pipe. It backfired as it passed by the lot, the sound echoing like a gunshot through the air.

The sound startled Georgie, and he bolted up and jumped down from the truck bed. Limping toward Nathan, he yelped in pain from the impact of his jump and fear from the frightening noise.

"That your dog?" Schroeder asked.

"Yeah," Nathan grimaced. "He shouldn't have done that—he has some old injuries, and jumping off the bed like that is going to aggravate them. Excuse me a second."

Georgie whined loudly and shook visibly as he approached Nathan. "It's okay, boy," Nathan said soothingly as he kneeled to stroke the Malinois's tan fur, momentarily setting his other travails aside. "It was just a car, nothing more."

As Nathan wrapped his arms around Georgie to calm his anxious companion, his trouser hitched up, and Schroeder observed the chrome exterior of his prosthetic left leg gleaming in the sunlight.

"Mr. Wilkinson, have we met before?" he asked, stroking his beard.

"I don't think so," Nathan answered, not looking at the man, still focused on calming Georgie's frayed nerves.

Then Schroeder noticed the collar embroidered with the army insignia wrapped around Georgie's neck.

"I do know you! I saw you on the local news. You're the soldier who was wounded in Iraq and was reunited with your war dog."

"He wasn't originally my dog. His handler was under my command and was killed in action. My unit wanted me to adopt him, and I was honored to do so."

Schroeder extended his right hand. "Mr. Wilkinson, it's an honor to meet you, and I want to thank you for your service to our country. And that goes for your dog as well."

"I appreciate your kind words." Nathan stood up. "So, tell me, what are we going to do about this water line issue?"

Schroeder paused a moment and, deep in contemplation, scratched his chin. Then he turned back to Nathan. "You know, most of us here live pretty quiet lives, doing our jobs, obeying the law, staying out of trouble. But sometimes we get so wrapped up in following the rules set out for us that we lose sight of the things that are truly important.

"Well, I'll tell you exactly what is important," he said, sounding like he'd made a big decision. "It's taking care of people like you, who risked so much and sacrificed so much so that we can live our quiet lives and follow our stupid rules."

Nathan felt hope rise within himself.

"I know what our ordinance says, and I know what our rules require. But I also know what is right and what is wrong. I'm going to see to it that we find a way to make sure you get your store built. After I tell the town council who you are and what you and your dog have done for our country, there won't be a single person in this city who will disagree with waiving these rules, I promise you."

"Mr. Schroeder, I can't tell you how much I appreciate this," a visibly moved Nathan said.

"Think nothing of it. It's the least I can do for you. Now if you'll excuse me, I need to get back to my office. I've got some work to do."

As Schroeder strode off to his car, Nathan turned again to his loyal companion. "Georgie," he said as he scratched the Malinois's head, "maybe someday you'll get tired of saving me. But I hope it isn't anytime soon."

* * * * * *

The meeting in Florence proved to be the turning point for Nathan's struggling start-up. That same evening, Harry Schroeder described to the Florence Town Council his encounter with Nathan and Georgie, and made an impassioned plea for the town to waive its line-extension reimbursement policy. Inspired by the pair's story of heroism, hardship, separation, and reunion, the council voted unanimously for the town to absorb the line cost.

Buoyed by the goodwill gesture, Nathan moved quickly to finalize the location's construction. The Florence SportsWorld opened in late 2009 to robust sales, despite the continuing recession, and Nathan breathed a sigh of relief as his cash-flow levels climbed back to sustainability. By early 2011, the economy had recovered to the point where he could begin planning for new stores in the towns of Oro Valley and Surprise. While nothing was ever certain in the business world, all indications were that Natana had weathered the storm.

His family life proved energetic and rewarding as well. Justin sprouted up in size and was toddling around on his own by twelve months. Ana returned to her job as assistant HR director at Van and Laurin Engineers, though leaving their son at daycare proved emotionally challenging. Both sets of grandparents made frequent visits to spend time with Justin, though Larry seemed to prefer the company of the two Wilkinson dogs.

Lindsay remained as healthy and energetic as ever, bounding up to Nathan when he returned home from work at night, constantly goading him into playing with one of her many stuffed toys, jumping on his lap whenever he found an unguarded moment to relax on the couch, and cuddling next to him in bed at night. Her limitless energy was matched only by her devotion to Nathan, though her exuberance made Georgie's struggle all the more heartbreaking.

As the months progressed, the General's medical challenges became more acute. The malnutrition had damaged his gastrointestinal system, and occasionally he would regurgitate his food or have an accident inside the house. He became more lethargic and spent days at a time curled up in his bed at the corner of the master bedroom. His rear legs had weakened from the lingering effects of the shrapnel wounds, and over time, severe arthritis settled in. He frequently required medical care, and Dr. Grittman prescribed a rigorous regimen of intravenous fluids, vitamin shots, and other medications.

But the most disturbing development was his immune system's gradual erosion. He became ill more frequently, his system unable to fend off the various bacteria and viruses.

It pained Nathan and Ana to witness Georgie's ongoing tribulations. It affected Lindsay as well—on those days when Georgie was unwell, Lindsay curled up against him, diffusing strength and support from her body into his. Georgie was her big brother, and she was determined to assist him in any way she could.

Georgie never lost his spirit, and on his good days, he ran buoyantly through the backyard chasing the squirrels that dared to venture into his territory. On these days Nathan made it a point to spend extra time with him, taking Georgie on walks through the neighborhood and bringing him along when he visited his stores. The SportsWorld employees knew the General's background and were always ready to greet him with treats and toys.

Those days became less frequent, and by early 2011, Georgie began to lose interest in leaving the house. His lethargy overwhelmed him, and when Nathan beckoned him to play or go for a walk, Georgie just gazed at him, a hint of sadness in his eyes, before shuffling over to his bed. Nathan and Ana sensed that Georgie's iron will was abating and returned to Dr. Grittman for a series of new tests.

The results revealed precisely what they had feared: stage two liver disease, a consequence of the weakened immune system and the lingering effects of the parasites and malnutrition. Dr. Grittman prescribed a regimen of antibiotics and steroids, which caused Georgie severe nausea but didn't prevent the disease from metastasizing to stage four by summer. Georgie's abdomen swelled, jaundice set in, and he suffered increasingly frequent seizures, the most violent of which caused him to collapse to the floor as his legs kicked involuntarily for two minutes. A tearful Nathan cradled Georgie's head for comfort while praying for the spasms to end quickly.

"It was the last seizure that did it," Nathan told Tom Manogue as the two sat in his living room. "We called Dr. Grittman again, and he told us that the pain and the seizures were going to get worse. He said that the best thing we can do for him is to end his suffering and to do it in a way that allows him to preserve his dignity."

"Couldn't have been easy for you to hear."

"No, it wasn't. We were both pretty shaken up after we got off the phone. Fortunately, Justin's too young to understand any of this."

"So, what are you going to do?"

"Saturday morning we're going to drive him up to Chino Valley, to Dr. Grittman's office, to have it done. But I have something special planned for him, and I was hoping you would be a part of it."

IV.10

Goodyear, Arizona—August 2011

It was the day that every dog owner knows will come but hopes inside that somehow it never will. The day when it becomes time to say good-bye.

* * * * * *

Saturday arrived far too quickly. Each day during that last week, Nathan came home early so that he could spend as much time as possible with his companion. Georgie rarely left his bed, so for hours Nathan sat beside him, stroking his tan fur and repeatedly telling him how much he loved him. He reminisced to Georgie about their service in Iraq, from the time he took down the fleeing insurgent to the fun they had in Camp War Eagle's main compound. Georgie occasionally rallied at the sound of the stories but more often faded away as Nathan spoke, laying his head back down as another wave of pain burned through his body.

On Friday evening, Nathan barbequed a T-bone steak and cut it into small pieces, which he sprinkled over Georgie's regular food. After Georgie finished his meal, Nathan gave him the bone and guided him out to the special spot in the backyard where he and Lindsay had chewed on the countless leftover bones given to them over the years. Watching Georgie lie in the grass and energetically gnaw on this last bone, Nathan knew that he would carry this memory of the General for the rest of his life.

Saturday morning, Sally drove down from Chino Valley to mind Justin for the day. Georgie watched Nathan in his bedroom with glassy eyes as he straightened his tie on the dress uniform he had not worn in many years. The Malinois whined anxiously as he sensed Nathan's apprehension. Nathan bent down and kissed him on his forehead.

"Are you okay?" Sally asked, sitting on the couch watching Justin play with a set of Legos in the corner of the living room.

"I think so. I'm just trying to get through this."

"It's for the best, and I think even Georgie knows that."

Nathan snapped the leash's hook into place on Georgie's collar and led him over to Sally. "You want to say anything to him before we go?"

"Yes." She leaned over to stroke Georgie's chin. "Thank you for protecting my son, both in Iraq and here. You're the bravest dog I've ever known, and I'll never forget you."

Then Nathan guided Georgie over to Justin, who was still absorbed in his Legos.

"Hey, kiddo," he said, "I'm going to be taking Georgie to a special place. You want to say goodbye to him?"

The three-year-old stared briefly at Georgie and patted him on the head. Then he turned back to his father. "When will he be back?" he asked.

"I'll talk to you about that later. It's important that you say goodbye to him now."

"Okay, see you later," Justin responded, then turned his attention back to the Legos.

Nathan led Georgie to the front door. Then he stopped at the sound of whining from behind him. Lindsay dashed out of the bedroom and up to Georgie, buried her head in his chest, and scratched at him with her paw.

"Easy now, Lindsay."

The schnauzer whined louder and reached up to give Georgie a kiss on his nose. Georgie yipped to acknowledge the gesture.

"I think she understands," Sally said.

Lindsay gave Nathan a look of fear and confusion. Nathan could see it in her eyes—*Don't take him from me!* He shook his head, the sadness in his own eyes telling her that there was no other alternative.

Her whining increasing into a pitched howl of despair, Lindsay pivoted about, ran back into the bedroom and hurled herself onto her bed.

* * * * * *

As the sun rose in the east, they drove in silence, Nathan and Ana lost in their innumerable memories. A still-anxious Georgie lay curled in the rear seat of the F150's cab. It seemed an eternity before they reached the familiar Highway 89, which navigated through Chino Valley's central district toward the complex that housed Dr. Grittman's office.

"Is everything ready?" Nathan asked Ana.

"Yes. Tom texted me and said it's all set."

Nathan parked the truck at the entrance to a suite of office condominiums. Dr. Grittman's veterinary hospital occupied a stand-alone building at the end of the complex.

Nathan turned to face Georgie. "This is for you, boy," was all he said. He opened the passenger door and carefully lifted the infirm and anxious Belgian Malinois to the pavement.

Dozens of soldiers in dress uniforms lined the sidewalk, accompanied by police officers from Chino Valley, nearby Prescott, Goodyear, and other Arizona communities. The mayors of Chino Valley and Goodyear approached the parked truck and shook Nathan's and Ana's hands. A color guard positioned itself behind the line, and a large gathering of citizens stood in the background.

As Nathan led Georgie along the sidewalk toward Dr. Grittman's office, the soldiers and police officers, many of whom had served in Afghanistan and Iraq, snapped to attention. Recognizing the show of respect, Georgie straightened his back and forced his failing body to walk as decorously as possible.

In front of the veterinarian's office stood Enrique Silva, Donnie Maurizio, James McCollom, and Ryan Hoff, like Nathan all clad in their dress uniforms. Nathan's father and Tom Manogue stood proudly beside them, Larry struggling to control his emotions as his own final moments with Shiloh flashed through his head.

In unison, the four veterans of Bravo Company Second Platoon saluted Georgie.

"Thanks for coming, guys," Nathan said to his comrades. "I know this means a lot to him."

"It was the least we could do," Silva replied, a tear rolling down his cheek. "He's one of us."

"And as you once said to Georgie," Hoff added, "'every one of us will be at your side, now and to the end'."

"You're a hero, General," Maurizio proclaimed, his perpetually stubbled cheeks also moist with tears. "In every way a hero can be described."

Nathan turned Georgie around, and the Malinois gazed a final time at the many who did not even know him yet had come to pay their respects. The crowd was silent and reserved; the soldiers and police officers remained at attention; the flags from the color guard flapped in the wind. It stirred within him a feeling of pride and gratitude.

And then, the black-and-white border beagle with the sparkling eyes appeared in front of him. It had been many years since his last visit, but Georgie recognized him instantly. The border beagle's transparent body glowed brightly, his expression one of warmth, benevolence, and understanding. His mere presence conveyed to Georgie an overwhelming comfort and reassurance.

I'm here for you. It's all going to be okay.

The visitor gestured toward Georgie, informing the Malinois that he would be waiting for him, to lead him on his next journey. Georgie nodded his gratitude. His spirits soothed, his anxiety melting away, he turned and followed his beloved Nathan through the clinic's door.

IV.11

Goodyear Arizona – September 2011

"To General George S. Patton, the most loyal companion and the best friend a man could ever have."

Nathan, Enrique, Tom, and Darrian clinked their Sam Adams bottles and took lengthy swigs. The late-afternoon sun shone brightly through the open curtains, bathing the living room in a vivid glow.

"I appreciate you guys coming over today," Nathan said. "It's been awfully quiet around here the last few weeks. After seven years, this place doesn't feel the same without Georgie."

"He was a helluva dog," Tom declared.

"And a helluva soldier," Silva added. "I'll never forget the moment Herrington went down. Georgie charged right into the line of fire to go after the shooter. No regard at all for his own personal safety. That, gentlemen, is the textbook definition of valor."

"So, how's Ana taking it?" Darrian asked.

"She's doing okay, I guess. She's been pretty quiet, and at times she goes off to the bedroom to be by herself. I can hear her crying, and sometimes I try to comfort her, but other times I leave her alone so she can work through it herself."

"It's got to be tough on her."

"It is. But she's strong – the strongest woman I've ever met. She'll get through this." Nathan brushed his hand against his chin and pondered his next words momentarily. "Dogs are more than just animals wandering through your house; they really and truly are members of your family. And they really do

~ 171 ~

love you more than anything else, even themselves. When they see you walk in the door, they jump up and run around in a state of complete and utter joy, as if it is the single greatest occasion in the history of the world. There is no place on Earth they would rather be than by your side. They keep you company when you're feeling down, and they always let you know that no matter how much of a failure you might think you are, you will always be their hero. Losing one can hurt bad. I don't want to equate it to losing a parent or a child, but it's still awfully painful, one of the toughest things a family will have to deal with. I don't even want to think about how Ana is going to handle it when this one goes." He pointed to Lindsay, who lay sullenly near the fireplace, and for a moment the room went quiet.

"I shouldn't be drinking this," Darrian blurted out, attempting to lighten the mood. "I've got to play the Eagles on Sunday."

"You don't need to be sober to beat the Eagles," Tom quipped.

"Says you. I've got to stay in shape, and I'm not as young as I used to be. The hits I've been taking are hurting a lot more than they used to."

"All the more reason to have a few of these before kickoff." Tom pointed to his Sam Adams. "That should dull the pain a bit. You should have done that before the Dallas game last week, could have been your excuse for that pic-six you threw in the fourth quarter."

"Be nice, Tom," Ana teased as she came into the room and parked herself on Nathan's lap.

"Darrian knows I love him. Of course, I'd love him more if he were Tom Brady."

"So, Darrian, you starting to think about life after football?" Silva asked.

"Yeah, more and more." He paused, twirling the diamond-studded trinket affixed to his right ring finger. "I'm thirty-six now, I've got my ring, and I'm starting to think that I might want to get out while I'm still healthy."

"I don't know what the Cardinals are going to do without you," Enrique said.

"Thanks, Enrique." Darrian patted Silva on the knee. "I appreciate that. But once I retire, I'm going to need to figure out something else to do. I've been thinking that I might start investing in some new businesses. In fact, I have one in mind right now."

"Oh? What's that?" Enrique asked.

Darrian glanced over to Nathan. "You mind if I tell him?"

"Go right ahead."

"I thought I would invest in this up-and-coming chain of sporting goods stores."

"That's great to hear!" Silva exclaimed.

"We've been talking about it for a while," Nathan said. "Now that the economy's better and my three stores are all making a profit, I'm considering another expansion. Darrian's going to provide the seed capital, and Tom's financial advisory company is going to arrange the long-term financing."

"And Darrian has also agreed to be SportsWorld's official spokesman," Ana said.

"When Darrian showed up at the store openings, it really spiked public interest," Tom added. "As formal spokesman for the chain, he should drive customer turnout even higher."

"But Natana Holdings is still a small company, and once we expand, I'm not going to be able to supervise all of the stores myself," Nathan continued. "I'm going to need to add staff. The first thing I need to do is hire someone I trust to oversee all operations."

Ana smiled as Nathan turned to his friend.

"Enrique, I know you're about to be discharged and are looking for something to do with your life. I'd like for you to join Natana as chief operating officer."

"Are you serious?"

"Of course we are," Darrian said. "I can't think of anyone I would trust more with my investment than you."

Enrique did not answer right way. He opened his mouth as though to speak, then shut it again. Finally, he shook his head and said in a rush, "But I don't have much business experience." He held up his palms as though to tell his friends to slow down. "You know I only had two years of college before I joined the army."

Nathan sighed deeply before responding. "First of all, you are smart, and you're not afraid of challenges. Second, you commanded soldiers in combat. You're a natural leader, and that's something you don't learn in college.

"The business isn't difficult, Shiv. I can teach you what you need to know. It's character that matters, and that's something you have in abundance."

"My husband trusted you with his life," Ana said. "So of course he's going to trust you with his business."

"I don't know what to say."

"How about yes?" Tom suggested.

"Well, then, I guess I'll be moving to Phoenix."

Ana threw her arms around Silva and hugged him.

"Now, remember," Nathan said, smiling, "I'll still be your boss, but at least this time I won't be ordering you into a line of enemy fire."

"I just hope I don't let all of you down."

"Not a chance," Darrian responded. "Unless, of course, you become an Eagles fan."

* * * * * *

True to form, Silva proved to be an exceptionally fast learner. After leasing an apartment in nearby Glendale, he energetically threw himself into his new responsibilities, visiting the existing stores to learn the general operations, identifying those products that attracted maximum customer interest and others that were candidates for discontinuance. He reviewed the new locations' sites, architectural plans, and community demographics. He ascended the learning curve rapidly, and within a matter of months, Nathan had entrusted him to oversee the construction of the Yuma and Tucson locations. Nathan took great pride in Silva's progress, and before long, he began to wonder how he had managed his operation before Enrique had joined up.

Customer interest surged thanks to Darrian's ads, which blanketed the local airwaves, and each of the new stores opened to robust sales. Natana's rocky kickoff and brush with bankruptcy became more and more of a fading memory as the company's now-rapid expansion opened the potential for still more new markets.

As 2012 faded into 2013, Nathan's family life further blossomed with the revelation that he and Ana would once again become parents. Larry, Sally, and their friends all met Nathan and Ana at their favorite Mexican restaurant in Goodyear to celebrate the news with dinner and, for all except Ana, a round of margaritas. It was a joyous evening, a commemoration of friendship, family, success, and the good fortune with which all had been blessed.

But as is all too commonplace in the magical journey of life, it was the happiness that the Wilkinsons were enjoying at that moment that made the impending heartbreak that much more difficult to bear.

IV.12

Goodyear, Arizona—October 2013

It had been thirteen years since Nathan rescued the lost and frightened miniature schnauzer from her makeshift shelter in the local park. Thirteen years since he took her home, bathed her, fed her, and contacted her owner with the good news that she had been found. Thirteen years since he heard the knock on his apartment door, opened it, and found himself gazing at the auburn-skinned woman with the flowing black hair who would forever change his life.

He had never known Ana without Lindsay. Through all their years together, and despite her advancing age, Lindsay retained the vigor, the passion, the enthusiasm, and the attitude of a puppy. Her devotion to Nathan remained absolute. In the mornings when he left, she retreated morosely to her bed, and when he returned at night, she greeted his arrival with delirious, unrequited love. She parked herself next to him on the couch, frequently rolling on her back to demand belly rubs, and at night she clambered onto the bed to sleep nestled between them. His tours of duty were difficult for her, and when he returned wounded and disconsolate, it was Lindsay as much as Ana whose devotion lifted Nathan's spirits and helped navigate him through that dark period of his life.

Though irrevocably bound to Nathan, Lindsay admired and revered her adopted older brother. She had just turned thirteen when Georgie passed, and as Nathan and Ana feared, it impacted her immeasurably. In the weeks following that sad day, she often wandered through the house, sniffing in vain for any evidence of her brother. In the evenings, when the family congregated in the living room, she occasionally sat on the floor and gazed toward the foyer, as if trying through sheer force of will to make Georgie appear at the front door. As it slowly dawned on her that she would not be seeing him again, her infectious exuberance and zest for life abated. Her movement slackened; she became more reserved, the sadness and resignation within her more and more perceptible.

Nathan and Ana tried to rally her spirits, playing her favorite games, taking her on walks, cuddling with her and letting her know that they were there for her. Their efforts were unrewarded, as Lindsay's transformation from youthful and energetic to aged and tentative accelerated alarmingly as the months wore on.

"It isn't right," Ana bemoaned. "Why do our dogs have to get old before we do? Why do they have to leave us? Why can't she always be with me?"

"I wish I knew," Nathan answered, taking her in his arms and gently rubbing her back.. All I do know is that it's part of a plan that we can't possibly hope to understand. We have to just love her and treasure her for whatever time she has left with us."

Lindsay's decline hastened as Ana's second pregnancy progressed. Her celebrations upon Nathan's arrival home lessened in intensity, and she lost interest in chasing the squirrels that lurked in the backyard. She even stopped sleeping with Ana and Nathan, the pain to her joints from mounting and dismounting their bed becoming too inhibiting. She spent most days lying in her bed in the corner of the living room, occasionally meandering aimlessly around the house, yelping in frustration when she lost track of where she was. Cataracts impaired her vision, and most disturbingly, she began to have difficulty recognizing her parents.

It was as if she was giving up.

* * * * * *

The chilly October morning air breezed through the open driver's-side window as Nathan steered the family's SUV into their garage. Ana hopped out and held the door to the kitchen open; he detached the gray, reinforced portable car seat and carried it through the entryway into the living room, where Larry and Sally sat watching a Gameboy-obsessed Justin. Nathan placed the carrier on the living room carpet, and the grandparents gazed admiringly at the sleeping infant, a ray of sunlight shining on her face. Nathan gently lifted Katherine Lynn Wilkinson out of the carrier and handed her to Larry, who sat down on the couch and cradled her in his arms.

"She's a beauty," Sally said.

"She sure is," Larry added. "Just like her grandmother."

"Larry! You keep talking like that and you might get rewarded later."

"Mom!" Nathan groaned. "Stop putting those images in my head! I want to be able to have more children some day!" Despite his purported annoyance at his parents, Nathan felt quiet satisfaction. *How far they've come!*

Ana peered at Lindsay, who was lying in her bed in the corner, barely noticing the commotion. "Lindsay girl!" she called. "Come over here and meet your new sister."

Lindsay lifted her head, glanced at Ana with expression of imperception and confusion, and laid her head back down.

"Oh, come here, girl." Ana took a step toward her.

"Honey, maybe you shouldn't disturb her," Nathan cautioned.

As Ana approached, Lindsay lifted her head and emitted a low growl. "Lindsay, it's me, Mommy," Ana said. Lindsay squinted at her, pulled herself out of her bed, and shuffled over to the couch by Larry.

"Dad, let her see Katie," Nathan said. Larry gently extended the sleeping child toward Lindsay. The schnauzer sniffed and squinted at the infant, then growled again.

"Lindsay…" Nathan took a step toward her. Lindsay barked angrily and flashed her teeth.

"Lindsay!" Nathan yelled and moved between them. The schnauzer backed up and snapped at him.

"Outside, now!" Nathan commanded. Disoriented, Lindsay paused a moment, steadied herself, and shuffled toward the door Ana had opened to the backyard.

Moments passed before Justin broke the silence. "Why is Lindsay so upset?"

"I don't know, buddy," Nathan answered.

"I think you do know," Larry said. "She's senile and suffering from dementia. She barely even knows who you guys are now."

"I don't get it. This has all happened so fast. It's like she's aged a decade in the last year."

"Her baser instincts are starting to take over," Larry said. "If she can't see something or doesn't recognize it, she feels threatened. And if that happens, she may get aggressive. I know it's been hard for you two, but now, with a newborn in the house, you can't take any chances."

"What are you saying?" Ana asked, though she already knew the answer.

"Just this." Larry gazed sympathetically at his daughter-in-law. "You know it's time."

* * * * * *

"So soon after Georgie," Ana sobbed. "I don't know if I can take this."

"It'll be okay." Nathan rubbed his wife's shoulder. "We'll get through this together."

Dr. Grittman had generously agreed to drive from Chino Valley to the Wilkinsons' home to perform the procedure. It seemed to be the right place to have it done. Lindsay had lived all her life in this house, first alone with Ana and then together with Nathan and their growing family. A lifetime of cherished memories was embedded within those four walls and yard, in this modest dwelling where she could always be safe and secure.

"Thanks for coming." Nathan greeted the family's long-time friend, shaking Dr. Grittman's hand and guiding him into the foyer, Ana by his side.

"Think nothing of it," Grittman replied, gripping his leather physician's bag. He paused to give Ana a hug. "How are you guys holding up?"

"We've been better."

"Are your parents here?"

"No. Dad said he thought it should be just us. But I really think that after Shiloh and Georgie, he couldn't bear to be here."

"I understand. As long as her immediate family is here, that's what matters most. Where would you like to have it done?"

"We thought we would do it in the backyard. There's a special spot where she and Georgie would chew on the steak bones I gave them after our family barbeques. I think it's the one place more than anywhere else where she was the most content."

"Okay. Let's bring her outside."

"I-I don't think I can watch," Ana said sheepishly. "Maybe you should do it without me."

Dr. Grittman placed his hand on Ana's shoulder. "Ana, I know this is tough for you. But it's important that you be at her side when she passes. There have been many times where families have brought their dogs into my office and then stayed in the waiting room while I performed the procedure. Lying alone on the gurney, the dogs become frightened and confused. They search frantically for their loved ones and pass away feeling abandoned by their family. That's no way for them to spend their final moments.

"So be there for Lindsay. Tell her it's okay, that you love her, and that you'll see her again soon. Your presence and the sound of your voice will make all the difference in the world to her, and she'll be at peace when she lets go. It may be one of the most difficult things you ever do, but do it for her."

"You're right." Ana sighed, patting Grittman's hand. "For all that she's given me the last fifteen years, it's the least I can give back to her."

Lindsay lay in her bed as the family gathered by the door to the backyard. Nathan cautiously approached her, taking care not to make any sudden moves or otherwise startle her. "Lindsay, sweet girl," he said soothingly, "come with Daddy, okay?"

She gazed incomprehensively for a moment, then shook her head, sat up, and hopped out of her bed. She glanced about in befuddlement, then slowly shuffled to the door and followed the family into the sunlit backyard. Ana placed the carrier holding a sleeping Katie on the grass beside Lindsay's special spot, and she and Justin kneeled next to Dr. Grittman, who pulled a syringe out of his leather physician's bag.

Nathan took hold of Lindsay's collar and guided her to the spot. Oblivious at first, when she saw that she was surrounded by her family, she felt an unease arise within her; she yelped nervously and began to shake visibly.

"It's okay, girl," Nathan said reassuringly, stroking her matted fur. "Don't be scared. We're here with you."

"We should all take a moment," Dr. Grittman said. "Is there anything you'd like to say to her?"

Nathan turned to his wife. "Honey?"

"Lindsay, you're the greatest. I love you so much." She began, her voice shaky, tears rolling down her reddened cheeks. "I can't imagine having spent the last fifteen years without you. You're the best friend I could ever have. Don't be afraid, girl; everything will be better in just a moment."

"Justin?" Nathan turned to his son. "Would you like to say something?"

"Is Lindsay going to go to heaven?" Justin asked. Ana nodded and sobbed again.

"Nathan, what about you?" Dr. Grittman asked.

Nathan gazed into Lindsay's eyes as he gently stroked her head. He strained to kneel in front of her, never easy with his prosthetic leg. "I'll always love you, girl. The day I found you was the day you made my family possible. You taught me loyalty and forgiveness, and you loved me unconditionally, even when I didn't deserve it. Thank you for being there for me and for loving me always."

Ana placed her hand on Lindsay's back, and Nathan cupped his hands around her head. Soothed by their touch, Lindsay ceased shaking, though her anxiety remained acute. Nathan nodded at Dr. Grittman, and the portly veterinarian leaned over and injected the syringe into Lindsay's foreleg just above the joint. Lindsay looked up at Nathan, and for a moment he saw an expression of youthful vigor and full recognition. She softly kissed his hand.

Then, as her eyelids became heavy, she saw sitting behind Nathan the black-and-white border beagle with the sparkling eyes. The one from the park, those many, many years ago. A bright light glowed above the transparent visitor, who beckoned to Lindsay, his expression conveying a message she instantly understood.

It's time to return to the Meadow.

Lindsay whined softly, sending the border beagle a message of her own.

I'm scared.

It's okay, the border beagle responded in that language understandable only to them. *I'm here for you now.*

I don't want to leave my family. I want to be with Nathan.

You will be again. Soon.

It was the last message that affected her, that gave her the comfort and strength she needed. The remaining fear and apprehension inside her dissipated; She let out a soft sigh, closed her eyes for the last time, and followed the border beagle into the light.

~ 181 ~

* * * * * *

It was odd, hearing the knock on the front door unaccompanied by ear-splitting barking and clamorous scurrying through the house.

"Good to see you, Dad."

Larry stepped inside, and Nathan closed the door behind them. Ana came into the foyer, holding a squirming Katie in her arms. "Hi, Larry. What brings you here?"

"I knew you would want to have this as soon as possible," Larry answered soberly. "Dr. Grittman delivered it to me earlier today, so I thought I would bring it to you."

Larry handed Nathan a small object wrapped in cloth. Nathan unraveled the fabric to reveal a silver urn with a single name inscribed on the base:

LINDSAY

"It's just the way we wanted it. Thanks again, Dad." Ana teared up as she reached out to gently stroke the shiny object.

"You okay, sweetie?" Larry asked her.

"Yeah, I guess so," she sighed and paused to search for her next words. "It's just that I miss her so much. I adopted her when she was nine weeks old. For fifteen years, she's been a central part of my life. I miss having her curled up with us in bed. I miss feeding her dinner scraps. And I miss fighting with her for Nathan's attention. I still can't believe she's gone."

"It's okay to mourn her. At least now she'll always be near you."

Nathan placed the urn on the built-in bookcase near the fireplace, next to two others—one inscribed **SHILOH** and the other **GEORGIE**.

"The three of them are all together now," he said mournfully.

"Listen guys," Larry said, "I know it hurts, but give it time. Eventually you'll get over it."

Nathan and Ana exchanged glances. Sometimes Larry spoke clumsily, but he meant well. "Maybe so," Ana responded. "But after losing both Lindsay and Georgie in the last two years, I don't think I can go through this again. I think our days of owning dogs are over."

~ 182 ~

V.

THE CRAZIES

V.1

Goodyear, Arizona—April 2015

"I'm home!"

A weary Nathan Wilkinson called out to his wife as he pushed open the garage's back entrance and stepped into the kitchen. The setting sun cast a dull glow across the gated neighborhood and through the windows, barely affecting the spacious new house's darkened interior. He flipped on the light switch adjacent to the door and placed his computer bag on the mammoth island in the kitchen center.

"Honey?" Still no answer. *That's odd—she's usually home this time of day.* He took a deep breath, enjoying the unique new-construction scent still detectable despite the family having moved in six months earlier.

Nathan loosened his tie as he strode into the living room and fumbled for the switch on the end table lamp. The silence seemed unnatural for this home that typically burst with thunderous family energy. Something did not feel right.

Now a different perception arose within him. Though Ana and the children were absent, he sensed that he was not alone, and his gut told him he was being targeted.

He glanced about; there were four entrances to the living room: from the kitchen, foyer, master bedroom, and outdoor deck. His military training kicked in as he assessed the threat level. An assailant could reach him in an instant from any direction; he was vulnerable and defenseless.

But it was already too late. The bedroom door burst open, and two figures rushed through the darkness into the living room. Nathan whirled about and desperately attempted to assume a defensive position. The two aggressors plowed into him, and the force of the collision knocked him to the floor and onto his back.

"Boomer! Zoey! Get off me!" But the Labradors, the eighty-pound black male Boomer and the sixty-pound blond female Zoey, ignored his pleas and set themselves on top of his sprawled body. Zoey cried out with delight while Boomer showered Nathan's face with sloppy wet kisses.

Ana, laughing uproariously, emerged from the bedroom with Katie in her arms.

"You set me up!" Nathan grunted, immediately regretting opening his mouth as Boomer persisted with the relentless deluge of affection over his face.

"Now would I, your loving wife, do something like that?"

It took effort to extract himself from the energized dogs, but Nathan finally managed to sit upright. Boomer and Zoey scampered throughout the living room, dining room, and kitchen, wailing with delight at their master's return.

"Ugh, now I know how Fred Flintstone felt," he muttered as he wiped his face and tried to collect himself.

"They missed you."

"Yeah, I haven't seen them in, like, eight hours. It must have been pure torture for them."

Zoey returned to Nathan and tried again to jump onto him, but she was dissuaded by a stern growl from Boomer. The brother and sister began to snarl at each other and then embarked on a playful wrestling match.

"Guys!" Nathan hollered over the barking and howling. "Take it outside!" He opened the door, and the two dogs shot into the spacious backyard, circling the swimming pool and commencing with yet another spirited tussle in the grass.

"Have I ever told you how crazy I think they are?" Nathan shook his head.

"Only about a hundred times."

Nathan watched Zoey chase after Boomer, nipping at his tail before plowing into him and sending them both to the ground in a jumble of paws, ears and tails. "I'm amazed they have enough brain power to fuel those big goofy bodies."

"Nathan! Don't say that about your newest family members."

"Yeah, yeah, sorry, whatever. Now how about a kiss for your battered husband?"

"Not until you wash your face, buster."

* * * * * *

While the Wilkinsons had been sincere in her intention to refrain from adopting another dog, circumstances, and fate, harbored other plans. The family's heartbreak over losing Lindsay and Georgie endured; a day rarely passed when Nathan and Ana didn't find their minds replaying happy memories of past times with their pets. A task as simple as gathering the morning newspaper or washing an old blanket under which they had snuggled during the chillier months could trigger such memories, some pleasant, others painful. Their home seemed a little quieter, a little emptier without their presence. Eventually, the tears ceased, but the heartache never would.

A few months later, as fate would have it, one of Ana's colleagues at Van and Laurin announced that she would be leaving the company to take a new job in South Korea. Newly promoted to vice president and director of human resources, Ana listened while the young, single woman explained that she would have to liquidate most of her belongings, as they would not fit into her diminutive new apartment on the outskirts of Seoul. Most importantly, her new living arrangements would not be appropriate for the young rambunctious Labrador puppies she had recently adopted, so she inquired as to whether anyone in the company might be looking for two new additions to their home.

Ana inquired throughout the company but could find no takers for the pups. The woman was distraught; none of her friends or acquaintances wanted them either, and the only remaining option would be the local shelter, where an uncertain fate awaited. She showed Ana more photos of the siblings; taken with their playful expressions and innocent eyes, to her own surprise, Ana told the woman that she would consider adopting them herself.

The next day she led a somewhat reluctant Nathan to the woman's townhome for a get-acquainted visit. As they sat together in the woman's den, Ana felt an immediate bond with the siblings. Their perpetual cycle of kisses, wrestling, chase games, and rolls onto their backs to solicit belly rubs charmed her, as did their infectious combination of youthful stamina and zest for life.

~ 186 ~

For Ana, it served as a powerful elixir that stemmed the pain from their recent loss.

Though Nathan had long remained open to the possibility of a new adoption, Labradors were not a breed that he had previously considered. The siblings seemed the polar opposite in intelligence and demeanor from the wizened Shiloh, the diminutive Lindsay, and the regal Georgie; nonetheless, Nathan too felt charmed and amused by their enthusiasm and limitless energy. So, they agreed to take the dogs, to the relief and delight of Ana's colleague. Nathan led them out of the townhome and into the cab of his truck, and together they journeyed to their new home in east Goodyear.

With the addition of Katie, they had finally outgrown Ana's dwelling, their home of so many years. Fortunately, Nathan's bourgeoning company enabled him to afford a larger house, which they designed and built on a corner lot in a brand-new master-planned community. It was their dream home—four bedrooms, two stories, and a half-acre backyard complete with swimming pool. Coincidentally or not, the house in general and the backyard in particular proved to be an ideal environment for two lively and energetic Labrador retrievers.

The antics began as soon as the two settled into their new home. Used to living in the confined setting of a townhome, when they realized that this spacious home and backyard were theirs, they unleashed an even greater torrent of pent-up energy. Chasing each other through the house and backyard, jumping into the pool for no reason other than it was there, furiously digging holes and then just as quickly abandoning them, engaging in wrestling matches with each other and with Nathan, they left hardly ever a moment of peace and quiet.

Inside the house, freshly made beds seldom survived the siblings' quest for a comfortable spot to lounge. Squeak toys lasted barely a week before being torn to shreds, and occasionally the wayward shoe served as an impromptu substitute. Satisfying their voracious appetites required frequent excursions to the grocery store or pet warehouse. And family members could not relax on the couch without at least one, and often both, settling beside them and demanding affection in the form of belly rubs, pets, or scratches underneath the chin.

And then there were the hunts. Because the subdivision bordered hundreds of acres of undeveloped land, the occasional field cottontail or squirrel would have the misfortune of wandering into the Wilkinsons' backyard. Any encounter with the siblings would inevitably end badly for the interlopers, thanks to Zoey, who, while smaller than her brother, possessed a far more lethal combination of swiftness and guile. She would glow with pride as she delivered her prize to the back door, only to be confused and disappointed when Ana recoiled at the sight.

Often Nathan would shake his head in amusement at their outrageous yet endearing antics. But they also serve as a salve that healed his wounded heart. Though he feared that it would be as if he were replacing his beloved Lindsay and Georgie, he quickly realized that Boomer and Zoey were fully independent members of the family, not replacements for those who had departed. That brought both to Nathan and Ana the closure they needed from a difficult and sorrowful period of their lives.

Before long the crazies, as Nathan affectionately referred to them, had fully integrated themselves into the Wilkinson household. Seven-year-old Justin enjoyed playing with them on those occasions when he wasn't engrossed in video games. Katie began to walk at thirteen months and thereafter rarely settled in one place; like her father at that age, she constantly toddled about the house seeking new frontiers to explore. She loved to play chase games with the dogs and often would try to climb the stairs on her own, which particularly exasperated Nathan. But she adored her father, and on those rare occasions when the dogs left him alone on the couch, she would climb into his lap and fall asleep against his chest. Holding his slumbering daughter helped Nathan realize that whatever the stress and challenges of family and everyday life, it was moments like this that made it all worthwhile.

V.2

Goodyear, Arizona—May 2016

"Justin, where's your father?" Ana asked as she entered the living room from the garage, clad in a Darrian Lawrence number ten Cardinals jersey, her hair entwined in a ponytail.

"I dunno," Justin mumbled, parked on the spacious couch, engulfed in his Gameboy. "Outside, I think."

Ana strode past Katie, who sat in front of the television, a pacifier in her mouth, watching a rerun of *Blues Clues*, and peered through the back-door's blinds to see Nathan trimming a hedge by the swimming pool. He was wearing an ASU baseball cap, a white tank top, and uncommonly for him, shorts that exposed his prosthetic left leg. But the springtime morning Arizona heat rendered yardwork intolerable in anything other than shorts, and no one else could see him in the fenced-in backyard. Boomer and Zoey wandered about the half-acre lot, sniffing for interlopers and occasionally barking and snapping at each other for no discernible reason.

"Nate, could you come here a minute?" Ana called out after cracking open the door.

"Just a sec." Nathan finished shearing an unkempt hedge, laid down his clippers, and ambled past the pool toward the back door. As he stepped inside, the Labradors shot past him and into the house, knocking the door wide open.

"Don't mind me!" Nathan groused, glancing to see the door bounce back from the doorstop and close behind him but not noticing that the child safety latch had failed to secure.

"What do you need, honey?" he asked, removing his cap and wiping the sweat from his forehead.

"I've been rearranging the garage shelves, but some of that stuff is too heavy for me to lift. Would you give me a hand for a minute?"

"Yeah, sure." He turned to Justin. "C'mon, pal, you can help out too."

"Ahhh, Dad," Justin grunted, eyes still affixed to his Gameboy.

"Don't 'Ahhh, Dad' me. You need to do some chores around this house too."

"Fine." Justin made a show of putting down his Gameboy before rising from the couch. No sooner had he vacated his spot than Boomer and Zoey hopped onto the couch and flopped down onto the still-warm cushions.

"Make yourselves comfortable, goofballs," Nathan snorted. "Don't you guys worry about a thing—we'll do all the work." Boomer stared at Nathan a moment and let out a loud yawn; Zoey shook her head violently, sending saliva smattering onto the cushions.

"Okay, now they're mocking me."

"You deserved it. Now, come with me."

"What about Katie?"

"She'll be fine." Ana gestured toward the toddler, who remained engrossed in her television show. "This should only take a couple of minutes." The three started to make their way toward the door to the garage. "Now, I want to put the garden tools on the top shelf and the leaf blower on the bottom…"

* * * * * *

Katie nibbled on her pacifier as she continued to sit in front of the television. On the couch, Boomer scratched himself, and Zoey lay on her side, staring ahead, a blank expression on her face.

A moment later, the show paused for a commercial. Uninterested in the advertisement, Katie glanced around for her mother and father. She saw the dogs, but there was no sign of any other family members. She rose to her feet and toddled into the kitchen. Her parents and brother weren't there either.

Confused, she returned to the living room and then approached the door to the back yard, parted the blinds, and peered through the window. Her short stature limited her field of vision, and she could see only a portion of the yard. She grasped the doorknob and gave it a tug; to her surprise, it swung open.

She stepped onto the porch and glanced about the half-acre backyard for her parents. She gazed to her right, fascinated by the sunlight reflecting off the cabana as she toddled forward, failing to notice that the swimming pool lay directly ahead of her.

* * * * * *

Boomer and Zoey had been watching with detached amusement as their young sister toddled from room to room on her mysterious journey. But that amusement transformed into alarm when they witnessed her open the door and step onto the back porch. Boomer shot Zoey a look of concern and distress; Zoey yelped her agreement, and the Labradors leapt off the couch and darted through the still-open door.

A distracted Katie was now only a few steps from the pool. The dogs sprinted past her, stopped, and pivoted about, using their bodies to block her pathway. Katie stopped abruptly, startled by their maneuver.

Standing together between her and the pool, the dogs stared at her for a moment, then let out low-pitched growls. They moved forward in sync; Boomer nudged her chest with his snout, and she backed up a step. He nudged her again, and she retreated further from the pool.

Zoey gently grasped Katie's shirt with her teeth and pulled on it to pivot her around back toward the still open door, as Boomer nudged her again from behind. Guided by the dogs, she toddled back to the doorway and stepped inside the house. Zoey led her into the living room as Boomer pawed at the open door, swinging it shut. The lock once again failed to secure.

* * * * * *

"I'll take the rest of it to the dumpster by my office later," Nathan said as he, Ana, and Justin stepped through the garage door a few moments later. "We should have gotten rid of that stuff during the move."

They entered the living room to find the dogs lying in the same spot on the couch, with Katie seated in front of the television.

"Okay, I get my seat back now." Justin shooed Zoey with his open hand; she and her brother reluctantly rose and hopped off the couch.

"Justin, you shouldn't have," Ana scolded him. "They were comfortable there."

"Somehow I bet they'll find another place to get comfortable," Nathan muttered. "That's the only thing they're talented at." Nathan turned back to the dogs. "C'mon, numskulls, let's go back outside. And try to stay out of trouble for once."

Zoey gave Boomer a knowing look, and they followed Nathan to the door. Nathan grasped the doorknob and noticed that the child safety latch was not secure. He glanced back at Katie, who remained captivated by her program. Then he shrugged, opened the door, and watched as the dogs scampered out into the backyard to play.

V.3

Goodyear, Arizona—August 2018

"Thanks for organizing this, Shiv. It's going to be a lot of fun for everyone."

"No problem. It's a great way to thank our employees for everything they've done for us."

Silva and Darrian sat across from Nathan in his modestly decorated office, reviewing the final invoices for the upcoming Natana Holdings Camping Weekend. Nathan knew the downtime would be good for employee morale. Without the tireless effort of the store managers and assistants, they would never have reached ten stores as quickly as they had. He felt a couple of days of quality time with their families was the least SportsWorld could give them.

The blistering late-afternoon Arizona sun glistened through the window behind Nathan's desk, reflecting off the autographed Cardinals helmet on his hutch and the Purple Heart medal and citation framed on his wall. Nathan scribbled his signature on the invoices to authorize payment of the reservation fees to Greenhollow National Park and handed the documents back to Silva.

"I'm just glad we could do it in August, before I'm needed at ESPN," Darrian said.

"I can't wait to see you on *SportsCenter*," Silva said. "You're a natural on TV."

"Thanks, Enrique. Every guy in the NFL wants to land that gig after retirement. I'm glad they went with me."

"So, Nate, has Ana warmed up to the idea of a camping weekend yet?" Silva asked.

"She's getting there. She's never gone camping before, and of course she's worried about whether the kids are going to like it. She told me she'd go as long as I rented an RV, so she could sleep in an actual bed at night."

"Always the city girl." Darrian laughed.

"When are your parents going to get there?" Silva asked.

"They should already be at the park by the time we arrive on Friday. Unfortunately, Charles Fletcher can't come. He's been having some health issues, and he said he's not up to it."

"That's too bad. But thanks for inviting Diesel, J-Run, and Airmail to join us," Silva said. "It'll be great to see them again."

"Think nothing of it. All the families are invited, and those guys are family too."

* * * * * *

Friday morning Nathan and Silva picked up the RV; Silva, who had piloted Bradleys and Humvees through countless firefights in Iraq, volunteered to do the driving. His muscular arms strained to steer the lumbering vehicle though Nathan's neighborhood, until they finally pulled it into his driveway, where the family stood in the garage ready to load their suitcases and supplies.

"Daddy, it's awesome!" Katie exclaimed, her bright-green eyes wide as she marveled at the RV. The five-year-old had blossomed into a rambunctious, spirited young girl, with pristine auburn skin and flowing jet-black hair like her mother. Justin stood beside her, baseball cap on backward, too engrossed in the music streaming from his iPhone into his AirPods to acknowledge either the RV or his father. Boomer and Zoey held back, gazing in bewilderment at the strange-looking vehicle.

"They can't wrap their brains around it," Nathan pointed at the dogs. "But then again, considering their brain power, that's not saying much." As usual, Nathan's good-natured taunt drew a sharp glance from his wife.

Boomer approached the sedentary vehicle, eyeing it suspiciously and sniffing at the tires. He let out a low growl; then he and Zoey crouched into an attack position and barked raucously at it.

"Guys!" Nathan hollered as Silva burst into laughter. "It's an RV! It's not going to attack you!"

The siblings paused, glanced at each other, and growled once more at the peculiar vehicle. Then they stopped again as they heard a red-tailed hawk flapping its wings overhead. The bird sailed gracefully past them and perched itself on the crest of the front yard's nine-foot saguaro cactus. Boomer and Zoey pivoted and scampered over to the cactus, barking and jumping up and down in a fruitless attempt to reach the bird, who gazed at them with an expression Nathan was convinced combined condescension and contempt.

"Uh, do they really think they're going to catch that hawk?" Silva asked.

"What do you think?" Nathan shrugged. "At least they've moved on from the threat of the RV. Let's get this thing loaded, so we can be on our way."

* * * * * *

An hour later, they departed for Greenhollow National Park, in central Arizona near the town of Payson. Silva steered the RV eastbound on Interstate 10 and then north on Highway 67, as Nathan relaxed in the passenger seat. The RV featured a small couch that folded into a bed, a tiny kitchenette, a double bed in the rear, and an open space in the center. Ana sat on the couch; Justin and Katie lay on the bed. The dogs nervously paced back and forth, first jumping on the bed and then retreating to the floor but never remaining still for more than a fleeting moment.

"They still can't figure this out," Ana said. "It's like a house, but it's moving. They aren't sure whether to be scared or excited. None of this makes any sense to them."

"Few things do," Nathan remarked.

They pulled into the park just after two in the afternoon. The large open grounds overlooked a lakefront with RVs, tents, picnic tables and firepits dotting the landscape. Hiking trails through the surrounding dense forest snaked deep into the Mogollon Rim. The scenery affirmed Greenhollow's well-earned reputation as one of the most picturesque locations in the state of Arizona.

Tom and Miranda had already arrived, as had Nathan's parents. Most of the store managers were there with their families, and Darrian planned to arrive later in the afternoon. After Silva parked at their designated slot, Nathan hopped out to greet the attendees. Ana helped the kids out of the RV, and their grandparents greeted them with warm hugs. The Labradors darted out the still-open door, relieved that their confinement was at an end and anxious to explore the rich smells and sights of their new surroundings.

"Boomer! Zoey! Stay close!" Nathan called out. But they ignored him, bounding jubilantly through the open campground and toward the lake, stopping at times to introduce themselves to the other guests with yelps and kisses.

"Obedient as usual," Silva remarked.

"It is a beautiful park," Ana said. "The lake and the forest are gorgeous."

"The hiking trails are great too," Silva said. "But the forest is pretty dense, so we need to make sure to keep everyone together. You wander off the trail more than a few yards into the forest, and you could lose your bearings really quick."

"I'll pass on the hiking." Nathan sighed, patting below his left knee. "I don't think the old peg leg here can take it."

"Don't worry, I'll take the kids out onto the trails later on," Ana said. "You stay here and fish with the other guys."

"You heard her, Shiv. And let it be known that I always do what my wife says."

* * * * * *

"And this, young lady, is how you properly toast a marshmallow."

The Wilkinsons and their friends had settled around the smoldering campfire, enjoying the clear and crisp evening air. As was typical for the altitude and time of year, the temperature had dropped precipitously, inducing the group to bundle into sweatshirts and trousers. Hoots from an owl perched in a nearby tree echoed through the campground.

The park bustled with activity. Families bounced a volleyball back and forth across the net of a makeshift court. Guests strolled lazily about the open area. A teenage boy sat on a bench playing a guitar while a group of youths listened as they gazed at the stars dotting the evening sky.

Darrian, Tom and Miranda, Maurizio, McCollom, and Hoff sat around the fire with Nathan and his family. Sally leaned against her husband, sipping a beer from a koozie-encased can.

"Sure got cold quick," Maurizio observed, moving closer to the fire.

"Everybody thinks *hot* when they think *desert*," Larry said. "And yeah, it does get hot during the day. But this place is five thousand feet above sea level, and even during the summer it gets down to the forties and fifties at night."

"That shouldn't be such a big deal to you, Jersey boy," Silva said to Maurizio.

"I spent too much time in Iraq. I don't care too much for cold weather anymore."

As Katie eagerly devoured the marshmallow that her father had toasted for her, Darrian tried to save his own drooping marshmallow, but it caught fire and dropped into the cinders.

"And another fumble by number ten," McCollom joked, drawing hearty laughter from the group.

"Oh, did you say something?" Darrian asked, waving his right hand at McCollom. "I didn't hear you. I was too busy admiring my Super Bowl ring."

"And Darrian Lawrence for the win." Hoff laughed.

"So, you enjoying life after the NFL, Darrian?" Maurizio asked.

"Well, I've got lots of money, I work one day a week at ESPN, and I'm no longer dodging three-hundred-pound linebackers who are trying to take my head off. So, yeah, I guess I'm making it work."

"Now all we need to do is find you a wife," Sally said.

"Only if she's as pretty as you, Mrs. Wilkinson."

Nathan turned to Katie. "You know, honey, I used to play football with Uncle Darrian."

"I know that, Daddy," the five-year-old responded, black hair dangling in front of her green eyes.

"Oh, you do? What else do you know about my past?"

"That you and Uncle Darrian and Uncle Tom went to school together."

"That's right, sweetie," Tom said.

"And that you used to beat Uncle Tom up."

Ana frowned at Katie while the rest of the gang again broke into laughter.

"To set the record straight, it was only once," Tom chuckled. "And I was outnumbered, two to one."

"Who helped you?" Katie asked her father.

"My dog," Nathan answered, a little more somberly. "His name was Shiloh. Someday I'll tell you all about him."

"Okay, Daddy."

"I miss that dog," Tom said. "He made our friendship possible. And he helped me straighten out a few things in my own life."

"Yeah." Larry nodded. "He meant a lot to all of us."

Nathan turned back to his daughter. "And after that, I'll tell you about Lindsay and Georgie too." Nathan jabbed his stick into the fire, pierced what was left of Darrian's marshmallow, and pulled it out relatively intact. "Speaking of dogs...Boomer! Zoey!" The Labradors scurried out of the darkness and up to Nathan as he split the marshmallow in half. "Why waste a perfectly good burnt marshmallow?" Nathan held the marshmallow's halves in front of them, and the dogs snatched them, the loud smacking of their mouths and tongues sparking titters among the group. It took them but a moment to consume their treat, after which they flipped about and scampered right back into the darkness.

"Those guys will eat anything that isn't moving, and more than a few things that do," Nathan remarked. Then he glanced around for Justin, who had not joined the group. He saw the boy sitting by himself on a tree stump a few feet away, eyes closed and listening to music through his AirPods, a dour look splashed across his face.

"Hey, buddy, why don't you join us?" Nathan called out to him. Justin remained motionless.

"Justin?" Still no answer. Nathan grabbed a pebble and tossed it at the tree stump; he opened his eyes and glanced about. Nathan motioned for him to remove the AirPod from his left ear.

"Why don't you come over here for a while?"

"I'm fine."

"C'mon, don't be that way. Spend some time with us. That's what this vacation is all about."

"Maybe I don't want to," he snapped. "I didn't even want to come here. You could have asked me, but you didn't." He shoved the AirPod back into his ear, hopped off the stump, and stalked off toward the RV.

"Ah, ten-year-olds." Nathan sighed. "Such a joy to be around."

"I thought they weren't supposed to start being a true pain in the butt until they reached puberty," Tom remarked.

"Looks like he's off to an early start."

"Leave him be," Sally urged. "He'll come around." Then she stood and turned to her granddaughter. "Katie, honey, Grandma wants to stretch her legs. You want to take a walk down by the lake with me?"

"Sure!" she said. "Can we look for the big fishes?" Miranda and Ana got up as well. "We'll join you too, so the guys can have some time to talk about whatever it is that they talk about when they're together."

"It'll be about you!" Nathan said.

Darrian extracted a six-pack of Budweiser from the cooler and passed the cans around. All took one except for Larry, who politely declined. "So, Enrique," Darrian said as he handed a can to Silva, "there's something I've been meaning to ask you for the longest time. How did you get the nickname Shiv?"

Enrique popped open his can and smiled at his comrades. "You sure you want to know?"

"Of course."

"Well, you know that my first deployment was in Afghanistan. When we would go out on patrols, most of the guys strapped sidearms to their legs, just in case their M4s needed a little, uh, supplement. I preferred a blade, like the one I used to carry in high school. The other guys gave me a lot of grief, told me knives are no good in a gunfight. But our second week there, we got into close quarters with a band of Taliban fighters in a marketplace outside of Kandahar. One of them jumped me from behind and took me to the ground."

Silva took a long drink from his Budweiser, then reached down and pulled a four-inch blade out from a holder strapped to the inside of his leg. "Lucky I had this little baby with me." The spine glistened in the moonlight as he waved it in front of Darrian. "I cut the guy from his throat all the way down to his sack."

Darrian's mouth fell open, and his eyes widened.

"He's telling it like it is," Hoff said. "We all saw it."

"And we stopped giving him grief after that," Maurizio added.

"And that's when we started calling him Shiv," McCollom said.

"I thought it would be best to call him Mr. Shiv," Hoff ventured.

~ 199 ~

Silva said no more; he just flashed a mischievous grin at Darrian.

"Okay, then." Darrian grimaced. "Dodging those three-hundred-pound linebackers doesn't sound so bad right now."

* * * * * *

"All right, everybody, gather round!" Nathan called out to the employees and their families milling about the camp. The clear weather had lingered into the next morning, and the rising sunbathed the park in bright, warm light. He was dressed in a gray T-shirt bearing an image of famed sniper Chris Kyle and seven-pocket hikers' pants. Ana and the children accompanied him, while the Labradors ran aimlessly through the grounds, scavenging for discarded food.

"Today's our fun day!" Nathan began. "We have a lot of different activities available for you to choose from. You can go boating on the lake, do some fishing at the pier, take a hike along some of the trails, or, if you don't have enough energy for any of that, just have a seat here at the lakefront and enjoy the scenery. Let's divide into groups for each activity. We'll plan on meeting back here around three so we can fire up the barbeques for tonight's cookout. Sound like a plan?"

As the employees divided into groups by respective activity, Ana and Katie briefly huddled and then made their way over to Nathan.

"Katie and I are going to head off on the nature hike," Ana told him. "She's real excited; she said she wants to look for deer and rabbits."

"There ought to be plenty of wildlife near the trails." Then Nathan turned to address his son. "Justin, Mom and Katie are going hiking, and I'm going to fish with the guys. Which one do you want to do?"

"How about neither?"

"How about one of the two?" Nathan said, a little more sternly.

"Okay, fishing then."

"That's my guy." Nathan tousled his son's hair, then turned back to his wife. "Now, you and Katie have fun. We'll go out and catch our dinner."

* * * * * *

Prior to departing for the fishing pier, Nathan rounded up Boomer and Zoey,

~ 200 ~

led them inside the RV, fired up the air-conditioning, and locked the door behind him. The siblings whined at the prospect of being cooped up inside the strange vehicle, but since the guests had departed from the main area on their excursions, no one was left to watch over them.

The friends parked themselves near the end of the long wooden pier and commenced with their afternoon of fishing. Maurizio and Hoff had never tried it, and their clumsy casting attempts brought some amusement to the rest of the party. They came up empty but didn't seem to mind, since even though it was still morning, they had already dipped into the beer chest.

The rest of the group were much more experienced anglers. Darrian snared a sizable tiger trout, and Justin's eyes grew wide when the retired quarterback reeled it in and let it flap around on the pier. Nathan showed Justin how to attach a worm to the hook, and he patiently worked with his son on the casting technique. It took a couple of hours, but Justin grew excited when he felt his first line tug. All the guys cheered as he reeled in an eight-inch carp, a minor prize but a victory nonetheless.

A few hours later they packed their catches in the Coleman cooler and collected their equipment. Nathan made sure to let Justin position his prize carp right at the very top, so he could show it to his mother and sister.

"That's a good-looking fish," Tom said to Justin as he snapped the cooler's lid shut. "It'll look even better on our dinner plates tonight. When we get back to camp, I'll show you how to gut, clean, and fry them."

"That'll be great."

Nathan beamed with pride and relief that the boy was finally enjoying himself.

Suddenly they heard frantic commotion behind him.

"Nathan!"

He turned to see Ana running in from one of the trails, a distraught expression on her face.

"Honey? What's wrong?" he asked.

"It's Katie!" Ana cried, her voice cracking. *"I can't find her!"*

V.4

Mogollon Rim, Arizona—August 2018

"All right, Ms. Wilkinson, you need to tell me everything that happened."

Gila County Sheriff Donald McClendon stood over a distraught Ana as she sat on a park bench in the open central camping area. The five-foot eleven inch, broad-shouldered lawman was dressed in full uniform and sported a bushy brown mustache that partially hid the scar on his right cheek. Sheriff's deputies and local police from the town of Payson milled about the grounds. Police cars and rescue vehicles filled the northern sector parking lot. The Natana employees and their families huddled together in groups, whispering anxiously among themselves, awaiting instructions on how they could assist in the rescue efforts.

Nathan sat next to Ana, holding her hand, and his parents stood behind them, Larry's arm draped over his wife's shoulders, both pale with fear, Larry visibly trembling.

Nathan tightened his grip on his wife's hand. *Be strong. They all need you now.* Fear tore through him as well. It would be as difficult as anything he had ever done, but he had to hold together, to be the symbol of strength his family needed.

"I-I don't know how it happened," Ana stammered. "There were about a dozen of us hiking along the trail. The forest was really dense, just like they told us. Katie had her heart set on seeing a deer and other wildlife, and every few minutes we stopped so she could look into the woods for them.

"One of the people with us knew a lot about the plant life here, and she was pointing out the different wildflowers along the route. At one point we kneeled in front of a cluster of, I think she called them, western yarrow, and she showed us some of the plant's features.

"When she finished, I stood up, and Katie was gone!" Ana started to sob. "I swear I didn't have my eye off of her for more than a minute!"

"Sheriff, our daughter has always been a fireball," Nathan added. "She's full of energy and loves to run around, climb stairs, explore, all of that. She must have seen something in the woods, maybe a rabbit or deer, and took off after it."

"She may be full of energy, but she's still five years old," the sheriff said in a calm tone. "She won't get very far. At best, she wandered maybe a mile or two, which means that we're working with a pretty narrow search grid."

"All of us in the group went into the woods to look for her," Ana continued, as though unable to hear her husband or the sheriff. "But it was so dark. We couldn't find any trace of her."

"That's understandable," Sheriff McClendon said. "You can lose sight of another person even if they're no more than ten yards off the trail.

"Listen," he said, "it's four thirty now, and that gives us time to conduct an initial sweep before nightfall. A lot of my deputies grew up around here, so they know their way around this forest. We've already dispatched the first two search parties, one of which is meeting up with the group you left behind at the point she disappeared, and three more are getting organized now.

"Count us in, Sheriff," Darrian said, pointing to Silva, Tom, Maurizio, Hoff, and McCollom.

"Great, we need all the warm bodies we can get."

Nathan stood up. "I'm going too."

"Mr. Wilkinson," the sheriff said to him, "can I talk to you a minute?" He motioned for Nathan to follow him out to his parked cruiser in the lot; though reluctant to leave his distraught wife, Nathan complied.

"Listen, Nathan—Can I call you that?" the sheriff asked as he braced his arm against his vehicle. Nathan nodded. "I didn't want to say this in front of your wife, given the state she's in right now. But the Rim country is pretty rugged. The forest is filled with steep inclines and drop-offs, and there are some pretty unfriendly animals out there. I don't think someone with your, uh, condition, should be trying to navigate your way through that."

"But she's my daughter, damnit!"

"I understand that. And I'm going to do everything in my power to find her. But I can't have one of my search parties hampered because someone can't keep up with them, even if that someone is her father. The best thing you can do is stay with your wife and keep her together. She's never needed you more than she needs you now."

"All right," Nathan reluctantly agreed. "But you're going to find her, and soon, right?"

"We're going to do the best we can," the sheriff replied.

"That wasn't a yes."

"I said, we'll do the best we can."

* * * * * *

Most of the Natana employees joined the search teams, each of which was led by a ranger or deputy, with a few adults remaining behind to watch the children. Other guests at the park offered to join in the search as well, along with police officers from Payson and Star Valley. Within an hour, five different search teams composed of over one hundred individuals were poised and ready to enter the dense woods surrounding the camp.

"Okay, everybody, it's five thirty now," Sheriff McClendon addressed the group. "We only have about two hours of daylight left, so we are going to have to move quickly. I want each of the teams to cover a different sector of the park. Two teams are to proceed to the spot where the girl was last seen, and I want one team on each of the three other trails.

"All of you volunteers are to do exactly what your team leaders tell you to do. And team leaders, you are to stay in constant radio contact both with the command center and with each other. Keep your GPS on, move quickly, and don't hesitate for any reason. I want that girl back with her parents before nightfall."

One by one, the groups moved toward their designated trails and disappeared into the dense forest. Nathan, Ana, Larry, Sally, and Justin remained at the main campground by the picnic table near the makeshift command center. Darrian and Silva gave Ana a hug before they joined their group.

"Don't worry," Darrian told her, "we'll find your little lady."

Ana sat back down on the picnic bench next to Justin, who was immersed in a game of Angry Birds on his iPhone. "This is all my fault," she said, her eyes filling with tears.

Nathan embraced his wife. "Don't do that to yourself. This wasn't your fault."

"Yeah, it's Katie's fault; she should have stayed near you," Justin muttered.

"Justin!" Nathan snapped. "Keep your opinions to yourself!"

"Sor-ry," he said snidely, then returned to his game.

"I guess all we can do now is wait," Larry said. "We might as well make ourselves comfortable."

"Good idea," Nathan agreed. "But this picnic table isn't big enough for all of us. I've got some folding chairs in my RV that we can use. Let me go get them."

He headed across the lot to his parked RV and opened the door; in an instant, Boomer and Zoey bounded out and onto the lot.

"Oh, sorry, guys. With all that's going on, I forgot that I left you in there before we went fishing. You need some outside time now anyway. Wait for me a second."

He disappeared inside the vehicle and reemerged a moment later carrying two folding chairs. He locked the RV's door and started back to the main campground, the Labradors bounding happily beside him, looping around the parking lot and pausing to playfully snap at each other.

After arriving back at the picnic table, Nathan unfolded the chairs and motioned for his parents to sit. Larry wearily settled into one of the chairs; Sally sat down next to him and rested her head on his shoulder, exhausted from the stress. Boomer and Zoey trotted up to the group, and Zoey attempted to climb into Larry's lap.

"Not now, girl." Larry abruptly pushed her away. Startled at the rebuff, Zoey glanced first at her brother and then around the campground, seeing the police officers, park rangers, and other officials roving about. She raised her paw and, sensing the tension, gestured at Boomer in puzzlement.

Something's not right.

The two dogs took a seat on the ground next to Nathan, their cheery dispositions vanishing. Boomer surveyed the family, then the others in the campground. His sister was correct; something was definitely wrong.

Uniformed strangers lurking throughout the campground, nervous and restrained exchanges of words, the apprehension in the family's voices, stress emanating from everyone, the repeated references to Katie.

Then it all came together. Boomer yipped knowingly at Zoey, who yipped back at her. They leapt to their feet, and in a flash they had dashed through the campground and off toward the trails.

"Hey! Come back here!" Nathan hollered at them, but it was too late; they had reached the main trail, and a moment later, they disappeared into the forest.

"What's gotten into them?" Sally inquired.

"Don't know, but then again, I never know with them," Nathan responded. "They probably just have to find some place to do their business. But whatever, we all have more important things to worry about than those two."

* * * * * *

The two Labradors galloped at full speed along the trail, maintaining their frantic pace until they reached the point where Katie went missing. Darrian had arrived there minutes earlier with the initial search party and now watched in amazement as Boomer stopped and sniffed anxiously while Zoey scrutinized the forest. They yipped at each other again, in that language understandable only to them, and together plunged into the woods.

As Sheriff McClendon had described, the terrain was rocky and strewn with sharp, spindled brush highly treacherous to human and canine alike. The towering forestry blocked nearly all the waning sunlight, casting a pall of darkness over the region even during the daytime. Chirps and tweets from the birds, insects, and other inhabitants echoed through the forest. Tree squirrels and wild hares bandied about, but the siblings ignored them, focusing single-mindedly on their mission.

An hour passed, and then a second, as the two navigated their way through the dense and hazardous landscape. They found the smells and scents frustratingly difficult to decipher. Periodically the dogs split up, each taking a circuitous route to increase their coverage before meeting up at a designated point. But the forest was so heavy, and the territory so vast, that despite all their efforts, they repeatedly came up empty.

Finally, they reached a river that flowed through a valley carved within the forest. Her throat dry from the nonstop hyperactivity, Zoey took a moment to refresh herself from the cool water; Boomer paused to take a drink as well. For a moment the two Labradors faced each other next to the waterway with concern and distress at their lack of progress.

Then they heard steps lumbering across the terrain, crunching through the spindly brush. Zoey pivoted toward the source and froze in fear at the sight.

It was a large black bear, six feet long, at least three hundred pounds, patches of gray in its fur, sharp and menacing claws, marching toward the stream less than twenty yards from them. Zoey nudged her brother, who recoiled when he sighted the predator.

In its single-minded resolve to quench its thirst, the bear failed to notice the Labradors standing in the open valley. Quietly Boomer and Zoey backed away from the stream, toward brush that they hoped, in the darkened area, would shield them from view. The bear reached the stream and lowered its head to take a drink, still oblivious to the siblings' presence.

Boomer reached the safeguard first and nodded, gesturing for Zoey to follow. Zoey ever so cautiously stepped forward. But in the gathering darkness she failed to notice a twig lying on the ground, and when she stepped on it, a loud crack echoed through the valley.

The bear pivoted toward the sound as Zoey threw herself behind the thicket. Zoey crouched behind Boomer, hoping that her brother's larger body and darker fur would shield her more visible blond coat. They held their breath as the bear stared in their direction for what seemed like an eternity.

Then the bear lowered its head, took another drink, turned around, and wandered off in the direction from where it had come.

Boomer and Zoey lingered for a moment to ensure that the coast was clear, then lifted themselves up and prepared to resume their search. But their relief at avoiding the predator was matched by their increasing anxiety over the multiple dangers imperiling their young sister.

* * * * * *

"Okay, teams, pull out now and report back to command," Sheriff McLendon barked into his walkie-talkie. A helicopter flew overhead, beaming a search light over the camp and the forest.

An agitated Nathan marched over to confront the sheriff. "Did I just hear you give the order to suspend the search?"

"I'm sorry, Nathan, but it's sunset now. The search parties aren't going to accomplish anything out there at night, and someone might get hurt if they stumble over a rock or get caught in one of those thickets."

"It's going to get cold tonight, and Katie's only in shorts and a T-shirt."

McLendon pointed to one of the helicopters circling overhead. "You see those choppers? They are going to spend the entire night sweeping the region with those spotlights. We're hoping that one of them will get lucky and spot her. If not, we'll start up with the search parties again first thing in the morning."

"There has to be something else I can do."

"There is one thing," McLendon replied somewhat tentatively. "Call your pediatrician and tell him to courier up to us all Katie's medical records. And her dental records too. Tell him it's just a precaution, standard procedure in these circumstances."

As he contemplated the meaning of the sheriff's request, Nathan's stomach knotted, and his blood turned cold.

* * * * * *

They were tired, hungry, and cold, having covered several miles in the past three hours. But still nothing—no scent, no trail, no sign of Katie. Zoey gestured to her brother, suggesting they return to camp for food and rest. But Boomer stood firm. He glared at his sister for a moment, communicating through his expression that he wasn't going anywhere. Taken aback at first, she found inspiration in her brother's strength and determination; she yipped to convey her new resolve and followed him into the forest to resume the search.

Darkness gradually enveloped the Rim as more hours passed. The moon was absent, and the stars bestowed a dull and muted illumination upon the forest. Occasionally Boomer and Zoey heard the churning sound of a helicopter passing through the evening sky, its floodlights beaming down over the mammoth forest, the spasmodic and scattered lighting serving only to illustrate the monumental challenge of their mission.

The Labradors proceeded cautiously, feeling their way along the terrain, their progress slower and more laborious in the gathering darkness. Fatigue seared through their bodies, and a combination of exhaustion, vexation, and disappointment drained their spirits while fueling an increasing fear of failure and tragedy.

And then...

Zoey yelped excitedly at her brother. *A scent!*

Boomer yapped back at her. *Are you sure?* Zoey squealed again, her snout aimed to the north. Powered by little more than adrenaline and resolve, they galloped toward the source. It was reckless, and dangerous, as they brushed against the sharp thickets and nearly stumbled over the countless protruding rocks. But they kept pushing forward and forward, until...

They stopped when they heard the sound, separate and distinct from the nighttime clatters of the forest life. The sound of gentle sobbing.

They moved forward cautiously, entering a clearing past yet another cluster of trees and brush. Despite the murky darkness, they instantly recognized the figure perched on a mammoth rock, shivering, her face buried in her hands as she shed tears of pain and fright.

It was Katie.

* * * * * *

The five-year-old jumped off the rock when she heard the brush rustling in the distance.

"Who's there?" Katie cried out, wiping tears from her eyes, fear audible in her young voice as she peered into the darkness. "I'm not afraid!"

The siblings emerged from the brush and approached her, illumination from the starlight revealing their identities.

"Zoey! Boomer!" she cried, then ran over and embraced them. She was dirty, her T-shirt torn and her shorts covered with burrs. Her matted black hair partially covered her eyes, and her face was stained from the frightened tears. She smiled weakly as the siblings showered her with kisses of joy and relief.

"Where's Mommy and Daddy?"

Zoey whined and set her paw on Katie's shoulder.

"But I want them!"

She sat down on an adjacent rock and wept again in frustration. The dogs closed in around her; Zoey placed her head on Katie's thigh to rally her spirits. She wiped the new tears from her eyes and stood up again.

"Let's go find them!" she declared, then stepped toward the brush at the edge of the clearing. The dogs sat motionless.

"C'mon," she said more forcefully, but the siblings remained stationary.

As she took another step, Boomer darted past Katie and spun around, positioning his body to block her path.

"You don't want me to go?"

Boomer yelped a single time.

"Okay. It's dark and scary out there anyway."

She folded her arms across her body and started to shiver. "I'm cold. I don't want to be cold."

Zoey took hold of Katie's shirt with her teeth and guided her back to the rock. She jumped up on her hind legs and positioned her front paws on Katie's shoulders, gently pushing her down to the soil. Zoey then dropped to the ground and set her body against the child's chest. Boomer took position behind her, also lying down and pressing his body against her back. The dogs' cradling bodies provided the girl a comforting and needed warmth against the plunging temperature.

"I'm tired now," she whimpered, laying her head on the dirt. Zoey gave Katie another kiss on the cheek, and both she and Boomer shut their eyes.

For the first time in hours, Katie felt relief and encouragement. She yawned and closed her eyes as well. Then she abruptly sat upright.

"Thank you for staying with me and keeping me company," she said to the figure in the distance. "But my friends are here to take care of me now. You can go home if you want. I won't mind."

And with that, Katie watched as the black-and-white border beagle with the sparkling eyes yelped at her in a tone of comfort and reassurance before fading into the night.

V.5

Mogollon Rim, Arizona—August 2018

"Did you get any sleep at all?" Nathan asked his wife.

"Maybe a few minutes here or there."

He was sitting on one of the folding chairs next to the picnic table, while Ana was curled on the ground over a makeshift bed of blankets. The sun peered over the forest-laden foothills of the Rim, bathing the campground in warm morning light. Several of the volunteers dozed on sleeping bags while police officers and park rangers relieved those who had manned the command center through the night.

Nathan ran his fingers through Ana's hair and kissed her gently on the forehead. "You should have gone back to the RV."

"I want to be here, in case something happens. And I wouldn't have gotten any more sleep there anyway."

In the distance, Sheriff McClendon huddled with his deputies, poring over geologic maps and satellite images of the region. TV news crews parked their vans at the periphery of the RV lot, as close to the campground as the deputies would allow them. Local pilots circled their planes overhead as they swept the area in tactical and logical support for the search effort.

"How you guys doing?" Silva asked as he, Maurizio, and Darrian approached Nathan and Ana.

"About as well as can be expected," Nathan responded, rubbing the stubble on his face.

"You want us to get you something to eat?" Darrian asked.

"Thanks, but no, I'm not hungry," Ana answered.

Nathan shook his head as well.

A moment later Sheriff McClendon joined them. "Okay, guys, we're getting ready to organize a new set of search teams. We're going to pick up right where we left off at nightfall yesterday. The good news is that we have a slew of additional volunteers who have come here from as far away as Show Low to aid in the search. Seems that this story was all over the news last night, and lots of people want to help."

"Be sure to tell everyone how much we appreciate their support," Nathan said.

"But there's something I need you to know," the sheriff continued. "I debated with myself about how much I was going to tell you, but you're her parents and you have a right to know. Last night it got down to fifty degrees, and the forecast is for it to get even colder tonight. That makes today the most critical day for the search. A small child like Katie is not going to be able to withstand more than one or two nights exposed to this kind of weather, especially since she doesn't have a coat or a sweatshirt. And the Rim is filled with other threats as well—snakes, bears, cliffs and drop-offs. Every hour she spends out there is an hour that puts her more in peril."

Nathan's stomach tightened again, and Ana's face turned ashen. Darrian kneeled in front of her and looked into her eyes. "Keep the faith, sweetheart," he said. "We'll find her." Ana buried her head in Darrian's shoulder.

Over the past hours Nathan had struggled to maintain his composure, to be the source of strength on which his parents, his son, and his wife could rely. But this latest news proved too much for him to bear. Stressed, exhausted, and emotionally spent, he bent over, placed his elbows on his knees, and covered his face in his hands as the tears began to flow. He felt a hand on his shoulder.

"It'll be okay," Justin said to him. "Katie's a fighter, and I know she'll come through this. Don't you worry about it."

Heartened by his son's words of encouragement, Nathan reached up and patted Justin's hand.

"C'mon guys," the sheriff said to Darrian, Silva, and Maurizio. "Let's get to work."

* * * * * *

Katie had yearned for it to have been nothing more than a bad dream, that she would wake in the comfort of her bed, surrounded by her beloved stuffed animals. She would leap out of bed and dash to the kitchen, to find her mother and father preparing the usual breakfast of scrambled eggs and bacon. She would sit down at the table and eagerly devour the always-delicious meal, after which she would kiss her mother and father before heading back to her bedroom to get dressed for the coming day.

But when she opened her eyes, she saw only rocks protruding from the dirt, reflecting the glare of the morning sun, and the surrounding forest trees fluttering in the wind. She shielded her eyes from the bright light and glanced about the terrain, the painful reality of her predicament returning to her.

Zoey remained nestled against her, motionless in her slumber. But Boomer had disappeared.

"Zoey!" Katie jostled the blond Labrador. "Where's Boomer?"

Zoey stood, shook herself, and anxiously looked for her brother.

Then they both glanced toward a rustling emanating from the brush at the edge of the clearing. Boomer emerged from behind it and strode up to them.

"Where did you go?" Katie asked. Boomer turned to the path from which he had emerged, then pivoted again to face them.

"You want us to follow you?"

Boomer yelped a single time. Katie rose to her feet and brushed the dirt from her clothes. In unison she and Zoey joined up with Boomer.

"Okay," she said. "I'm hungry, and I'm thirsty, and I want to go home." Boomer took the lead, marching toward the path leading from the clearing, as Zoey remained at Katie's side.

* * * * * *

Boomer took position a few feet ahead of Zoey and Katie as they made their way through the dense forest. He could not discern if they were heading in the direction from which they had come, given that much of their previous day's trek had been at dusk. The morning sun had rapidly warmed the forest, though the foliage still impeded their visibility and navigation. Boomer scanned the terrain, scouting for the clearest path forward, while Zoey flanked Katie, guarding her from the forest's numerous unseen threats. They listened for the sound of rescuers but heard only the occasional clatter of the woodland creatures.

Weakened from hunger and thirst, Katie often paused to rest. Aware of her diminished physical state, the dogs patiently waited for her to gather her strength before proceeding with their journey.

Several hours passed. Boomer relentlessly combed the terrain for any familiar landmarks but still found nothing recognizable. Neither he nor Zoey picked up any familiar scents. The forest was a labyrinth of nature, so confounding, so unforgiving in its convolution. They could only continue their advance and hope to detect something, anything, that would lead them to safety.

Finally, their first break, as they sighted the valley with the narrow river. Boomer galloped down to the waterway's bank, while Zoey gestured at Katie to follow her brother. Approaching the river, Katie gazed at the pure water flowing along the fifty-foot wide stream.

"Can I drink from it?" she asked.

Boomer answered by lowering his snout and lapping up the cool liquid; Zoey joined him a moment later. Katie fell to her knees between them and dipped her cupped hands into the water. She brought the liquid to her lips, slurped heartily, and smiled at the two Labradors, already feeling more energized as the water flowed down her throat.

Then she heard a sound, a muffled yelp, emanating from the river's center. She turned to her right and saw a small gray wolf cub in the river's mid-center thrashing about in the churning flow, struggling to keep its head above the water's edge. It cried out in terror as the currents repeatedly pulled it under the surface.

Zoey saw it too. She glanced at Boomer; intention already clear; her brother's return glance conveyed his own appeal.

Don't do it!

Without hesitation, Zoey jumped into the water and frantically paddled toward the cub. Despite its narrow width, the river was deep, its currents powerful and unforgiving. Zoey too felt the undertow conspiring to drag her below the surface; she fought back with every muscle in her fatigued body. Within moments, she reached the cub; she clamped her mouth tightly around its neck, then pivoted to paddle back to the shoreline.

~ 214 ~

At first the cub tried to wriggle free, as terrified of Zoey as it was of the river. It ceased resisting when it realized the Labrador was there to assist, remaining in Zoey's grasp as the pair advanced to the river's edge.

Katie breathed a sigh of relief when the two finally emerged from the water. Zoey released the cub, who fell to the ground, exhausted from its terrifying ordeal. As it lay panting in the dirt, the siblings sniffed and nudged its diminutive body, checking for visible wounds. Seeing none, they backed up to give it space to rest and gather itself.

Katie approached the cub, extended her hand, and stroked its head. The cub glanced up at her and gave Katie's hand a kiss. Katie smiled and reached down to rub its belly.

Then she, Boomer, and Zoey all heard the crunch of steps behind them. In unison, the three companions spun about toward the source.

It was an adult gray wolf.

* * * * * *

Katie shrieked at the sight of the frightening creature. It glowered at the group; provoked further by the girl's squeal, it growled and took a step toward them.

Katie, Zoey, and Boomer backed away from the cub as the gray wolf flashed its teeth. Zoey and Boomer quickly positioned themselves in front of the terrified Katie.

Then the cub rose to its feet, shook the water off its damp fur, and, still exhausted from its ordeal, made its way over to the adult wolf. The wolf sniffed it, turned it with its snout and carefully eyed it, seeing no injuries.

Zoey moved forward, positioning herself nose to nose with the wolf. The wolf snarled, and Zoey growled back. For the longest time, the two stared at each other in silence. Then, ever so imperceptibly, the wolf nodded at Zoey. It backed up, turned around, and cub in tow, gestured with its head at the other three. Zoey gave Boomer and Katie a look of reassurance and strode toward the wolf.

Katie glanced at Boomer. "I think she wants us to go with her." Boomer yelped his agreement, and the trio followed the wolf away from the river and into the forest.

* * * * * *

"I don't care how tired they are, tell them to keep searching!" Sheriff McClendon bellowed into his walkie-talkie. He clenched his sizable fists in frustration; it was now 4:00 p.m., and the little girl had been gone for over a day now. They had three more hours of sunlight at best, with another dangerously cold evening approaching.

One of his deputies approached McClendon. "Sheriff, the media reps want a statement for the evening news."

"Tell them the search is ongoing. Nothing else."

"But, sir, this is going to be the lead story on all the cable channels tonight. We need to give them some more details."

"The hell we do. You go tell those reporters that if they want to be useful, they can join one of the search parties."

"Yes, sir." As the deputy trotted off, McClendon glanced over to the park bench where the parents and their family remained encamped. They were good people, and none of this was their fault. People had gotten lost before in the Mogollon Rim, though no one as young as little Katie. He felt especially bad for Nathan, whom he knew was itching to join the search parties. But his injury, incurred in the defense of all Americans, was preventing him from coming to the assistance of that young American whom he loved the most.

McClendon loved being sheriff of Gila County. He had lived here all his life and since middle school had aspired for a career in law enforcement. He found the job as rewarding as he had hoped, and his tough but fair administration had markedly improved the quality of life in his community. But there was one aspect of the job he did not relish, an obligation as heart-wrenching as it was inevitable in the field of public service. That was the occasional requirement to inform a family member that a loved one was gone. Whether through accident, homicide, or other tragedy, to see the anguish in the relatives' eyes as his words sank in, to witness the slow-motion collapse of their world around them... Few things were more haunting, even to a seasoned veteran like him. And to share such news about a five-year-old child with her parents...

He turned to observe a visibly shaken Nathan comforting his equally distressed wife. They were good people, those two, so undeserving of the predicament in which they found themselves. He checked his watch again; time was running out. They needed a break, and soon.

* * * * * *

Her stomach ached from hunger, her lips were dry and cracking, and her legs burned from fatigue. But Katie persisted, straining herself to keep up with her two best friends and their new companions. She could tell that Boomer and Zoey were equally weary. But the sun was waning, and she feared the prospect of spending another night in the cold outdoors.

As they walked, the cub occasionally circled back to Katie, playfully jumping up at her. Katie smiled and stroked its fur, but she found it increasingly difficult to engage in playtime as the exhaustion and despair sapped away her energy.

Confident in her familiarity with the terrain, as resolute in her determination as Boomer and Zoey, the gray wolf lead the group forward relentlessly. She rarely communicated with Zoey, having already established an understanding with the Labradors that this was now her pack and her responsibility. The tree-studded terrain was so repetitious, so alike, so interchangeable; Katie's frustration and anxiety rose as she feared they would never find their way back home.

And then, the gray wolf stopped. She yelped once at Zoey, then pointed ahead with her snout. Katie picked up on the gesture and strained her eyes to see what had captured the wolf's attention.

Fifty yards ahead lay an opening in the forest, a hiking trail.

"That's the road back to Mommy and Daddy!" Katie shouted. Zoey and Boomer yelped and set off toward it, while the wolf and her cub remained.

Boomer stopped and turned to acknowledge the wolf's generosity and invaluable assistance. But his blood ran cold as behind the wolf and her cub stood a familiar and frightening sight.

It was the black bear.

* * * * * *

At first it just stood erect, staring at the group. Then it sniffed and roared menacingly upon making eye contact with Boomer. Katie screamed; her shriek agitated the predator and it suddenly moved toward them, its lithe and agile body closing ground rapidly.

The gray wolf emitted a piercing howl that echoed through the forest, then grabbed her cub and disappeared behind a cluster of trees. Zoey yelped at her, pleading for her to return, to no avail. Zoey grunted in frustration and took position next to Boomer, both in front of Katie.

At once Boomer realized that they could never hope to outrun the bear. Though frightened by the beast's size and bulk, he knew that there could be no backing down. There was only one course of action. He yapped at Zoey, who nodded, and together they charged forward.

The bear halted, startled by the bold advance. The Labradors stopped a few yards from it, and the adversaries tensely faced each other.

Boomer and Zoey growled and flashed their teeth, attempting to intimidate their much larger foe. Unimpressed, the bear roared back at them. Katie cowered and sobbed in terror.

For the longest moment, the adversaries persisted with their standoff. The siblings watched the bear rise to its hind legs and eye Katie, its ultimate prey. No matter the cost, it had to be stopped.

Boomer glanced at Zoey, and again they burst forward, Zoey zagging to the left and Boomer to the right. In unison they lunged at the bear from opposite sides.

Boomer made contact first, sinking his teeth into the bear's left hind leg. The bear howled in pain and slashed at Boomer with its left front paw. Boomer let go and dove toward the ground, barely dodging the razor-sharp claw. Zoey hurled her body into the bear's right midsection, attempting to knock it to the ground. But the predator was too large, and too muscular; Zoey bounced off it and tumbled to the dirt.

The bear pounced at Zoey; she rolled to the right, avoiding its lethal jaws. Seeing the bear thrusting forward, Boomer seized the opportunity, hurdled himself onto its back, and buried his teeth into its neck. Again the bear shrieked in agony and flailed about in an attempt to shed the attacking Labrador. Boomer held on for dear life until the bear's violent thrusts sent him crashing to the ground as well.

Then the bear changed tactics, turning suddenly and charging, its speed and agility catching Zoey off guard. Zoey pivoted to her right but saw her escape route cut off by a cluster of trees. She was trapped.

Boomer scrambled to his feet and, in a desperate attempt to save his sister, lunged again at the bear. The bear saw Boomer's attack coming and swiped its front right paw at him, its sharp claws gashed deep into and across the Labrador's underside. Boomer again plummeted to the ground, yelping in severe pain and unable to right himself.

Zoey slipped by the bear and darted over to her brother. The bear roared again and closed on them. Bleeding and unable to rise to his feet, Boomer braced himself for the assault. Zoey refused to leave her brother's side; together the siblings prepared for their last stand.

Then the combatants were startled by a high-pitched chorus of howls in the distance. A pack of a dozen adult wolves emerged from the dense foliage, led by the mother wolf and her cub. In an instant they surrounded the bear, cutting off his route to the Labradors, their teeth flashing and their fur standing on end.

Though the bear was larger and more ferocious than any one of them, the pack's collective strength gave it pause. It roared again, but the wolves stood firm, resolved and unyielding. Then, assessing the changed circumstances, the bear stepped back and turned about. The pack opened up a pathway in the circle; it lumbered through it and off into the forest.

Katie jumped to her feed and darted over to Zoey and Boomer. "Are you okay?" she asked, kneeling in front of Boomer. He whined, kissed Katie's hand, and struggled to his feet. Blood stained his dark fur, but he still managed to steady himself.

The other wolves positioned themselves behind the mother and her cub, and in unison they approached the three companions. Zoey inched forward to face the mother wolf, and they yipped at each other. Then the wolf howled and, together with her cub and the rest of her pack, turned and disappeared into the forest.

"Thank you," Katie called out to them.

Zoey nudged Katie with her head. "I know," she said to the Labrador. "Boomer's hurt. We have to get him to Mommy and Daddy."

Katie placed her arm around Boomer's torso, bracing his body with her own, leaning him against her, holding him upright. His legs wobbly, pain shooting through his body, it took all his remaining strength to step forward. Together they slowly made their way toward the trail.

* * * * * *

"But, Sheriff, you can't!" Ana pleaded, her voice cracking.

Justin sat in her lap at the picnic table that Ana had not left since the day before, his Gameboy gone as he focused on consoling his mother. A somber Nathan sat by her side, his parents with him, as were Darrian, Silva, Maurizio, Hoff, and McCollom, who had just returned with their search groups.

"I'm afraid I don't have a choice," Sheriff McClendon responded. "I've had teams out in the forest for over twelve hours now. Sunset is in half an hour, and I need to call the rest of them back now."

"Katie can't spend another night out there!" Larry implored as Sally wiped tears from her eyes. "You yourself said that she may not be able to survive a second night!"

"Mr. Wilkinson, this is one of the toughest calls I've ever had to make. But we are in the same position that we were in yesterday. The volunteers can't conduct an effective search in a dense forest at night; all they will do is risk injuring themselves. I have to pull them out. Believe me, I wish I had another option right now, any option at all. But I just don't."

"Oh God, no!" Ana wept.

"This is ridiculous!" Darrian snarled. "We can handle ourselves just fine in the dark. These guys are combat veterans, for God's sake. Give us a couple of flashlights, and we'll go right back out there now."

"Oh no, you won't, Mr. Lawrence," the sheriff responded. "I don't need you and your friends trying to play hero and ending up getting lost too. You're staying right here with the parents. That's where you can do the most good."

Nathan sat silently, too distraught to speak. The commotion throughout the campsite flashed in and out of his consciousness in a smoky haze. Barely aware of his surroundings, his mind overwhelmed; he saw himself holding his newborn daughter, the first tooth splitting through her gum, her first smile, her tentative first steps, and the first time he heard her call him Daddy. Tucking her into bed at night while she told him she loved him; wiping away her tears when she fell and scraped her knee; watching her face light up as she opened her presents on Christmas morning; all the memories that burn into a father's soul. His precious daughter, lost now in that unforgiving forest, and gone, maybe forever...

"Sheriff!" a deputy shouted, pointing toward the entrance to the main trail. All movement at the camp came to a sudden halt.

An exhausted Katie Wilkinson emerged from the woods flanked by her beloved Labrador retrievers. Katie's arm remained firmly wrapped around the torso of a visibly hobbling Boomer as she guided him, while Zoey strode at their side.

"Katie!" Ana screamed, scarcely believing her eyes. She dashed toward her daughter. Nathan was dumbstruck, gazing in astonishment at his daughter and at the two savior dogs standing proudly beside her.

"Thank you, God, thank you!" Ana wept as she grabbed the girl and lifted her into a hug.

"I'll be utterly damned!" Sheriff McClendon exclaimed. He motioned to the deputy who had alerted him. "Get the paramedics here right now!"

In an instant Katie was surrounded by Larry, Sally, and others. It took Nathan a moment to recover from his paralysis and reach her as well, but when he did, he threw his arms around his daughter and refused to let go.

"My little punkin! I missed you so much!"

"I'm hungry, Daddy," she said softly.

"Don't you worry—we'll get you your favorite meal right away. All the mac and cheese you can eat and ice cream for dessert. But, honey, how did you find your way back here?"

"It was Boomer and Zoey. They found me and brought me back."

It seemed impossible for Nathan to believe, that these two Labradors could have accomplished something at which no one else, not Sheriff McClendon nor his deputies nor Katie's family or friends nor the dozens of other volunteers, had been successful. But there was the proof, right before his eyes, the very girl whose life they had saved.

Nathan handed his daughter back to Ana and bent down over his two dogs. "You guys!" he exclaimed. "You are the greatest!"

As Nathan reached over to embrace them, Boomer collapsed to the ground, and Nathan gasped in horror at the sight of the Labrador's blood-soaked underbelly.

* * * * * *

"I'll be right behind you," Nathan said to Ana as she sat in the ambulance beside Katie. Two paramedics were still examining the young girl, who was strapped onto a stretcher, intravenous tubes inserted into her arms. Nathan stood next to the open door, his prosthetic leg resting on the ambulance's bumper.

"How is she?" Ana asked one of the paramedics.

"She's tired and malnourished but otherwise in remarkably good shape. We'll take good care of her. She's going to be fine."

Ana stroked Katie's hair and adjusted the breathing mask. "Did you hear that, honey? Everything's going to be okay."

"I know, Mommy."

One of the paramedics slid the door shut, and the ambulance screeched forward, its lights flashing, through the gauntlet of media vans toward the county general hospital.

"Mommy," Katie said to Ana, "when I get better, will I be able to come back here to say thank you to the wolf and the dog with the sparkly eyes?"

* * * * * *

As the ambulance disappeared, Nathan headed over to Sheriff McClendon, who was initialing documents at the makeshift command post.

"Damned paperwork," McClendon muttered as he signed another form. "Follows you everywhere, even into the middle of the forest."

"Sheriff, do you know where Zoey is?" Nathan asked.

He pointed to his right. "Over there. She hasn't left your other dog's body."

"They've always been close."

"I'm sorry for your loss, Nathan."

"Thank you." Nathan paused a moment, fighting to restrain the bereavement tugging at his soul. "Let me ask you... Do you have any idea what happened to Boomer?"

"Yes, as a matter of fact I do. While you were tending to your daughter, we took a close look at his wounds. All indications are that the lacerations were caused by the claws of a bear."

"A bear?" Nathan sputtered.

"Yes. I think your dog fought off one of the black bears that populate the Rim country. No doubt saved your daughter's life."

Nathan stood silently, his mind struggling to process the full force of the words he had just heard.

"The wounds were so deep that he pretty much bled out on the way back here. I don't know how he made it this far, given the pain and the loss of blood—must have been sheer force of will."

"I guess he wanted to make sure Katie got back here safely."

"You are a fortunate man, to have had these two dogs in your family."

"I certainly know that now, Sheriff."

One of McClendon's deputies approached the two men. "Sheriff," he said, "I hate to keep bringing this up, but the media is all over me for a statement from you."

"Well, now that I've got something good to say, I guess I'll go talk to them. You want to join me, Nathan?"

"If you don't mind, I think I'll be getting to the hospital."

As the sheriff took position behind the gaggle of hastily set microphones and cameras, Nathan approached his two dogs. Boomer lay on the ground, his torso covered by a soft wool blanket. His eyes were closed; a peaceful look enveloped his face. Zoey continued her vigil next to him, whining in sorrow, unbearable anguish etched across her face.

Nathan kneeled next to Zoey and stroked her matted blond hair. "How you doing, girl?"

She whimpered faintly.

"I'm so sorry," Nathan stammered through his own tears. "There's nothing any of us could have done for him. But I'm just so proud of you and your brother. I can never repay either of you for what you did for Katie."

He reached down and placed his hand on top of the lifeless Boomer's head. "Boomer, you crazy, silly pup," he sobbed, tears flowing down his face. "You are a true hero. I mean that. And believe me, I know what it's like for a dog to be a hero."

V.6

Goodyear, Arizona—August 2018

For the next several days, the story of Katie's dramatic rescue dominated the local and national news. The media gaggle that had swarmed the campground migrated to Gila County General Hospital, where the girl was recovering from her ordeal. Reporters pestered visitors at the front entrance, each hoping to secure an interview or at least a quote from a friend or relative that they could relay to a public captivated by the story of the young survivor. Nathan watched the antics with growing aggravation from the window of Katie's third-floor private room, shaking his head at their overbearing and discourteous tactics.

"Don't worry about them," Darrian assured Nathan. "In a couple of days, a hurricane will hit, or a politician will get caught sleeping with his babysitter, and they'll all lose interest in Katie."

Given his media experience, Darrian was the natural choice to assume the role of family spokesman. Each day he gave a brief statement to the assembled reporters on Katie's condition. He reminded them that the family sought privacy and would not be appearing before the cameras themselves. A few of the journalists inevitably sought his autograph or a quick selfie. Darrian always graciously agreed, knowing from his NFL days the value of keeping news organizations with access to millions of people on his good side.

Katie rallied quickly and within a few days regained much of her strength. The resident in charge confirmed the paramedics' initial diagnosis that she had suffered some malnourishment and exposure but no lasting damage. He also confirmed that she had been rescued just in time; she might not have withstood another night in sub-fifty-degree weather. At the end of the week, they discharged her, and carrying a stuffed penguin given by the staff as a farewell present, she hugged each of her nurses and doctors before she and her parents departed for home.

* * * * * *

The family's relief and exhilaration at the happy outcome was tempered by the pain of their tragic loss. They would all miss Boomer's limitless energy and enthusiasm, from his maniacal greetings upon their arrival home to his madcap chases after the field rodents that had the temerity to venture into his backyard. No more wrestling matches for spots on the couch or good-natured scolding over the occasional torn-up shoe. It made Nathan realize how special the last four years had been and how much the goofy Labrador had contributed to the healing of his family's hearts after the loss of Lindsay and Georgie. And now, just like that, he too was gone.

But no one took Boomer's death harder than his sister. In happier times, Zoey would bound alongside Boomer, sharing his unmitigated joy and passion for all things, from the acquisition of a stray sock with which to instigate a tug-of-war match to the outdoor rule-free chase games, followed by spontaneous vaults into the swimming pool. In the weeks after the family returned home from the Rim, Zoey appeared drained of that boundless energy for which she was so well known. She moped around the house and slept for hours on end. Sometimes when she woke, she searched for Boomer as if his loss had been nothing more than an unpleasant dream. Then reality would set in as she accepted that her brother was gone, and the melancholy would return. For Zoey, her reason for being was slowly but irrevocably fading away.

The whole family tried to rally her spirits. Nathan took her on his walks to the park, Ana attempted to initiate tug-of-war games using her various stuffed animals, and Justin and Katie cuddled with her and rubbed her underside. But nothing worked, and her frightening slide accelerated.

Most alarming, Zoey's appetite rapidly dissipated. Ana served her the highest quality dog food, but Zoey rarely touched it. Treats, chew toys, bacon sticks—she turned them all away. Katie's tableside scraps? Nope. Ana started

~ 225 ~

warming the dog food in the microwave and livening it up with a smattering of cottage cheese and boneless chicken. Still Zoey refused to eat.

"It's okay, girl," Nathan said, gesturing for her to join him on the couch. "You still have us. We'll always be here for you." But she sat unmoving on the floor, staring at him with sad, nearly lifeless eyes—her meaning was all too clear.

But I miss him so much!

"I know. We miss him too." Nathan tried to lift her onto the couch; it alarmed him to feel her ribcage. She resisted, struggled free, and stalked off to her bed in the corner of the living room.

In desperation, they brought her to Dr. Grittman, who conducted a thorough examination. "The problem is pretty straightforward," he told Nathan and Ana after finishing. "There's no physical condition here—no ulcers, tumors, or anything of that nature. Her issue is depression, nothing more. Dogs can get depressed, just like people, especially when they lose someone close to them."

"I remember that happened with Lindsay, after Georgie passed," Ana said.

"But this is worse. Boomer and Zoey were littermates. They had a special bond and were together every day, all day, for their entire lives. Now Zoey's brother is gone. Not only is she still mourning his death, she may even blame herself for not doing more to prevent it."

"So, what can we do to help her get through this?"

"I'm afraid that there isn't much you can do I'll prescribe a special anti-depressant and a few appetite-enhancing meds. Give her those, and just keep loving her and being there for her. But if she doesn't start eating again, and I mean soon, you may have to bring her back here one last time."

* * * * * *

Faced with that devastating pronouncement, and the six-year-old memory of saying goodbye to Lindsay still vivid and painful, Nathan was almost relieved at what happened next, just a few days later.

It was a crisp, late-November Saturday morning at the Wilkinsons' Goodyear home. An unshaven Nathan lounged in his study, perusing the morning newspaper on his iPad. Ana had just stepped out of the shower and was drying her hair, while Justin played with his Gameboy and Katie lounged on her parents' bed watching television. It was the weekend before Thanksgiving, and they all were looking forward to the onset of the holiday season, hoping it would brighten Zoey's spirits too.

Suddenly Nathan heard a piercing shriek from the center of the house. He burst from his chair and dashed into the living room to find Zoey on her side in her bed in the corner, unmoving.

In an instant, Ana had joined him. "Nate! What is it?"

Nathan reached down and gently caressed Zoey's skin. Then, he turned to his wife, his face ashen. "I'm sorry, honey."

A moment later Katie wandered into the living room and up to Ana, who lifted her up and buried her head into her shoulder.

"Don't look at her, baby," she whispered.

"It's all right, Mommy," Katie responded. "I'm sad, but she's with Boomer and the sparkly dog now."

"Yes, I'm sure she is," Ana said, stepping back toward the bedroom, still clutching Katie.

Katie turned her head to her right and smiled warmly at Zoey and Boomer, who stood in the center of living room with her friend, the black-and-white border beagle with the sparkling eyes. Zoey nuzzled against Boomer for a moment, a look of elation on her face. Then she and Boomer each yipped a single time at Katie, as if to say goodbye, before the three canines faded away.

* * * * * *

Immediately upon seeing Nathan carrying the blanket-covered bundle into his office, trailed by Ana, Justin, and Katie, Dr. Grittman knew. "Bring her into the examination room," he said somberly.

"It's so sad," Ana moaned as Grittman examined the lifeless Zoey. "She was only six. She had her whole life ahead of her."

"Yes, she did. But at some point, she decided that her life wasn't worth living without her brother. It's not a medically recognized diagnosis, but I have no doubt that she died of a broken heart."

"We owe her so much," Nathan said, still struggling to contain his grief. "She was every bit as courageous as Boomer."

They spent a few more minutes at the veterinarian's office, signing the appropriate forms. "This never gets any easier," Ana sighed, as she read and executed the final document.

"I know, honey. Every time we lose a dog, it feels like someone punched me right in the gut. I know I've said this before, but this time I mean it. I don't think we should get another dog. I don't want to go through this again."

As they exited into the outer lobby, Nathan's iPhone chirped.

"You're not going to answer that, are you?" Ana said incredulously.

Nathan shrugged, tapped the answer button, and withdrew into an adjoining examining room, leaving the door open behind him. "I'm sorry, what was that?" Ana heard him say. "You're from...*Hollywood*?"

V.7

Hollywood, California—March 2021

"**B**oomer, we have to find her!"

"I know, Zoey. Everything depends on us. We're the only ones who can save her!"

"But we can't do anything until we get out of this RV!"

"They may think they have us trapped in here, but I know how we can get out. Follow my lead!"

* * * * * *

"Wait a second," Nathan whispered to his wife. "They can...talk?"

"Of course they can!" bellowed Richard Weissman, the tan, immaculately coiffed executive producer sitting next to them. Other studio executives and cast members sat scattered throughout the darkened private theater, enthralled with the final cut unfolding in front of them.

Weissman gestured at the screen. "There's nothing audiences love more than talking animals. And look at the CGI effects—their mouths move in perfect sync with the dialogue. Believe you me, they'll have a lot more to say before the movie is over."

* * * * * *

Boomer squatted in front of the locked RV door and gestured to his sister. Zoey backed up and then sprinted toward her brother. Using his body as a springboard, she vaulted up to the door's window and collided with it headfirst; it shattered as she rebounded to the floor. Zoey picked herself up and hopped onto Boomer's back, then reached her front paw through the broken window and hooked the outside latch. She turned the latch counterclockwise, and the door sprang open.

"Good job, Zoey!" Boomer congratulated his sister. "We're free! Now, would you get off me already?"

* * * * * *

"Ah, they can open doors too," Nathan muttered. "You know those Labrador paws, real nimble. So realistic."

"Quiet!" Ana shushed. "Just enjoy the movie."

* * * * * *

Zoey and Boomer scrambled outside the trailer to see dozens of police officers milling about the campground, airplanes flying overhead, a tank parked near the RV, and armed soldiers patrolling in combat gear.

"I think I know where she might be!" Zoey exclaimed. "C'mon Boomer, let's go! There's no time to lose!"

The two dogs took off, shooting past their owner, a heavyset man in torn jeans and sporting a baseball cap.

"Hey, you two!" he shouted. "Come back here! Leave this up to us humans!" But the siblings ignored him as they single-mindedly set forth on their mission, disappearing into the forest.

"Let them go, Nathaniel," his wife said.

"I should go with them, Amy, but…I'm just not up to it." He patted his copious midsection, and his wife nodded sympathetically.

"Don't you worry, Nathaniel," she said. "If anyone can find little Kathy, it's Boomer and Zoey! They're the bravest dogs in the world!" She placed her arm around him, and together they turned to gaze at the setting sun.

* * * * * *

~ 230 ~

"Funny," Nathan said, "I don't remember seeing any tanks or armed soldiers at the campgrounds."

"Details, details," Ana smirked.

"And that dialogue. Not exactly Shakespeare, is it?"

"It's supposed to be a family movie. At least there aren't any swear words in it."

"You mean like the ones rolling around in my head while I watch this?"

"Nathan! Be nice!"

"And what's with them casting someone who weighs three hundred pounds as me?"

"It's Eddie Wemberly!" Ana exclaimed, as though Nathan was supposed to care the country's comedian du jour was playing him.

"Yeah, whatever. But I couldn't join the search parties because I lost my leg in Iraq, not because I was too fat to walk through the forest."

"Sitting right here, Nate," came a voice two rows down from him.

"Sorry, Eddie," Nathan said sheepishly.

"That's okay," Eddie responded good-naturedly. "People make fun of my weight all the time. When they do, I just remind them who's bank account is fatter."

"Point taken." Nathan laughed.

"Remember, honey," Ana chimed in, "this is just a movie. It's not intended to be 100 percent accurate."

"That's easy for you to say. They cast Kristie Graham as you. She's the hottest actress in Hollywood."

"Thank you, Nate," came a voice next to Eddie.

"I knew you were there, Kristie; that's why I said it," Nathan responded, earning a playful smack on the shoulder from his wife.

* * * * * *

Boomer lay on the ground, dazed by the bear's punch. He struggled to lift himself up as the bear roared, flashed its claws, and moved in for the kill.

"Not so fast, buster!" Zoey exclaimed. "You want to mess with my brother? You have to go through me first!"

She curled her paw into a fist and landed a haymaker to the bear's jaw; it collapsed, stunned by the force. Zoey jumped on top of the bear and struck it repeatedly in the face.

"Enough!" the bear finally said. "I give up!"

Zoey hopped off the predator; it sat up and shook its head. She leaned in toward the bear until her nose was inches from its snout. "Now, you get lost, or I'll give it to you twice as bad!"

Conceding defeat, the bear scrambled to its feet and ran off whimpering.

"Are you okay?" Zoey said to Boomer.

"Yeah, thanks to you," Boomer said as he stood and dusted himself off. "You're the greatest, sis!"

* * * * * *

From her seat next to Justin, Katie leaned across Ana and pulled at her father's sleeve. "Daddy," she whispered, "that's not how it happened."

"Yeah, I kind of figured that."

* * * * * *

"So, what do we do now?" Zoey asked. "It's almost dark, and we still haven't found her."

"And this forest is way too large," Boomer responded. "We'll never find her if we stay on foot. There's only one thing left for us to do. We have to use our secret powers!"

"You're right, Boomer. Let's go!"

Together they broke into a gallop that propelled them into the air. Soaring above the trees, they gazed downward at the dense forest, continuing their desperate search and their race against time.

* * * * * *

"So, they can *fly* too?" Nathan groaned. "That's it; just kill me now."

* * * * * *

As the lights in the theater brightened, the small crowd of actors, producers, and studio executives burst into wild applause and took turns giving each other congratulatory hugs.

"So," Weissman said to Nathan and Ana, "what'd you think?'

"Well, I..." Nathan started.

"We loved it!" Ana interjected.

"Excellent!" Weissman exclaimed. "So did the test audiences. We're going to go into wide release in four weeks, but we think the film's tracking to be a major hit. I've already commissioned a script for a sequel."

"A sequel?"

"Yeah. In this one, Boomer and Zoey join the search for the president's young daughter after she gets lost in the desert."

"I see," Nathan said. "Doing the job those pesky Secret Service guys aren't up to."

"Show some vision, Nate! We're talking real franchise opportunity here. Not just movie receipts but merchandise too. I want every kid under seven to ask for Boomer and Zoey stuffed dolls for Christmas this year. Lunch boxes, T-shirts, pajamas, the whole nine yards. Could be very lucrative for you and your family, since you'll get a cut of the profits.

"Now, if you'll excuse me, I need to go kiss up to a few of the execs here. You gotta keep the money happy."

As Weissman wandered off, Nathan turned to his children. "How did you like the movie, guys?"

"It was cool," Justin said. "I loved the part where Boomer ended up driving one of the tanks right through the RV."

"Yeah, that added so much to the plot too." Nathan snorted. "Katie, honey, what did you think of it?"

"It makes me miss the real Boomer and Zoey," she answered, sadness in her voice.

"I know." Ana consoled her. "But this way everyone will know what they did for you."

"Mom's right," Nathan agreed. "After all, what better way is there to honor a couple of crazy, goofy dogs than with a crazy, goofy movie about them?"

VI.

REUNION

VI.1

Goodyear, Arizona—October 2021

"Honey, you want some more eggs?"

Nathan nodded as he sat at the kitchen table scanning the news summaries and half-listening to the flat-screen television in the living room blaring a cable morning news program. On this autumn Tuesday morning he was still recovering from his hectic weekend of yard work, a family outing to the local shopping mall, and a trip to Glendale for Sunday's Cardinals game. His body ached from the physical exertion, and he felt groggy from a subpar night of sleep.

"And now for more of our in-depth interview with Arkansas Governor William Thornhill."

Hearing his home state mentioned, Nathan glanced up and across the room at the screen. The young, platinum-blond, female host was seated on a couch next to a handsome, fit, gray-haired man in his mid-fifties who was clad in an impeccably tailored suit with a red tie and American flag lapel pin.

"Governor," the host began, "I know it's a little early to be talking about the next election, but according to conventional wisdom, if you are going to declare your candidacy for the presidential nomination, it will happen soon…"

Ana brought the skillet over to the table and scooped scrambled eggs onto Nathan's plate. "Where did you say you were going today?"

"Yuma. The chamber of commerce wants to give that SportsWorld a proclamation of appreciation for the jobs we brought to the city. You know the drill—they're going to make a couple of speeches, give me a plaque, and take a few pictures for the next day's newspaper."

"Maybe they're using it as an excuse to meet the guy who owned the super dogs."

"I hope not. I almost wish that movie hadn't turned out to be such a big hit. Now that Boomer and Zoey are household names, it's hard to go anywhere without people asking about them. At least the royalty checks make it all a little easier to tolerate."

"Will you be home in time for dinner?"

Nathan shook his head. "No. I won't be home till late tonight. They want to do the ceremony at the city council meeting, and that doesn't start until six. I'll drive home as soon as it's over."

"You should stay in Yuma tonight. It's a three-hour drive, and you shouldn't be doing that at night when you're tired."

"I have a meeting with the landowner for our proposed Chandler site at nine tomorrow morning." Nathan lifted his coffee mug in a weary cheer. "Don't worry. I'll be fine."

"So, Governor, tell us a little more about yourself," the anchor said. "What were you like as a teenager, growing up in Hot Springs?"

Nathan's focus again snapped to the TV.

"Well, Sandy, like a lot of kids in the 1970s, I had a bit of a wild streak. I was pretty irresponsible, and I didn't pay much attention to school or work. I was too busy having fun with my friends and with the local girls."

"But you ended up going to Harvard and getting a Rhodes Scholarship."

"Yes, I did manage to turn my life around. There were a lot of reasons for that. But I'd have to say that one incident, more than any other, changed me, made me the man I am today. My advisors have urged me not to speak publicly about it, but I believe that the American people have the right to know the person who they might be voting for."

"Oh?" The anchor's eyes widened. "By all means, tell us about it."

"Daddy, do you like this dress?" Katie asked as she appeared before her father. The eight-year-old was in second grade now and for the first time harbored a genuine concern about her appearance.

"It looks great," Nathan told her. "All the boys are going to love you."

"Gross!"

Nathan chuckled as she retreated, then turned back to the television.

"…was joy-riding with my girlfriend one morning, after having skipped school," the governor said. "I was driving really fast through a neighborhood, and I wasn't paying attention to the road. And then out of nowhere a dog appeared over a hill and in the middle of the street. I tried to avoid it, but I couldn't, and I ended up hitting and killing it. Turns out it belonged to a three-year-old boy who lived in the neighborhood. As long as I live, I will never forget the look of anguish on the boy's face when he saw his dog lying in the street. I knew it was my fault, and I tried to apologize, but I couldn't find the words."

Nathan leaned forward, listening more intently. The story seemed to have an odd effect on him; he did not know why though, but it was particularly gripping.

The governor teared up. "I'm not going to make any excuses for what I did. I accept full responsibility. But if there is anything good that could come out of something as horrible as this, it's that for the first time in my life I learned that actions have real-world consequences and that when I acted recklessly, it didn't just affect me, it affected other people as well. That day I vowed that I would get my life in order and I would try to become the best person I could be, so that I could make a difference for this world."

"Governor, that's an amazing confession," the host said. "Most politicians would never admit to such an incident from their past."

"I don't want to be like other candidates, who use double-talk to spin or explain away these things. I'm a human being, and I've made mistakes in my life. But what is important is to learn from those mistakes; that makes you a better person. I think this incident, and that dog's tragic sacrifice, taught me that."

"Did you ever see the boy again?"

"No." The governor turned his head to face the camera. "But if I could see him again, I would tell him how sorry I am and ask him if he could find it in his heart to forgive me."

* * * * * *

Nathan spent the morning at his office, meeting first with his accountants and then with his contractor to discuss the plans for the new Chandler SportsWorld. After grabbing a quick lunch, he departed for the long drive to

Yuma. The October climate was warm and humid, and as usual for Arizona, the sun shone brightly in the clear sky.

He arrived in Yuma late in the afternoon and dropped by the SportsWorld outlet to chat with the manager before proceeding to Yuma City Hall. The council meeting began at six, but the council abruptly adjourned into executive session to discuss a pending litigation against the city by an aggrieved developer. The executive session dragged on for almost three hours; Nathan passed the time by alternating between making small talk with the representatives of the chamber of commerce and surfing the web on his iPhone.

Finally, just past 10:00 p.m., the council reconvened into public session. Though everyone was tired, they forged ahead with the chamber's presentation. Nathan gave a brief speech thanking the chamber and the city on behalf of SportsWorld and then stood with the elected officials for the obligatory photos. By eleven, mentally and physically exhausted, he concluded his obligations and began the drive back to Goodyear.

He didn't like to drive late at night. He had already put in a fifteen-hour day, on top of a weekend of poor sleep. But he needed to be back for the meeting with the Chandler landowner the next morning. He cursed himself for both the overscheduling and the misfortune of having to wait out the executive session.

It was dark and quiet along Interstate 8; cloud cover impeded the moon and starlight. There was very little civilization to illuminate the landscape between Yuma and Phoenix, few rest stops from which to purchase a snack or a cup of coffee. It was road and desert, little more.

After ninety minutes, he turned off the interstate and onto Highway 85, northbound to Phoenix. Less than an hour from home now. He shook his head to remain alert. But, if anything, this road proved even more monotonous, mile after mile of Sonoran Desert, the trademark saguaro cactuses dotting the rocky terrain. The combination of it all produced an almost hypnotic effect. Fatigue had worn down his body; cobwebs dulled his senses; the landscape ahead started spinning; his heavy eyelids drooped…

* * * * * *

First a jolt. Then disorientation. His body jostled back and forth, side to side, straining at the seat belt. The world turned over. A bright flash, followed by searing pain, the sensation of simultaneously being punched and stabbed in the chest. Another rollover, then a final jolt before coming to a rest. A lengthy, eerie silence. A flashback to that horrible night with his unit in Nasifah. But this was worse. Much worse.

He drifted in and out of consciousness. While awake, he felt vaguely as though he were pinned behind the wheel of his car. Remains from the deployed airbag rested in his lap. Then darkness. Then momentary consciousness again, followed by voices—not complete sentences, just random words.

"Trapped…hurt badly…ambulance…hospital…"

He felt the liquid warmth of his blood-soaked shirt. Every breath shot waves of pain through his chest. Images flashed of firefighters working feverishly to extract him from his vehicle. Then, drifting away once more.

He woke again to find himself on a stretcher being guided by two nurses down a brightly lit corridor. He gagged on the tube inserted down his throat; waves of pain throbbed through his upper body. He saw the glistening stethoscope bouncing off a doctor's chest as he raced alongside him. The team plowed the stretcher through a doorway and into a surgical trauma chamber. Three more doctors and two ER nurses approached him, masked, gloved, and in scrubs, worry etched across their faces.

"Where are the X-rays?" one doctor demanded.

"Right here!" One of the nurses handed a packet to him, and he held it up to the light.

"We've got several broken ribs and a collapsed right lung. I'm going to have to open him up."

"You need to hurry. He's still losing blood, and his BP is declining."

"He's in severe shock. Pupils badly dilated."

"Doctor, heart is going into cardiac dysrhythmias!"

"Get the defibrillator over here!"

"We're losing him…"

"I can't detect a pulse…"

He felt the room spinning, first slowly and then faster and faster. His chest pain faded away. Then darkness.

* * * * * *

I don't understand… Is that me?

He found himself gazing down over a group of surgically clad medical professionals huddled over what appeared to be an operating table. A single bare leg protruded from one end of the table, but the gathered caregivers impeded his view of the patient's upper body.

He no longer felt any of the throbbing, crippling pain. So too was gone the fear and anxiety he had been experiencing; instead he felt calm, almost serene. He glanced about and found to his surprise that he was floating at the top of the chamber. The doctors were shouting instructions at each other over the shrill buzz of the heart monitor; Nathan could hear the alarm in their voices.

Now he felt himself floating involuntarily through the wall and down the brightly lit corridor, entering a waiting room filled with familiar faces.

Ana. Justin and Katie. Larry and Sally. Darrian. Tom and Miranda. Enrique.

Ana draped herself in Larry's arms, burying her head in his shoulder and crying hysterically. Sally held Katie tightly in her lap. A visibly shaken Darrian had his arm clasped around Justin. The others wore expressions of shock, fear, and apprehension.

Everybody! Don't be worried—I'm okay! Nathan tried to speak; they remained huddled together, all weighed down by the enormity of the circumstance.

Nathan floated down from the ceiling and over to Ana, reached out and gently stroked her cheek. She suddenly stopped crying and glanced about, a perplexed look on her face. He tried to turn toward his children, but without warning he felt an unidentified force pulling him away.

Now Nathan was outside, floating in the nighttime sky above the hospital. The stars and moonlight poked through the cloud cover and cast a haze over the hospital's rooftop. Something on the roof caught his eye: a tan backpack behind the air conditioner's ventilator near the fire escape, on which a single word was embroidered:

Bannockburn

For an instant Nathan contemplated the puzzling word; then he felt a warmth behind him. He pivoted to see a light radiating in the distance. It was brighter than anything he had ever seen, yet the heat and the intensity of the light conveyed an inexplicable comfort.

He floated toward it and into what he perceived to be a dark tunnel. The hospital, the city below him, the star-specked sky all faded from view. He could not ascertain the length of the tunnel or the distance he was traveling; all that mattered now was to reach the oncoming brightness. He willed himself to accelerate his pace until, with a combination of anticipation and foreboding, he plunged into the light.

VI.2

The Meadow

*B*reathtaking. There was no other description for it.

Nathan found himself standing alone in the center of an endless meadow sprinkled with patches of daffodils, chrysanthemums, and begonias. Warm light poured over the rolling hills, gentle winds swayed the luxuriant oak and magnolia trees, and in the distance, pristine, fresh water flowed lazily through a stream. Tall grasses glistened from the droplets of morning dew. The colors were indescribably vivid, overwhelming in their intensity and sheer beauty. He could see a range of mountains lining the distant horizon, a gateway to further meadows beyond the divide.

He gazed about, enveloped by a sense of peace and contentment. He inhaled the thick, moist air, then looked down and noticed that he was dressed all in white. Lengthy, lush blades of grass brushed against his bare feet—both of them. He wiggled his toes. He had ten again!

In the distance, he saw innumerable packs of animals scampering happily about the landscape. Dogs and cats played chase games together, horses meandered through the meadow, and birds flew overhead, letting the gentle breeze guide their paths. The playful barking and howling that echoed only intensified the meadow's serene and peaceful ambience.

He could see only one structure in the distance beyond the rolling hills—a magnificent golden bridge. The fifty-foot-wide entrance was supported by shimmering yellow suspension cables and resplendent girders; its pathway disappeared upward into a layer of clouds. To discover where it led, he would have to venture onto the bridge.

"Beautiful, isn't it?" came a voice at his side. Nathan turned to encounter an old man with a bushy white beard, dressed in plain brown tunic similar to those borne by medieval friars, held in place by a rope about his portly waist. Though Nathan had never seen him before, the man seemed oddly familiar.

"Yes, it is," he said to the old man. "This whole place ... I've never seen anything like it."

"Sometimes I just like to stand here and admire the sheer magnificence of it all."

"Like a painting come to life."

"Yes. But most of all, I love to watch the animals. Look at them. They don't have a care in the world. They have everything they need, and all they want is to relax, play, and make each other happy. When was the last time you felt that way, Nathan?"

Nathan was taken aback by the man's familiarity. "Do we know each other?"

"We always have."

"I don't understand."

"It's okay. You will soon enough."

"Can you tell me where I am?"

The man paused a moment and stroked his beard. "It's hard to describe. Some call it a way station. A staging area. A first stop."

"A first stop to where?"

"To home."

Nathan's mind raced as he assembled the pieces of the puzzle: the floating, the light, the tunnel, and now the meadow. "Can I ask you a question?"

"Of course."

"Am I dead?"

The old man paused again. "That remains to be seen, Nathan. Whether you stay or go back, it's not always a choice."

"Are you the one who decides?"

"Oh no." The old man laughed. "I'm just a caretaker, a custodian, if you will. I'm here to assist in the transition, for you and for the others."

"What others?"

The old man smiled and pointed to his right. "Those who wait for you."

In the distance, emerging from the plateau, Nathan saw them.

Two Labrador retrievers, one black and one blond, galloping full speed toward him through the tall grass.

"Boomer! Zoey!"

The dogs crashed into him, sending Nathan careening backward and onto the soft grass. The siblings jumped on him and showered his cheeks with wet kisses.

"I can't believe it's really you!" Overcome with emotion, he wrestled with the both of them, playfully pushing them away and letting them jump back on him as they whined and yipped with elation.

It took considerable effort to shed the jubilant canines, but Nathan finally managed to rise to his feet. He cupped the still-manic Boomer's head with his hands and looked directly into the Labrador's dark eyes.

"There's so much I've wanted to say to you, buddy," he said. "Things that I didn't have the chance to tell you before you died.

"Thank you, Boomer, for finding Katie in the forest and bringing her back to us."

And then he reached for Zoey, pulled her alongside her brother, and warmly hugged the two of them. "Thanks to both of you. You guys saved her life." Panting profusely, Boomer and Zoey whimpered their acknowledgment, and both kissed him on the cheek.

"It wasn't the only time," the old man said.

"What do you mean?"

The old man gestured at Zoey, and Nathan gazed deeply into her eyes. He saw it all—toddler Katie wandering into the backyard toward the pool, Zoey and her brother dashing outside to prevent an unspeakable tragedy.

"You two really are the greatest," Nathan said, his voice shaking with emotion. "I'm so proud of the both of you. I wish you could see how famous you both became back on earth."

"That's not important to them," the old man interjected. "They only wanted to be there for you and your family. That's all that ever mattered to them."

Zoey scratched at Nathan again, attempting to get his attention. "I wish you hadn't left us so soon," he said to her. "But I'm happy you're with your brother again. You two are soulmates, and you belong together. Now and forever."

The siblings broke away from him and scampered frantically into the meadow. Nathan took off after them; it felt so exhilarating to be running on both legs again. But as they had been in life, the Labradors proved far more speedy and agile. They circled about, jumped on him again, then sprinted away and back again, in that random pattern for which they had been so beloved. Before long they commenced with another of their spirited wrestling matches, growling and bouncing off each other until they tumbled to the ground in a tangle of paws and tails. Nathan laughed heartily as he watched them roll about in the grass.

The old man ambled up to Nathan. "They aren't the only ones who have been waiting for you," he said.

Then Nathan heard a soft yelping sound to his left. He looked down to see a black miniature schnauzer whining and squealing, desperately trying to garner his attention.

"Lindsay!"

There she was, that jubilant black bundle of radiant and unrestrained energy. The aged, infirm dog to whom he and his family had tearfully said their goodbyes in their backyard was gone, restored to the young, healthy, vigorous schnauzer from his happiest memories. He picked up the diminutive canine, and she scratched at him, whining and deluging him with love and affection.

"My sweet girl!" he sobbed, hugging her tightly. "I've missed you too!" Lindsay yelped in excitement at the sound of her beloved Nathan's voice, burrowing her head into his neck.

"This one was originally Ana's dog," Nathan said to the old man, wiping tears from his eyes as Lindsay closed her eyes and whimpered again. "But she and I formed a special bond, starting that day I found her in the park. She was always at my side, showing off to try to impress me, cuddling up to me on the couch or in our bed, getting jealous and snippy when I paid attention to anyone else. Whenever I was down, or feeling sorry for myself, she would show me that I mattered, that I was loved, and that everything would be okay."

"She loved you more than life itself; it's what we can say for so many of our pets. Given the choice, they would rather follow you out into a cold, wintry night than be alone inside by a warm fire.

"You see, Nathan, when they arrive here, they all are given the opportunity to continue their journey. But those who left someone special behind often

choose to wait here in this place. And when that someone special finally appears, they are reunited, and together they depart for their final destination."

"Where do they go?"

The old man pointed to the golden bridge. Nathan observed an older woman with short black-and-gray hair near the entrance surrounded by seven dogs and two cats of varying shapes and sizes. She took turns caressing and scratching each of them as they whimpered with excitement and jumped on her legs. Nearby, a man stroked the mane of a brown horse that nuzzled against him. And off in the distance a young girl sat in the grass, surrounded by puppies who jumped into and out of her lap, while adult dogs stood in the background watching over them.

"The woman fostered many dogs and cats throughout her life," the man said. "They were souls no one else wanted, and she rescued all of them from certain death. Thanks to her, they were able to have full and happy lives. Ever since they arrived here, they have waited for the chance to show her how grateful they were for the lives she gave them.

"The man was a rancher, and that was his favorite horse. They were inseparable for over thirty years, and neither could fathom making the final journey without the other. So, as you can see, it's not just dogs and cats who wait for us here. Our bond with all animals runs deep."

"What about the girl?"

"Her life ended tragically, and too soon. She was scared and alone when she arrived here. These dogs didn't know her on earth, but here they all bound together to ease her transition and guide her on her journey."

Nathan watched the older woman stand up, and in unison, she and her pets stepped onto the golden bridge, set forward together, and disappeared into the clouds. Moments later, the man and his horse followed her onto the bridge. The little girl seemed content to remain in the meadow playing with her new friends.

"The animals don't want to go alone," the old man said. "They want to be with their special friend. It gives both you and your pets great comfort, knowing that you will all make the journey together."

"So, you've been waiting for me girl?" Nathan said to Lindsay, who whined at him in response. Then he felt a scratching at his hip and turned to

see Boomer and Zoey staring at him, their mouths open and tongues hanging out. "I know, I know, you guys have been waiting too."

Lindsay yipped at Boomer and Zoey. Nathan set her down and she, Boomer and Zoey began yet another chase game, circling around Nathan and the old man, burning with energy and exultation.

"It's so great to see them playing together," Nathan said. "They never knew each other back on earth. We adopted Boomer and Zoey after Lindsay passed."

"All of your friends have formed a bond with each other here. A bond that centers around you."

"All of my friends?" Nathan asked, his breath catching. The old man smiled again at him.

Nathan heard a deep and distinctive bark, emanating from the golden bridge off in the distance. He squinted and saw emerging from the clouds and onto the bridge's pathway a magnificent tan Belgian Malinois.

"Georgie!"

Once again Nathan was overcome by a wave of emotion. "Come to me, boy!" he called out. But the General remained affixed on the bridge's pathway.

"He has already made the journey," the old man explained. "But he wanted to return for you."

Then Nathan saw another figure emerge from the clouds onto the golden bridge, a tall young man, blond and baby faced, dressed in white, and sporting a warm grin as he stopped next to Georgie.

It was Brian Herrington, the courageous private who had died saving Nathan in Nasifah.

Brian gestured to Georgie, and the Malinois dashed off the bridge and over to Nathan. He jumped up his hind legs and set his front paws on each of Nathan's shoulders as he too bestowed upon Nathan a succession of kisses. Laughing, Nathan reached down to scratch Georgie's favorite spot behind his shoulder.

Lindsay yelped excitedly at the sight of her long-time companion, and Georgie backed off Nathan to nuzzle her with his snout. Boomer and Zoey gaped in respect and awe at the courageous and valiant military war dog.

"When he arrived here," the old man said, "Brian was waiting. It gave Georgie great comfort to be reunited with him."

"I'm really happy to hear that. I loved Georgie, but I always knew that he and Brian had a special bond. Brian was taken from him way too soon."

"Now they will always be together. But Brian wants you to be with Georgie as well."

"Thank you for coming back to be with me," Nathan said to the general. "And thank you for always being there to protect me, at war and at home afterward."

He glanced back at Brian, who was still standing on the golden bridge in the distance. "And thank you too, Brian, for letting me be with him again."

Brian smiled and waved at Nathan, then turned and disappeared into the clouds.

Nathan kneeled, surrounded by Boomer, Zoey, Lindsay, and Georgie. They all yipped and scratched at him, each competing for his attention. He laughed as Georgie and Boomer rumbled and sniffed at each other while Lindsay and Zoey watched, bemusement on their faces.

"Boys will be boys, won't they?" Nathan remarked to his girls. Despite the yipping, there was an unmistakable familiarity among all of them, of purpose and body, of soul and spirit, Nathan as the focal point. The love, the content, the joy, it was almost perfect, yet not quite complete...

And then there was another.

Alone in the distance, under a voluptuous magnolia tree, Nathan saw a tan German shepherd with a black double-coat standing proudly in the illumination of the bright sunlight. The shepherd stared poignantly at Nathan, its ears pointed upward and its tail wagging furiously.

"Shiloh!"

The other dogs backed away so Shiloh could provide Nathan with his own special greeting. He bounded up to Nathan and circled him repeatedly, rubbing his body against him, before reaching up and raining yet more kisses on Nathan's face.

"It's been so long!" Nathan croaked. "Thirty years!" He ran his hands through Shiloh's soft double-coat; the dog whimpered at the touch of his reunited friend.

"I'll never forget the times we spent together when I was growing up. You were my best friend, the one I could always count on. When I thought I couldn't make it in my new home, you were there to cheer me up. You taught

me patience and resolve, honor and integrity, love and forgiveness. I wish you could have been there to see me become a man, to watch me marry Ana, and to meet my children."

Nathan stepped back from the shepherd, yet more tears welling in his eyes. "I'm so sorry I wasn't there for you at the end," he stammered. "I was so wrapped up in college, and football, and my own comings and goings that I didn't think about how much you needed me. Can you ever forgive me?"

Shiloh yipped a single time, then reached up and kissed Nathan again.

"Of course he can," the old man said. "His love for you is unconditional. Like all the others."

"Without you, Shiloh," Nathan said, "I never would have become the person I am. I know that now."

"He knows it too. Its why he was there. For you and your father."

"My father?"

"Sometimes a single gesture can make a defining impact on a person's life."

In the same manner as before, the old man gestured for Nathan to gaze into Shiloh's eyes. He saw his father in the shed, gun in his hand, Shiloh's intervention, the bonding between the two, and the new direction for Larry, all stemming from that act of compassion and kindness. Entirely without his knowledge, it was an act that prevented a tragedy that would have forever impacted his life.

"Every one of us was lucky to know you, Shiloh."

* * * * * *

Shiloh, Lindsay, Georgie, Boomer, and Zoey. All together, all with Nathan. Now it truly was perfect. He had never felt more gratified, more at peace, than he had at this very moment.

Together they explored, played games with each other and with the other animals wandering about the meadow, and stretched out beneath the trees, resting and enjoying the breathtaking scenery. Nathan watched countless others arrive and be reunited with their pets and then together make the journey across the golden bridge. There was no sense of passing time; it seemed to last both an instant and forever.

Later, he woke up from a nap underneath one of the sprawling magnolia trees, stretching and engrossing himself in the cool breeze and the warm sunlight. Lindsay was snuggled against him, her eyes closed, her open mouth emanating a soft whistle. Boomer and Zoey shunned the idea of napping, preferring to chase each other through the meadow, their energy as eternal as their enthusiasm. Georgie lapped water from the nearby stream, while Shiloh, upon seeing Nathan wake, fetched an errant stick, intending to goad him into their favorite pastime of tug-of-war. As Shiloh approached Nathan, stick in mouth, he was intercepted by Boomer, who grabbed the other end of the stick. Lindsay jumped up and bounded over to watch the friendly match, along with Georgie and Zoey. Nathan lay back, watching his dogs play together in the magnificent meadow, a feeling of peace and contentment filling his soul.

"It's what they've wanted, ever since they came here," the old man said as he approached Nathan. "To be with you and to be with each other."

"How long have I been here?" Nathan asked.

"It's not like that. What you refer to as time, in a linear sense, does not exist here."

Nathan rose to his feet. "It's wonderful here; it really is. And I can't tell you how much comfort it gives me to know that I meant so much to them."

"My son," the old man said somberly, "as I told you when you first arrived, not all who come here can return to their life. It depends on the circumstances behind their arrival. But you, Nathan, do have a choice."

"I do?"

"Yes. You have to decide whether you want to continue on your journey or go back."

Nathan sighed and paused to glance again at the spectacular scenery of the meadow. "This is such a beautiful place, everything I hoped heaven would be. But I don't want to be dead, not yet.

"I have so much left to do with my life. There are people who depend on me. And I have a family that's going to need me to be there for them. I want to watch my son become a man. I want to see my daughter graduate from college and walk her down the aisle on her wedding day. I want to hold my grandchildren in my arms. And I want to grow old with my wife.

"I can't stay here. So...I want to go back."

"I understand," the old man said.

As if on cue, the dogs ceased their games and circled around Nathan. They gazed at him, pained expressions emerging on their faces.

"I'm sorry, all of you," Nathan said. "I hope you understand that I need to be with my family right now. But I promise that when I come back, I'll never leave any of you again."

"They'll be waiting here for you, Nathan," the old man said.

"I know. And I'll think of each of you every day."

The old man gestured behind Nathan. "Before you go, there is one other I would like to introduce you to. Though you have met him before."

On cue, a black-and-white mixed breed emerged from behind a spindly brush, its ears pointed upward, its back arched high, and its eyes sparkling brightly. It was predominantly beagle and border collie, though traces of Australian shepherd and Labrador were visible as well. Nathan's memory jogged as the dog approached him; something seemed familiar about this dog.

"I know you," he said, reaching down to stroke its exquisite double-coat. "Where have I seen you before?"

"Frisco here was your very first dog," the old man explained. "He was with you a short time, when you were very young. And he gave his life to save you." The old man gestured at Nathan to gaze into Frisco's sparkling eyes. And again Nathan saw it all—this time he was the toddler, wandering up the street and over the plateau, the car racing toward him, and Frisco's heroic act of sacrifice. He saw his mother's tears, the teenaged driver's angst, and his own questions about what had happened to his dog.

"I have a vague memory of a dog in our house when I was really young," Nathan stammered, "but I didn't remember that this happened to him."

"You were three years of age, not old enough for such memories to remain with you."

"My mother never talked about him. I guess now I know why."

Nathan turned to the border beagle, yet again overwhelmed with emotion. "All I have—my wife and children, my business, my friends, my other dogs, my very life—is because you sacrificed so I could live. How can I ever thank you?"

Frisco yelped and kissed Nathan on his nose.

"Though he was not able to spend much time with you," the old man said,

"Frisco has long been a presence in your life. He has watched over you and has aided your other dogs with their own journeys. He even provided comfort to Katie during her darkest hour.

"But now he wants to finish his time with you on earth. When you go back, will you allow him to do so?"

Nathan scratched Frisco again on his head. "I can't think of anything I'd want more."

* * * * * *

He sat with all his dogs in the meadow's grassy field a final time. For once, Boomer and Zoey were sitting still. Georgie and Shiloh were stoic and subdued, while Lindsay whimpered loudly. Frisco sat beside all of them wearing a pained expression.

"I'm sorry I have to leave," Nathan said to them. "I'll miss all of you, believe me, I will. But I have to return to my family. I hope you understand."

Despite their sadness, the dogs all knew in their souls that Nathan was making the right choice.

"I'm honored to know each of you," Nathan continued. "And when I return, we'll never be apart again. I promise you."

The dogs remained immobile, all whimpering as they watched Nathan walk over to the old man.

"Are you ready to go back?" the old man asked. Nathan nodded a single time.

The old man placed his hand on Nathan's shoulder. "Remember, someday you will return again, and when you do, they will all be here, waiting for you. As all wait for their special friends here at the Rainbow Bridge."

VI.3

Phoenix, Arizona—October 2021

"I've got a pulse!"

"Thank God!" the lead surgeon exclaimed as he held the defibrillator's paddles. "The last shock must have done it."

"Heart rate is increasing," one of the ER techs said. "BP sixty over thirty now and climbing."

"Okay, keep monitoring all vitals closely and notify me of any fluctuations. We're not out of the woods yet."

"How long was the patient flatlined?" asked another tech.

"About four minutes. Another minute and we wouldn't have been able to bring him back."

The team expressed audible relief as they worked to stabilize the still-unconscious Nathan Wilkinson.

"Great job to all of you," the lead surgeon said. "Way to work together to bring him back. Thanks to you, this guy's children are still going to have a father."

* * * * * *

"All of you must be getting tired of having to visit me in hospitals."

It was four days later, and Nathan was sitting up in his bed, intravenous tubes inserted in his arms, his chest secured in a compressive brace. Despite the seriousness of his injuries, his strength was rapidly returning, his discomfort remarkably minimal.

His loved ones had all joined him in the private room—Ana, Justin, Katie, Larry, Sally, Tom, Miranda, Darrian, and Enrique. A vase filled with flowers sat on the dresser alongside a cookie-and-balloon basket.

"Well, at least it wasn't an IED," Silva noted dryly.

"I almost wish it had been. Falling asleep at the wheel—what a boneheaded thing to do."

"It's okay, honey," Ana chimed in. "It was an accident—that's all."

"So, how many times are you going to remind me that I should have stayed the night at a hotel in Yuma?"

"Once a day for the rest of your life." She grinned, and the others burst into laughter. "The important thing is that you're going to make a full recovery."

"Yes, you will," came a voice at the door. All turned to see the doctor who had overseen Nathan's emergency room treatment. His stethoscope dangled from his neck, and behind him stood a pretty, young brunette scribe, carrying an iPad onto which she was transcribing medical notes.

"You're one tough dude, Mr. Wilkinson," the doctor said as he approached Nathan. "A lot of people wouldn't have survived your injuries."

"You should have seen some of the hits he took on the field during our college days," Darrian remarked. "He's plenty tough, let me tell you."

The doctor smiled and took a pause to say, "I'm a big fan of yours, Mr. Lawrence."

"I'm an even bigger fan of you. You saved my friend's life."

"How long will he have to stay here in the hospital?" Sally asked.

"Probably about another week. Then he should rest at home for a while, maybe another two weeks. After that he should have regained most of his mobility."

Then the doctor addressed Nathan. "Mr. Wilkinson, the fact that you are going to recover from this mishap without any permanent damage is pretty remarkable in and of itself. However, you're going to be awfully sore for a while. So, take it easy. No heavy lifting or strenuous physical activity for at least the next three months."

"I'll see to that, Doctor," Sally said. "I'll take care of him myself."

"Oh, Mom, you don't need to do that."

"Son," Larry added, "I learned a long time ago that when your mother says she's going to do something, it's going to happen. So, you better embrace it."

"I'd take that advice if I were you," Tom said.

"Now if the rest of you don't mind," the doctor said, "I'd like to speak to Mr. and Ms. Wilkinson privately for a few minutes.'

Sally took Justin and Katie by the hand as the visitors shuffled out and into the corridor. "C'mon, guys, let's see if they have ice cream in the cafeteria."

"Okay, Grandma!" Katie said excitedly.

"Now, Mr. Wilkinson," the doctor said, "I wanted to talk to you about another matter. You have been through a very traumatic experience, one that has not only affected your body but your brain as well. This can have a lasting impact on you, and so you may want to consider speaking with someone about it."

"Why would I need to do that?" Nathan asked, a low testiness in his voice.

"It's just that brains tend to have a very unique reaction to trauma, especially when it involves oxygen deprivation, like yours was. It may have caused you to hallucinate, and that can be very disturbing to a lot of people.

"As an ER physician, I've encountered a lot of patients who have been on the brink, who have flatlined like you did. They've told me some pretty implausible stories about what they experienced when they were in that state."

"Did you have something like that happen to you, honey?" Ana asked.

"We'll talk about it later." Nathan turned back to the doctor. "So, you don't believe any of those experiences are real?"

"Of course not. The brain is a remarkable organ, capable of adapting to many different circumstances. If you experienced anything, it was probably a hallucination resulting from the trauma and the oxygen deprivation."

"I'll keep that in mind," Nathan said, amused by the doctor's smug self-assuredness. "By the way, Doctor, do you ever spend any time on the roof of the hospital?"

"Yes, I do on occasion," the doctor replied, taken aback by the seemingly random question. "Sometimes, especially after a stressful shift in the ER, I like to go up to the roof to unwind and get a breath of fresh air."

"Well, if you're missing your backpack, you might want to check for it up there, behind the primary ventilating unit."

"How did you know I lost my backpack?" the doctor asked incredulously.

"Oh, just a hunch. Anyway, thanks again for all you've done for my family and me, Dr. Bannockburn."

VII.

EPILOGUE

VII.1

Goodyear, Arizona—February 2022

"It's called Operation Kindness, honey, and it's a shelter for lost and abandoned dogs."

Nathan buttoned Katie's jacket as they stood together in the living room. He unfolded the hood for extra protection from the chilly Saturday morning. Justin stood impatiently by the door, already clad in his overcoat.

"But the best thing about it," Nathan continued, "is that it's a no-kill shelter. That means they won't put a dog down unless it's very sick and can't be nursed back to health. They want all their dogs and cats to have new families to live with."

"That's where we're going to find our new dog?" Katie asked, her eyes bright.

"I hope so."

Ana emerged from the bedroom and came into the living room. "Okay, I'm all set to go. You feeling okay?"

"I'm fine. It feels good to have all my mobility back and to be getting out of the house again. I've been cooped up way too long. Thank goodness Enrique has everything under control at the company."

"What I meant was, are you sure you're ready to do …this?" she asked as she buttoned up her own jacket.

Nathan glanced at the wall shelving next to the fireplace. They were there, as they always were, the five shiny, silver urns:

SHILOH

LINDSAY

GEORGIE

BOOMER

ZOEY

"Absolutely," he answered without hesitation.

* * * * * *

"Thank you for coming, Mr. and Ms. Wilkinson. Welcome to Operation Kindness. I'm the director. My name's Angie and I hope I can help you find what you are looking for."

The spacious, single-story facility bustled with activity. Families, couples, and individuals milled about the open reception area. There was a play zone outdoors and several get-acquainted rooms off the reception area in which families could be introduced to potential adoptees. The boarding rooms were in the back; the sounds of intermittent barking echoed through the facility. Justin wandered about the reception area, watching other families interact with the animals, while Katie remained close to her parents.

"Do you have any idea what kind of dog you would like to adopt?" Angie asked. "Large or small? Puppy or adult?"

"I want one who's never been loved," Katie said. Ana squeezed her hand.

"We have a few of those, I'm sorry to say. Come with me."

She led them through a doorway and into a kennel housing a dozen mature dogs. The cages lined a pathway that ran down the middle of the kennel. The room was hygienic and sanitary; empty dog dishes inside the generally clean cages awaited collection by the staff. The pathway led to a separate doorway that opened to a fenced-in outdoor play zone that sported grassy turf and a splash pond.

"We feed the dogs twice a day, and we try to give them at least an hour of exercise, with less outdoor time on those days when it's particularly hot."

"We have a few of those days here in Arizona," Ana said.

The family strolled through the kennel, pausing to observe each of the dogs. They were all kinds—large and small, quiet and loud, calm and anxious. A Dalmatian sat subdued in the back of its cage; a pit bull slept soundly in its bed; and an Australian shepherd paced back and forth, whimpering softly.

"Most of these dogs are two to four years old," Angie explained. "Some were dropped off here by owners who couldn't take care of them. Others were abandoned or were picked up as strays. And some were mistreated by their previous owners."

"I hate to hear that," Nathan grunted.

"I wish I could take them all home," Katie said.

Nathan glanced at the last cage on the right. In the corner sat a black-and-white mixed breed, which looked to be fifty pounds. Its fur was patchy, portions having been ripped away from the skin. It was shivering, its eyes desolate and a pleading expression on its face. Instantly Nathan felt drawn to it.

"What about that one?" he asked.

"We got him in a few weeks ago," Angie replied. "He's pretty young, although we don't know precisely how old he is. He was badly abused by his previous owner—he had been beaten and left chained outdoors for weeks at a time, even in the middle of the summer. The neighbors finally called animal control, and when they found him, he was on the verge of starvation. The officers immediately placed him under their custody, but he was in such bad shape that they took him to the city pound and were going to have him put down. Fortunately, one of my people was making the rounds at the pound that day and insisted that he be brought here. We've been trying to nurse him back to health."

"That is just awful," Ana moaned. "Your organization deserves so much credit for all you do for these dogs."

"What kind of dog is he?" Justin asked.

"He's a pretty classic mutt, best we can tell. We think he's got some beagle and shepherd in him, and maybe even some border collie and Labrador as well. The sad thing is that a lot of people don't want mutts or mixed breeds; they prefer purebreds.

"Now I can let you inside the pen to get acquainted with him. But given his history with people, he isn't likely to be very sociable."

The Wilkinsons approached the pen, and Angie unlocked the door. Ana and

Justin stood back while Nathan and Katie stepped inside. The dog lingered in the corner, whining and shivering and staring warily at them.

"It's okay, boy," Nathan said in a soothing voice. "You want to come say hello?"

"Here, give him this." Angie handed Katie a biscuit, and Katie crouched, cautiously extending the treat. He leaned forward, sniffed it, then carefully took it from Katie's hand with his teeth and bit into it with a loud crunching sound that echoed through the chamber.

He sniffed at Katie's still-extended hand. He rose to his feet, took a step toward her, and gave her hand a kiss.

"You're welcome," Katie said, a grin spreading across her face.

The dog extended his paws into her lap, and Katie scratched him behind the ears. He stopped shivering and nuzzled against Katie, kissing her again, this time on her cheek.

"Wow!" Angie said. "I haven't seen him take to anyone like that. It's as if he already knows you."

"Daddy, I want him!" Katie said.

"Honey, he's the first dog we've seen. Maybe we should see a few more…"

And then Nathan stopped. The mixed breed was gazing at him, and for a brief moment, and visible only to Nathan, his eyes sparkled with a bright white glow.

Nathan turned to Ana. "Or maybe we should take him now. I want this one too."

"I guess that settles it." Ana smiled. "We have ourselves a new family member."

"That's wonderful!" Angie said. "I know you'll give him a great home. You guys stay here and keep getting acquainted with him while I go to my office and get started on the paperwork."

As Angie departed, Nathan kneeled and placed his hands on his daughter's shoulders. "Honey, he's a very special dog, and he's meant for us. But he's been badly abused his whole life. He's very sad and vulnerable, and he's going to need someone to love him and take good care of him. Are you up for that?"

"Of course!"

"And if you do that, you will have a loyal friend for life, someone completely devoted to you and to all of us." With those words, he gave his daughter a hug.

"What should we name him?" Katie asked.

"I have a suggestion," Nathan answered. "I think we should name him…Frisco."

ABOUT THE AUTHOR

Dan V. Jackson is a writer, a family man, and a dog owner. He earned his BA in 1982 and an MBA in 1984, both from the University of Chicago, and has over thirty-five years' experience as a financial consultant. He was a cofounder of the international consulting firm Economists.com LLC, which was acquired by California-based Willdan Financial Services in 2015, and now Mr. Jackson serves as a Willdan vice president.

Rainbow Bridge is Mr. Jackson's second publication. His first novel, *The Forgotten Men*, was published by Mediaguruz in 2012.

Mr. Jackson lives outside of Dallas, Texas, in the fast-growing community of Frisco, with his wife, Cheryl. Their two daughters, Melissa and Rachel, live out of state. Fortunately, his three dogs, Abby, Bella, and Sammie, are there to provide companionship and entertainment. He enjoys running, golf, and football, and is a lifelong Dallas Cowboys fan.

He can be reached at djackson@economists.com, on Twitter at DanVJWrites, or at his website, www.danvjackson.com.